Justice For All

Justice For All

Murder New York Style 5

Edited By

D.M. Barr & Joseph R.G. De Marco

LEVEL
BEST BOOKS

Disclaimer

As per the theme of Murder New York Style: Justice for All, readers should be advised that in this anthology, many authors chose to tackle sensitive social justice issues and in doing so, may have included scenes of violence and some strong language. Please proceed accordingly.

First edition

ISBN: 978-1-68512-005-4

Cover art by Level Best Designs

This book was professionally typeset on Reedsy.
Find out more at reedsy.com

For everyone fighting for a kinder, more just, and equitable world.

Contents

Introduction

While we can't say for sure when each of the talented authors of the New York/Tri-State Chapter of Sisters in Crime wrote the stories we've presented in this anthology, we do know that the Chapter conceived the theme for *Murder New York Style: Justice for All* during a time of great political, social, and physical turmoil. The United States had just come out of its most contentious election in decades; a global pandemic threatened the lives of the world population just as the resulting recession affected their wallets; hate crimes were on a disturbing rise; and outraged citizens crowded city streets worldwide, decrying bias against race, immigration, and sexual orientation. It was hard not to be consumed by themes of justice when so much happening in the world was frustratingly beyond our control.

The ongoing battle for equality, integrity, and fairness reverberates in each of the sixteen thought-provoking stories that our panel of judges chose for inclusion, their diversity covering the spectrum of mystery and suspense subgenres.

Along with more traditional mysteries that demand justice against all odds are Lori Robbins' comic tale "Leading Ladies," in which an octogenarian with a love of gambling and Broadway musicals recruits her home stager granddaughter to investigate the entirely plausible albeit sudden death of her best friend; and Cathi Stoler's "The Art of Payback," in which a woman whose late mother was swindled out of a precious Picasso won't rest until she exacts an artistic revenge on the art broker responsible.

Others of our stories poke at the most pressing social issues of our time.

Both Anne-Marie Sutton in "The New Guy," and Elle Hartford in "Harbor Life and City Silt," take up the issue of race relations. Sutton describes a New York insurance company in the early seventies, where one of its veteran employees hasn't yet embraced the civil rights movement, as shown by his reluctance to work alongside a minority intern; while Hartford tackles the universal desire for co-existence in her futuristic tale of a city inhabited by both "landfolk" and "merfolk" where a string of murders threatens the peace.

Both Kathleen Marple Kalb and Catherine Siemann deliver period pieces that remind us the quest for justice is nothing new. Kalb's story, "The Thanksgiving Ragamuffin," describes an assault outside an opera singer's Washington Square townhouse that raises the ongoing issue of antisemitism, while Siemann's tale, "The Teacup," follows an immigrant woman living on the Lower East Side who faces eviction and possible domestic abuse. Immigration also plays a part in "Injustice in Brooklyn" by Stephanie Wilson-Flaherty, set in modern-day Bay Ridge, where a self-proclaimed busybody helps a Latino family whose son has been accused of gun possession and attempted murder. And LGBTQIA issues are addressed by Mary Jo Robertiello in "Family Matters," in which a newly married gay minister with a gambling problem and a homophobic stepfather is suspected in the strangulation of his mother.

Nina Mansfield wrestles with financial abandonment and drug abuse in "Windy Willows," in which a desolate mom who's lost her son to drugs decides to secretly help another mother who's been abandoned by her baby daddy. Privilege raises its ugly head in two stories; first, Nancy Good's "What Matters Most," where a Manhattan mom who doesn't fit in with the socialite crowd at her daughter's private school suspects another mother of murder; and second, Catherine Maiorisi's "When the Caged Bird Flies," where a terror-stricken Black victim deals with the aftermath of rape by a white member of Congress. And sex trafficking looms large in "The World According to Lucy" by Susie Case, where a hardworking college student with an apparent secret life collapses in class, prompting her professor to launch an investigation that includes the local tattoo parlor and her fellow classmates.

Ageism—at both ends of the spectrum—plays heavily in both Ellen Quint's "Risky Assumptions," the tale of an older female attorney and her P.I. who investigate the murder of a modeling agency owner suspected of sexual abuse; and Nina Wachsman's YA tale, "Laundry after Midnight," where a twelve-year-old boy witnesses a murder through this apartment peephole and investigates when the authorities and his parents seem too keen to chalk it up to an accident. The fate of another pre-teen leads to murder in Roz Siegel's "David and the Garmento," in which the daughter of immigrants plots to murder the husband who has not only abandoned her but plans to lure their son to his polygamous cult in India.

And for the writers among our readers, D.M. Barr tackles literary justice in the ironic "A Trial for the Books," in which a jury of publishers put a blogger-slash-amateur book critic on trial for his arbitrary one-star reviews.

The satisfying endings of all sixteen tales mirror the universal feeling of hope in the world, especially the ubiquitous prayer that once the COVID-19 virus is contained, we can resume our normal lives. As editors, that desire inspires us as we rush to publication so *Murder New York Style: Justice for All* can make its debut at what we have faith will be an in-person Brooklyn Book Fair later this year.

To our authors, please know that editing this book has been a wonderful reminder of the great talent that resides in our Chapter. Thanks for your cooperation in so gracefully and graciously accepting most of our proposed edits, though ultimately, the storylines and resolutions remained yours. Many thanks to our judges and to Elizabeth Mannion for her proofreading and photography contributions. Thanks also to Level Best Books for their excellent editing, cover art, and production. And to our readers, if these tales of murder and mayhem inspire you, please consider joining our ranks at Sisters in Crime, or perhaps purchasing others of our authors' books. But above all, stay safe. It can be a dangerous world out there.

—D.M. Barr and Joseph R.G. De Marco
   Editors

LEADING LADIES

by Lori Robbins

W hen Olga Tabatchnik died, Nana got suspicious. I pointed out, as diplomatically as I could, that Mrs. Tabatchnik was eighty-seven.

Never one to allow rational details to get in the way of an emotional argument, my grandmother was unimpressed. "Listen to me, Julie. You're missing the big picture. Other than the diabetes and heart disease, Olga was in perfect health. She ate a lot better than I do, that's for sure."

Truer words were never spoken. Nana subsisted mostly on candy and coffee. Her only known source of protein came from peanut brittle. When I was a kid, her apartment seemed magical. She kept lollipops behind the bed, licorice in every drawer, and chocolates in the living room.

I was in a rush to leave and put the phone on speaker. "New York City rats eat better than you. Are you suggesting the doctors missed some other underlying condition?"

She hummed a few bars of "Just You Wait" from her favorite musical, *My Fair Lady*. According to her, most of the wisdom of the world was contained in Alan Jay Lerner's iconic lyrics. Her qualms concerning Mrs. Tabatchnik, however, dealt with far darker matters than Eliza Doolittle's woes regarding the rain in Spain.

"I think the doctor missed the fact that she was murdered."

I sighed. For all her quirks, she was the sanest person I knew. "How did you come to this conclusion?"

There was a brief silence. In the background, I heard Henry Higgins declaiming the marvels of the English language. Thanks to my grandmother's love of theater, I knew every note of every Broadway musical from the last sixty years.

I could almost hear her thinking. When she did speak, it was much slower than the staccato rhythm of the song. "Olga and I met early. We had just begun constructing a new cryptic crossword puzzle that we hoped to sell to the *Times*. Olga was distracted and forgetful—not at all her usual self. She kept coming up with the most improbable clues. I know she was still quite upset about her housekeeper, who died in that awful subway accident. I thought if she went to the Las Vegas night at the new senior center it would cheer her up." She added, with some satisfaction, "I made a bundle."

I groaned. "I hope you were discreet. If you're not careful, you'll get blacklisted at every poker night in the tri-state area."

You wouldn't think it to look at her, but my grandmother was a card shark. She met Mrs. Tabatchnik five years ago, over a blackjack table in Atlantic City, and the two bonded over their love of gambling, puzzles, and games.

Mrs. Tabatchnik resided on Park Avenue, and Nana in Brooklyn, but they were as close as if they'd grown up together. I'd met Mrs. Tabatchnik only once when she soundly defeated me at Scrabble. As a consolation prize, she sent me a Scrabble dictionary, heavily annotated.

Nana dismissed my worries. "I was very careful. I only took a few big hands. But even at amateur night, surrounded by gullible marks, counting cards takes concentration. I noticed Olga still didn't seem herself. She was thirsty and drank a lot of water, in addition to two vodka martinis."

Her suspicions regarding Mrs. Tabatchnik's death were getting less and less credible. Mrs. Tabatchnik had diabetes, and her thirst was a definite warning sign—not of murder, but of physical distress.

She spoke faster, as if in anticipation of more objections. "Olga left to go to the ladies' room. When she didn't return, I went to check on her. Someone had already called nine-one-one. The ambulance arrived and took her away." Her voice became tearful. "But it was too late. And I-I never saw her again."

Despite my haste to get to my appointment, I was gentle. "I'm so sorry you lost your friend. But I doubt any of those elderly gamblers murdered Mrs. Tabatchnik, no matter how high the stakes."

"Correct. But Bradley and Ramona, her son and daughter-in-law, were there. All night, they never left her side. Maybe they were trying to protect her. Naturally, everyone concluded, as you did, that an old woman died of natural causes. But that's not what happened. Olga said her drink didn't taste right. I'm certain she was poisoned."

While I pondered my grandmother's unlikely theory, I donned three more layers of clothing as insurance against the bitterly cold day. I stuffed a pair of high-heeled shoes in my bag and pulled thick boots on my feet. I wanted to make a good impression on my new client but saw no reason to suffer the indignities of fashion for the rush hour crowd on the Lexington Avenue local.

I cast about for some way to help her through her grief. "It makes sense that you're in shock. You weren't expecting Mrs. Tabatchnik to die so suddenly. Have you called Mom?"

She gave a derisive laugh. "Your mother, who has no trouble believing in the existence of an astral plane, doesn't believe Olga was murdered. She doesn't even want to go to the funeral, where we can confront all the suspects." Her tone became more urgent. "Old people deserve justice as much as anyone. Olga and I were a team. She didn't have to die. Not like that. Help me find out what really happened."

With as much sympathy as I could convey over the phone, I said, "I'll call you later, after I meet with my new client. Did I tell you about her? Ramona Dimon. Very ritzy—Park Avenue address."

She cleared her throat. "I know. Ramona was Olga's daughter-in-law, the one I mentioned earlier." Her voice broke again. "Olga turned the deed to the apartment over to her son last year, after she had that bout with pneumonia." With more firmness, she continued, "I told Ramona and Bradley you were the best at staging homes, and you wouldn't charge them an arm and a leg. It would break Olga's heart to know they're selling it. She wanted it to stay in the family."

I tripled locked my door and headed down the stairs. "Thanks for the recommendation. I'm glad you got around to telling me."

Nana was uncharacteristically grim. "You don't have to thank me. You have to get this job and then search the apartment for clues. Keep your wits about you. It could be dangerous."

There wasn't the slightest chance I could change her mind, but I had to try. "Would it kill you to at least consider the possibility your friend died a natural death?"

Her voice was firm. "Yes."

* * *

Unlike the glitzy glass and steel behemoths that had come to dominate the cityscape, Mrs. Tabatchnik's building whispered, rather than screamed, money. The doorman opened the gilt and glass entrance, and I entered a lobby with rose-colored walls and subdued furnishings. I sat on a sofa to change my shoes before giving my name to the receptionist. He gave me a friendly nod and directed me to the appropriate elevator, where yet another employee took me to the topmost floor.

A short woman in a maid's uniform opened the door to Penthouse B and greeted me without enthusiasm. In stark contrast to her taciturnity, a thin, blonde woman rushed toward me.

"Julie! I've been waiting for ages!"

Although I'd managed to arrive five minutes before the appointed time, I didn't correct her. My goal was to get Ramona to part with a small portion of her large inheritance, not score points for accuracy.

The apartment was a spacious, if gloomy, time capsule. The appraisers on *Antiques Roadshow* would have had a field day pontificating upon the history of the heavy, marble-topped furniture, elaborately patterned rugs, and etageres crammed with silver and crystal. I photographed each room from multiple angles and took careful measurements. Staging the apartment would take a lot of work, but if I got the job, and the place sold quickly, my fledgling design company might actually begin supporting me, instead of the other way around. It was no fun waitressing at night in order to stay in business during the day.

The only modern item in the apartment, aside from several books of crossword puzzles, was Ramona herself. Dressed all in white, her tall, lanky figure provided a stark contrast to the heavy, dark décor. I guessed she was in her late forties or early fifties, but I wasn't sure. She had the kind of angular beauty usually assigned to runway models, but her skin was tighter than was strictly consistent with how nature normally arranged facial features.

"Well? What do you think?" Ramona looked far from confident in my abilities.

I was used to dealing with anxious clients, although up to this point, none had the kind of money that afforded life on Park Avenue. But the people who employed me to stage their modest homes were no different from Ramona. They all wanted to sell quickly, preferably for more than the place was worth. That desire didn't mean they weren't emotionally attached to their possessions. I'd seen grown men and women get teary-eyed—or personally offended—when I suggested Aunt Barbie's prized collection of china dogs was unlikely to appeal to the uninformed eye. Or that their kids' framed report cards, circa 1985, didn't substantially add to the already doubtful charm of a cluttered and hopelessly dated kitchen.

Mindful that Ramona, or her husband, might have sentimental associations to every mincing porcelain figurine, I started small. "I suggest painting every room and removing all the personal items." I paused. "Most of this lovely furniture should probably go into storage. I'll bring in some more modern pieces we can use to redecorate. You don't want anything damaged during the open house."

Her expression lost some of its initial friendliness. "I know you're cheap, but is that all you have?" She added, with some tartness, "My broker has his own stagers and isn't thrilled I'm thinking of using you. As for open houses, there won't be any. He will show the apartment by appointment only, to qualified buyers. In the future, you'll be dealing with him."

I beat down the butterflies in my stomach and swept the heavy silk drapes to one side. Sunlight poured through the window, partially dispelling the damp chill. I drew some quick sketches to show her how the redecorated living room would look.

I spoke more authoritatively than I felt. "If you want a fast sale at the right price, we need to get rid of nearly everything and start over. My job is to turn this unique home into an apartment that will appeal to multiple buyers."

She winced at the bright light and reclosed the curtains. Leaning over my shoulder, she examined the drawings carefully, and her posture relaxed. "That's more like it. Perhaps I should have explained earlier we have no interest in this mausoleum, which has been in the Tabatchnik family since the beginning of time. Bradley and I can't wait to move."

I offered polite condolences, embarrassed I hadn't done so earlier.

She sighed and wiped her eyes. "Thank you, but it was a blessing in disguise. Sadly, in the last few months, her dementia got much worse, which wasn't surprising in a woman of her age." She pointed to the maid, standing guard in the doorway. "Mrs. Verdad was her housekeeper. Also, her caretaker."

Ramona winced again and dimmed the lights on the chandelier. "I feel a migraine coming on. Let's wrap this up."

Things proceeded smoothly after that. She called her broker, and we agreed to meet to discuss details. On the way out, I paused to admire a group of photographs in antique silver frames. The most prominent was of two old ladies, with big smiles and improbably bright blonde hair, standing behind a craps table. It rested on a book of crossword puzzles.

It was a picture I knew well. "My grandmother has the same photo in her apartment. They were best friends, as I'm sure you know."

Ramona picked it up, looking from the picture to me and back again. "You're welcome to it. Without the frame, of course."

I drew back. "Your husband may want it."

She handed it to me. "Doubtful. He's not the sentimental type."

I took the picture and carefully undid the fasteners while Ramona answered a phone call. A small square of paper, which had been wedged between the photograph and the backing, fell to the floor.

I should have handed the paper to her. But I didn't. I slipped it into my pocket. The only thing Ramona wanted from the apartment was money. But Nana would treasure that scrap of paper from Olga.

Ramona finished her call. "It would be delightful to continue chatting, but we both have work to do." She gestured to the maid, who had followed us. "Mrs. Verdad will take care of you. So, if there's nothing else?"

I pointed to the book of crossword puzzles. "If you don't mind, I'd like to take this with me. I'm a big fan of puzzles."

She was busy sending a text. "Uh-huh, sure," she said, without looking up.

I thanked her and left.

* * *

The next day, I unwillingly emerged from a deep slumber to fumble for my phone.

My grandmother's loud greeting punctured any hope I had of getting back to sleep. "Julie! Guess what? I made coffee cake. We can celebrate your new job."

I squinted at the phone. "It's six o'clock. In the morning."

She sounded hurt. "You told me you wake up early."

This was true. However, I'd had my heart broken the night before, which had put a serious dent in my usual sleep cycle.

"If you must, you can bring that boyfriend of yours," she said, presumably to sweeten the deal.

I declined her half-hearted offer. "You know the song from *My Fair Lady* called 'Show Me'?"

Nana snorted her assent. "I taught it to you."

I stared at the ceiling. "After I asked him to show me where the relationship was going, he ended it. That's the last time I take advice from a Broadway play."

She didn't bother with condolences. "It's all for the best. I never liked him anyway. Come now and I'll throw in a cup of coffee."

I cocooned myself in two sweaters and a puffy brown winter coat. I was nearly as short as my grandmother, and the getup made me look like an ambulatory potato, with long dark hair and brown eyes in place of sour cream and chives.

Nana's kitchen smelled of coffee, cinnamon, and sugar. In response to her eager questions, I withdrew the book of crossword puzzles and the square of paper that had been hidden behind the photograph and handed both to her.

She was thrilled. While she hunted for her reading glasses, I read, for the tenth time, the neatly printed message. I'd inherited my grandmother's love of puzzles, but the words made no sense to me. *"Clearly not a girl's best friend."* I looked up from the page. "Was Mrs. Tabatchnik getting senile? Ramona said she was having some mental problems."

Nana was outraged. "Certainly not. She was a lot sharper and a lot smarter than Ramona." She opened her laptop. "Olga and I were constructing a new crossword." She pointed to the screen. The same clue was inscribed there as well. I got chills looking at it.

Her voice shook. "Remember when I told you Olga was putting in all these weird clues? She was sending me a message—one that she couldn't say out loud. We have to figure out what it was."

I waited for Nana to compose herself before trying to get her to see reason.

"Mrs. Tabatchnik could not possibly have anticipated having me find this note, which was hidden inside a photograph."

Nana was undaunted. "Of course not. That's why she wrote the message in multiple places. Olga told me many times that if she died before me, she wanted me to have whatever photographs I wanted. And her books. It was your cleverness that got us this clue so quickly."

I forked up the last crumbs of cake. "But now that we have this theoretical clue, what do we do? I have no idea what it means."

Nana shook her head. "Me either. But I'll figure it out." She looked off into the distance. "I'll ask around at the funeral. It's scheduled for one o'clock today. That'll be the perfect time for you to examine Olga's apartment for more clues."

I hugged her. "Do us both a favor and tread lightly. If you're right—and I'm not yet convinced you are—we're tracking a killer. I hope neither Bradley nor Ramona is involved. I want them to recommend me to their rich friends, and I don't think their endorsement will carry as much weight from jail as it would from Park Avenue."

* * *

Mrs. Verdad, the housekeeper, let me in and followed me from room to room. She eyed me as I examined a bookshelf. In an accusatory tone, she said, "Mrs. Tabatchnik loved her books."

Her intense scrutiny made me nervous. "Nearly everything is going to be moved in a few days. I'm deciding which things will stay when we stage the apartment. I'm sure that's what Mrs. Tabatchnik would have wanted."

She was not persuaded. "How would you know what Mrs. Tabatchnik would have wanted? You only know what Ms. Dimon wanted. You should bring your grandmother with you the next time you come. She would know what to do."

Unlike Ramona, Mrs. Verdad seemed deeply attached to the apartment. "I'm so sorry for your loss. Were you with Mrs. Tabatchnik for long?"

As unwillingly as if she were giving away state secrets, Mrs. Verdad said,

"Not long."

Under my two wool sweaters, I felt cold. Not simply from the chill in the air, but from the atmosphere in the room. Mrs. Verdad's unsmiling demeanor was giving me the creeps. She did nothing threatening, but her unflinching gaze felt menacing. I remembered that Mrs. Tabatchnik's previous housekeeper had died—thrown onto the subway tracks in what the police termed a tragic accident.

I turned my back to her, trying to break the spell she'd cast. I had a job to do. Two jobs, if I included Nana's quixotic injunction to investigate Mrs. Tabatchnik's death.

I was drawn to Mrs. Tabatchnik's collection of first edition children's books. Those would definitely stay. But wedged between a set of Beverly Cleary books, and every single Nancy Drew mystery, was a tattered songbook from the musical *Gentlemen Prefer Blondes*.

The intercom buzzed, breaking our silence. Mrs. Verdad left to answer it.

My heart was pounding. With shaky fingers, I put the songbook in my bag. As thefts go, it wasn't serious. But it was unethical. Feeling guilty, I was about to put it back when Mrs. Verdad returned.

She stared at me with even greater intensity. I was terrified she'd seen me.

"We'll probably be spending quite a bit of time together over the next few days," I said. "What's your first name? I'm Julie."

She stiffened. "Clara. But I prefer Mrs. Verdad."

My nervous attempt at camaraderie did little to thaw Mrs. Verdad's icy demeanor. With her response, the cold apartment got too hot for me. I grabbed my coat and headed for the door. Mrs. Verdad followed on my heels. I swung open the door and screamed when a tall guy in a dark coat blocked my way.

He turned pale. "What the hell is going on here?"

Mrs. Verdad pointed to me. "This is the decorator Ms. Dimon hired." She grimaced as she completed the introduction. "This is Matt Laurent, the real estate agent."

I mumbled an apology for yelling loud enough to shatter glass and edged into the hallway.

The real estate agent followed me into the elevator. "I didn't mean to startle you. Let me make it up to you by buying lunch. We can talk about the apartment."

I was still shaky. Also, embarrassed. "Thanks, but I, uh, I have another appointment.

He would not be put off. "I have a car waiting. I'll give you a lift."

I inspected him. Thirty-ish, dark-haired, and good-looking, Matt Laurent seemed normal, but I trusted no one. I made my way home. And not via the subway.

* * *

I called my mother as soon as I got back to my apartment. "Don't you see? If Nana is right, Mrs. Verdad is a prime suspect!" A new thought, worse than the first, occurred to me. "What if she tries to kill me? Or Nana? Maybe she's conspiring with the real estate agent."

My mother was her usual detached self. "This whole plot, as you call it, is a figment of your—and your grandmother's—overactive imaginations. Do the design job and forget everything else. Otherwise, you'll be waitressing for the rest of your life. That's what I call scary."

I didn't answer her, worried she was right. And equally worried she was wrong.

She sighed. "This craziness is blocking my chakras. I'm going to a yoga class, and you should come with me. It'll do you good."

I could barely swallow. "Screw the yoga. Mrs. Verdad's first name is *Clara*. Get it? The first part of the clue is the word *clear*—which is what Clara means. And the second part, *best friend*, applies to her last name."

With another long-suffering sigh, she said, "Verdad doesn't mean best friend It means true."

"Yes! And who's truer than a best friend?"

Mom had one final argument. "Why didn't Mrs. Tabatchnik just tell your grandmother she felt threatened? Or tell her kids? Why would she make up this lame clue?"

I was unnerved by her logic, as well as the fact this was the very argument I'd posed to my grandmother. "Ramona said she was showing signs of dementia. Maybe Mrs. Tabatchnik was leaving the clues for herself, so she wouldn't forget. Or maybe she wasn't certain she was in danger but left the clues in case she died suddenly. If that's what happened, her plan worked, since Nana is on the case. She counted on Nana to figure it out."

I checked my phone for what felt like the hundredth time that day. The funeral had to have ended hours earlier. Where was Nana?

* * *

Several tense hours elapsed before I learned Nana was in the hospital. She was injured, but more than that, she was furious. "These doctors think I twisted my ankle. They talked to me as if I were a child. But I know what happened. I was pushed."

Her right foot was heavily bandaged, but the rest of her appeared unharmed, and she was discharged with a bottle of painkillers and instructions to rest.

I had a cab waiting. Nana's gait was unsteady, but her gaze was as sharp as ever.

"We have to move quickly. Bradley Tabatchnik is still at large. He shoved me into the street. Tried to kill me. If one of those crazy cyclists hadn't hit me first, I would have ended up under a bus."

"Are you sure it was Mrs. Tabatchnik's son who went after you?" I explained how the crossword clue pointed to Mrs. Verdad.

She frowned. "I didn't see who pushed me. But I googled the name 'Bradley.' It means clearing."

I tried to fit this information into what we already knew. "The clue had the word 'clearly' with the letter L in brackets. Clearly and clearing aren't at all the same."

She bit her lip. "I'm still working on it. Maybe it has something to do with that songbook from *Gentlemen Prefer Blondes*. I'll study the lyrics tonight."

I helped her out of the car. "You may be onto something. Ramona has blonde hair, which means Bradley is the gentleman who prefers blondes."

* * *

The next morning, Nana still wasn't well. The shock of her friend's death, combined with pain from the injuries she'd suffered the previous day, left her too weak to get out of bed.

To my horror, Bradley Tabatchnik called. His voice was urgent. "I need to see your grandmother."

I'd let the Wicked Witch of the West zoom through the window on a flaming broomstick before I allowed Bradley Tabatchnik anywhere near my Nana. "She's resting. She'll get back to you later."

As soon as I ended the call, my phone buzzed with a text from Ramona. *Moving men here. Need you ASAP.*

I left Nana with my mother, who had spent the night tending her, and headed to Mrs. Tabatchnik's apartment, arming myself with Nana's pepper spray. Despite this precaution, I decided if Mrs. Verdad, Matt Laurent, or Bradley Tabatchnik were there, I would run. I'm no hero.

Thankfully, it was Ramona who answered the door.

I looked around. "Where are the movers?"

She grimaced. "They're on the way."

The same uneasy feeling I'd had each time I was in the apartment returned. I followed her to the living room. She brushed back her long blonde hair. While she tended to the fire, I examined, once again, the bookshelves filled with children's literature. Beverly Cleary's Ramona book had pride of place. Staring at them, I realized Mrs. Tabatchnik's clues weren't hidden at all. They were right in front of me. Distracted by a furious buzzing, I fished my phone from my bag. Nana's message was two minutes too late. *RAMONA KILLED OLGA—RUN!!!*

I backed away. Ramona held an andiron in both hands. With a vicious swipe, she knocked the phone from my hands. "I know what you're up to. You and that snooping grandmother of yours." Her conversational tone was as horrifying as her look of implacable fury. "I waited and waited for Olga to

13

die. But she wouldn't. She was going to live to one hundred. Out of spite."

Ramona barked a short laugh. "Your granny gave Bradley the third degree at the funeral. As if that pathetic loser had the guts to kill his mother." She fixed me with an enraged stare. "A lot of good it did her. He told me all about it."

I turned and ran, toppling a glass case behind me in a bid to slow her down. Ramona sidestepped it. With bruised fingers, I fumbled for the pepper spray but couldn't get a clean hit in time to stop her. She slammed me again with the andiron. Not a direct hit. But hard enough that I collapsed in pain.

I kicked a table in front of her. "You're crazy! You'll never get away with it."

Her eyes were red and streaming, but she kept coming. "Oh, I think I will."

In that fraught moment, Nana's voice spoke to my unconscious. Channeling Eliza Doolittle from *My Fair Lady*, I hurled, not a slipper, but a brass figurine.

She screamed, and blood burst from her nose. But like some futuristic cyborg, she recovered and kept coming.

Until Mrs. Verdad crashed through the door and conked Ramona on the head with an eighteenth-century silver teapot.

* * *

After I recovered from my concussion and various other painful bruises, Nana invited me, Bradley Tabatchnik, and Mrs. Verdad for dinner. She also invited Matt Laurent.

Although Nana mostly ate candy, she was one hell of a good cook. Over dinner, we pieced together the ugly story of how two people died. And how Nana and I came very close to joining them.

Mrs. Verdad spoke first. "Ramona told me Mrs. Tabatchnik was getting senile. She said I shouldn't pay attention if she started talking crazy." Her eyes filled with tears. "Mrs. Tabatchnik wanted me to save her clues to give to you. I didn't know what that meant, and forgive me, I thought that was the dementia talking. Then, after she died, I wasn't so sure."

I mentally apologized to Mrs. Verdad for suspecting her of murder. "Was that why you watched me so carefully?"

Mrs. Verdad nodded. "Yes. I wanted to make sure you found whatever Mrs. Tabatchnik had left behind, so you could give it to your grandmother."

Bradley shuddered. "My mother hated Ramona, but I—I was in love with her. She was…so beautiful and so charming. But I'd be lying if I didn't admit there were signs she wasn't…well." He paused. "I adopted a puppy. She said he ran away. But her story didn't ring true. It was then I began to suspect she was…unbalanced."

Nana was gentle. "Tell us what happened next."

Bradley's voice was hoarse with emotion. "My mother was terribly shaken after her former housekeeper was pushed under a train, almost certainly by Ramona. After the accident, Ramona rarely left Mom's side, even after hiring Mrs. Verdad. Later, the medical examiners found large quantities of beta-blockers in her blood. That's what killed her."

Nana nodded. "Julie told me Ramona suffered from migraines."

Bradley stared at his wine without drinking it. "She poisoned my mother. I have no doubt I was next." His hands trembled. "After the funeral, Ramona questioned me about you. I told her what you said—that you were suspicious of how Mom died." He covered his face with his hands. "It's my fault she attacked you. I'm a fool. She married me for my money and got tired waiting for the payoff."

Matt asked, "What about the crossword puzzle clue? Did that mean anything?"

Nana smiled through her tears. "No one beat Olga at puzzles. I knew from the start that the brackets around the 'L' in the word 'clearly' meant something important."

I reminded my grandmother that not everyone at the table was a word nerd.

Nana explained, "The songbook Julie found was next to a set of books by Beverly *Cleary*. See? The word clearly without the L? Clear-y!" Seeing the baffled looks around the table, she added, "Beverly Cleary's most famous books are about a girl named Ramona."

I added. "And the blonde Ramona's last name, Dimon, relates to the second part of the clue."

Nana was pleased. "Exactly. My favorite song in that book you swiped—*Gentlemen Prefer Blondes*—is 'Diamonds are a Girl's Best Friend.' Diamonds—definitely *not* Dimon!"

* * *

The next few months were a busy time for all of us. Nana resumed her visits to the senior center. The executive board, instead of banning her from their next Las Vegas Night, enlisted her to organize it. It was their most successful fundraiser, and the Children's Hospital honored her at their annual dinner.

With Matt's help, I staged Mrs. Tabatchnik's apartment. It was a record sale for the building and was featured in the real estate section of several newspapers. We celebrated together. As we walked back to his apartment, all I could think of was my namesake, Julie Andrews, and the overpowering feeling that I could have danced all night.

* * *

Lori Robbins' debut novel, *Lesson Plan for Murder,* won the Silver Falchion Award for Best Cozy Mystery and was a finalist in the Readers' Choice and Indie Book Awards. It will be republished later this year as part of a new Master Class Mystery Series and will be followed in early 2022 with *Study Guide to Murder.* Lori's latest work, *Murder in First Position*, opens her On Pointe Mysteries; it tied for First Prize/ Best Mystery in the 2021 Indie Book Awards, was a finalist in the Silver Falchion Award for Best Cozy Mystery, and is on the long list for a Mystery and Mayhem Book Award. The sequel is due out in November. Another of her short stories, "Accidents Happen," was published this past May. She is a former vice president of the New York chapter of Sisters in Crime and a member of both Mystery Writers of America and International Thriller Writers.

THE TEACUP

by Catherine Siemann

I t was almost dark, that cold November in 1890, when I made my way up the four flights of stairs to the top floor of the tenement on Norfolk Street. While I'd had occasion to visit clients at home in the course of my work with the immigrant community on the Lower East Side, I hadn't become accustomed to their housing conditions. The stairway was narrow and unlit, so I clung tightly to the railing as I felt my way up the sloping steps, the worn wood uneven in places. Smells of cooking—meat, garlic, and unfamiliar spices with an ever-present undertone of cabbage—came from various apartments as I climbed.

I knocked on the apartment door. There was a scuffling and a pair of young voices. "Mama said not to open the door!"

"But there's a lady she's expecting!"

A heavier step and a moment later, Margarethe Baumann stood in an open doorway. She was with child, though not very far along. A pair of young ones peered out from behind her skirts. Her pretty blue eyes showed how tired she was, both in their expression and in the darkened skin underneath. Her light brown hair was swept up in a hasty knot. Her dull gray dress was mended in several places, and she straightened the apron that partly covered it.

"Oh, Miss Lockwood, it is so good of you to come." Her voice was soft, but she spoke quickly, as if she was afraid of interruption. "It's been hard to get anyone to mind the little ones since my neighbor took that factory job, and I wasn't sure that you'd want us all traipsing through your office. Bobby's got a nasty head cold, and now Annie and Benny do too." An emphatic sneeze from one of the children underlined the point. "The older children should be in school, but Rosie and I are looking after the others today, aren't we, dear?" She glanced back over her shoulder at an older girl, who'd quietly followed her siblings into the room. "You don't mind coming in, do you? I can give you a cup of tea." The smile that lit up her worn face transformed her into someone younger and more hopeful.

I entered a small, windowless kitchen, dominated by a cast-iron stove. It was a typical three-room tenement flat, with a dark bedroom to my left, and a front parlor to my right. Its windows, which faced out onto the noisy street, provided the only source of outside light or air.

No matter how often I visited my clients in the tenements of the Lower East Side, I was constantly amazed at how entire families managed to live in such small spaces; in fact, the airy bedroom of the uptown brownstone that I shared with my aunt and uncle was as large as this entire apartment. Yet a man and wife, and their four—soon to be five—children managed in these crowded rooms. Rooms they might soon lose.

The children retreated to the parlor, where the youngest boy and girl played with a wooden toy cart, occasionally raising their voices, and growing quiet again. The older boy looked idly at what was probably a schoolbook, and the eldest girl pulled out a sewing basket. She sat there mending, while her brother occasionally broke his silence to read aloud to her, too softly for me to hear more than a murmur.

I settled myself at the kitchen table and looked over my notes, while Margarethe Baumann put on the kettle. She lifted the lid of a large pot, and the marvelous smell of lamb, vegetables, and thyme escaped. The heat from the stove in the poorly ventilated room was oppressive. I tugged at the high lace collar of my blouse when my hostess wasn't looking.

"As you know, my name is Emma Lockwood, and I'm an attorney." This was when the questions usually began, but Mrs. Baumann simply smiled. "The law clinic at the Neighborhood Guild referred your case to my firm. I understand that you're three months behind on your rent, and your landlord is threatening eviction."

She nodded. "My husband was injured and unable to work for a couple of months. His boss thinks the world of him, so he held Peter's job for him, but we're so far behind that I can't help but worry about how we're going to make up the payments. The landlord sent someone around the other day. He didn't exactly threaten, but he made it clear that we're going to have to leave soon if we can't catch up on the rent."

"We can try to negotiate a payment schedule. If you've been good tenants, your landlord may think twice about losing you. Do you belong to a mutual aid society? Sometimes they have funds for situations like this."

She shook her head. "I don't think so. I'm certain Peter would have mentioned it." The kettle was coming to a boil, so she rose and went over to the stove. "A drop of milk?"

"No, thank you," I said. Better it go to the Baumann children. "I'm sure we'll manage something."

Margarethe Baumann handed me a cup of tea, white bone china, with a deep red-and-gold trim and a matching saucer. "It's so nice to use my good tea set. I save it for company, for fear the children might break something."

As if on cue, there was a cry of distress from the front room, and a voice calling, "She won't let me play."

"Annie, let your brother have his turn." She poured her own tea, also omitting milk. On the shelf there were two more matching cups and saucers, alongside the sturdy, workaday blue-and-white china found nearly everywhere in the city. "They were a gift from my last employer when I left her service to marry Peter. I ought to see if they're worth anything, really, but they have such lovely memories attached."

The delicate china cup looked familiar. Hadn't I drunk from similar ones before, somewhere? I blew cautiously into my tea and sipped. "It's delicious, thank you very much. And the tea service is very nice indeed."

"She felt bad about giving me something used, Mrs. Thompson did, but I'd always admired them so. And her married daughter had given her a new set, painted with roses and very cheerful. Anyway, she'd no need to give me anything at all, me leaving her like that, and good servants difficult to find. But she was always so kind, not like the other ladies I'd worked for."

The door opened and closed with a slam. "Gossiping with the neighbors?" Peter Baumann was a slim, even-featured man of middle height, whose sneering expression marred his good looks. He walked haltingly, as though he hadn't yet entirely recovered from the accident. "I hope supper's not going to be late."

"No, Peter. It's nearly done. Lamb stew, just the way you like it. This is Miss Emma Lockwood. She's here to help about the landlord."

"Miss Lockwood?" He looked me up and down, clearly predisposed to finding fault. To be inconspicuous, I'd chosen my dark blue coat and skirt, and a small, not particularly fashionable hat. But they'd also cost far more than anything the Baumanns could afford, and it seemed Peter Baumann could tell that. "Some uptown lady dispensing good works? Well, we don't need your kind around here, Miss Lockwood."

"She's going to talk to the landlord, about catching up with the rent, Peter. I thought you'd be pleased." Margarethe Baumann's gaze met neither her husband's nor mine.

"And why should this fine lady care whether we get thrown out on the

20

streets or not, Margarethe?"

"My firm provides legal services, for low or no cost, to people in the neighborhood who need them," I said.

He laughed. "A lady lawyer? Who ever heard of such a thing?"

"There are three…no, now it's four of us in New York State. And in California, where I come from, we've had women lawyers for over a decade. I trained there with my father."

Margarethe Baumann continued to look down at the table. "Miss Lockwood was just leaving," she said, meekly.

I set my cup down in its saucer, the tea only half-drunk. "Yes, I'll be on my way."

She reached out her hand to pick it up. It was then that I saw the bruising around her wrist.

The door closed behind me, and I was partway down the first flight of stairs, when I heard an angry voice, male, yelling: "Telling strangers our problems?" Margarethe responded, but her tone was quieter, and I couldn't tell what she was saying. If only there was something I could do for her. Would an eviction be a blessing in disguise, serving to break up an unhappy family?

* * *

I had several matters pending with the same landlord and secured an appointment for the middle of the following week. A few days after my visit to the Baumann home, I was out for a Saturday afternoon stroll uptown with Cecily Van Duyn, my dearest friend and, not coincidentally, my law partner's wife. She called my attention to a shop window as we passed. "Look! Exactly like those horrid things my mother gave me." It was a set of red-and-gold trimmed teacups just like Margarethe Baumann's.

"So that's where I've seen them." At Cecily and Will's home just off Fifth Avenue. "One of my clients has a set too. A gift from her old employer. I'm sure she has no idea how valuable they are, and I'd be curious to see what she could get for them."

Cecily nodded, as the two of us peered into the display window. "My mother brought them back from Paris or Vienna or somewhere of the sort. Apparently, they're Russian, and she says they're old and quite valuable. Mrs. Astor has a set and therefore everyone else wants one too."

"I'll never understand the hold that woman has on people."

"That's because you're sensible, Emma." My friend looked thoughtful. "Betsey, the parlormaid, broke one of the saucers the other day. She was certain I'd dismiss her—as if I cared about the ridiculous things. It's absurd that a perfectly good servant should live in fear of losing her job over something so unimportant, but Mama *will* ask about them when she comes to tea. Perhaps your client would like to sell hers to me at whatever old Mr. Farrington is asking. Then I'll have extras, and poor Betsey can rest easy."

I squinted at the china in the window. "He's bound to be charging something far beyond their true worth, considering this neighborhood."

Cecily laughed. "I can afford it."

We went inside, and our inquiry revealed a price far greater than I'd imagined a set of cups and saucers could possibly be worth. Cecily told the shopkeeper she'd have to think about it.

If Margarethe Baumann were willing to sell, she was going to have more than she'd need to pay her back rent. It wouldn't make her wealthy, but it would help.

* * *

The negotiations with the Baumanns' landlord were fairly routine; he'd allow an extension, and partial payments over the course of some months to come. The market was soft at the moment, and the Baumanns had been good tenants. He was equally willing to accommodate my other clients, all except for one family he'd found too troublesome because of their insistence on some rather necessary repairs.

Mrs. Baumann came to the office the next morning, her youngest child in tow. While Lucy, our clerk-typist, took it upon herself to amuse Benny by introducing him to the wonders of a desk chair on casters, I waved his mother to a chair by my desk.

"Good news," I said. "The landlord's willing to let you make up the payments over the next six months. I know it won't be easy, but spread out over that amount of time, it could be managed."

She nodded. "I used to do piecework. One of the garment factories sent me hand finishing to do at home. Peter was doing well enough that he wanted me to stop that, but I should be able to pick it up again."

"You might not have to. Those teacups of yours? A friend and I spotted some just like them in a shop uptown a few days ago. She's interested in buying yours, and she's willing to pay you what the shopkeeper was asking." I took a deep breath. "The price is more than you might imagine."

"How much?" Her tone was wary.

I told her.

Her eyes widened, and she twisted the end of her scarf tightly. "I suppose I ought to sell them then. If that's what they're worth, it will get us out of our troubles." The scarf shifted slightly, revealing marks on the side of her neck. A quick gesture and they were covered again. "Maybe even be enough to move us to a nicer neighborhood, up in Yorkville or out in Brooklyn. Only I'll miss them. It may seem foolish, but they remind me of such a lovely time."

I wanted to help with her other problem, but if she knew I'd seen the evidence of what her husband was doing to her, she might walk away and never come back. That had happened before. So, I simply smiled. "It's entirely up to you. I don't have the money now, and I'm in court for the next few days, but I could bring you the cash and pick up the cups on Friday."

She hesitated for just a moment. "Yes. But I have one question."

"Of course." I made a note in my diary, then looked back up.

"Peter always says that what's his is his and what's mine is also his. Is that true? If the cups were a gift to me, are they his too?"

"If the cups were a gift to you, then so is the money you'd get from selling them. That wouldn't be true everywhere. Traditionally, what belongs to the wife becomes the property of her husband. But forty years ago, New York was one of the first states to enact what's called a Married Women's Property Law. It means you can own things that are yours and yours alone."

Sometimes the law did the right thing; it was a shame more people didn't know about it.

She lit up. "Miss Lockwood, if I could ask…the other day, you said you came from California? People go there to start over, don't they?" She looked so hopeful.

"Yes," I said, trying to ignore the feeling in my chest that always came when I thought of home, of what I'd lost. "I came East for a new beginning, but most folks do it the other way around. There are plenty of opportunities in California." How much would cross-country train fare cost for a woman and her four children?

* * *

At the appointed time, I made my way up those dark and uneven stairs to the Baumann apartment. I knocked. The eldest girl opened the door, nodded at me, and stepped back to let me pass. "Mama, the lawyer-lady is here."

"Thank you, Rosie." Margarethe Baumann was sitting at the kitchen table, rolling out a lump of dough and collapsing it back together again. I watched as she repeated the process twice more before meeting my eyes with an expression of blank despair. "They're gone. The teacups, they're gone."

And with them, possibility. Something tightened inside me as I looked at the shelf where they'd been kept. There was an empty space, and the sturdy blue and white china stood alone. I could scarcely breathe. "Do you know when it happened?"

"I stepped out just before noon. I went around the corner to pick up some flour and eggs. When I returned, they were gone." Her eyes welled with tears.

"Were the children here?"

She shook her head. "They're at school, all except Rosie. She finally caught the cold that the others had. But she came along with me to see if the fresh air would make her feel better. We got caught up, chatting with the shopkeeper's wife about this and that, but we weren't gone more than fifteen or twenty minutes. When we came back, the cups and saucers were all missing."

"Was the door locked? Was anything else disturbed?"

"I locked it and pocketed the key on my way out. When we returned, the door was still locked, and everything was just as we'd left it. Everything except the one thing that was going to make all the difference." She abruptly resumed rolling out the dough.

"Did anyone know how valuable they were?"

"No. I only told Rosie." Rolling it out, again. "Not even her father. He… sometimes he can be foolish about money. I thought it was best."

After meeting Peter Baumann the previous week, I'd made some inquiries about him. An obliging friend, more familiar with the saloons and gaming rooms of the Bowery than I, discovered that Baumann was known to fancy his luck at faro and dice. His wife's caution was only sensible.

Margarethe Baumann frowned, a line forming between her eyes. "There was a man here the other day, a Russian, I think. He said the landlord had sent him. He admired my tea set, only because his mother had one like it. But he didn't say anything about it being valuable."

"If he works for the landlord, it's quite likely he has access to a passkey, which would let him into any apartment in the building. If he happened past and saw you were out, it would have been easy enough for him to run up, grab the dishes and…." But even as I said it, I saw the flaw in the argument. For safety in transporting the delicate china, he'd need a padded box, like the one I was carrying. He'd need to be prepared.

"He was so kind," she said. "He told me stories about back home." Her eyes misted a little. "And he asked about mine."

There was no point in contacting the police. On the Lower East Side, the theft of a household item was unlikely to place highly on their list of priorities. And they wouldn't be likely to believe its value. The poor woman, so close to something that could have meant such a difference to her, and then this.

I had other resources, however, and I wouldn't give up until I'd exhausted those.

* * *

25

In my line of work, it was useful to have a wide acquaintance in all walks of life. Ulysses Blake was a friend I'd known back home who'd come to New York and found himself in a city that only occasionally overlapped with mine. Not to put too fine a point on it, he was associated with, if not quite a member of, the Old Towners gang, a criminal organization with a wide and varied reach south of Fourteenth Street. A few days later, we were sitting in my office, with me at my desk and Blake in an armchair opposite, his long legs drawn up and his hat in his hands. His dark hair was slightly ruffled, and he wore his big city suit with an air that suggested he was just as likely to get on horseback and ride away as he was to catch the next streetcar.

"Any luck on the Baumann matter?" I asked.

He cracked a smile, which widened into a lopsided grin, and his broad shoulders shifted to a relaxed position. "Emma, you will be the death of me. I've just spent two days asking hardened criminals about teacups. You can imagine the kind of jokes that are going around about me now…or maybe you can't."

The door opened and Lucy came in with a tray. She handed me a cup—a quite ordinary one—and another to Blake.

"That's how you take it, Mister Blake, right? Milk, no sugar?" She stood, gazing at my visitor, who turned his dark eyes and impish smile on her but just nodded his response. Finally, as she showed no signs of leaving, I hinted that there were some documents on her desk that I needed sooner rather than later.

"Another victim of your manly charms," I winked.

Blake gave me a look. "She deserves better. Getting back to the matter at hand, nobody's seen any stolen dinnerware in the past few days. But Peter Baumann's been back to his old ways. He lost heavily at cards at The Blue Swan the other night."

"With money that belonged to his wife."

"Sounds like it."

I sighed. "At least they have an agreement with the landlord for now. But how long before Peter Baumann's gotten his family evicted permanently?"

Blake nodded. "Men shouldn't have families if they can't do right by them.

I'll stop by tomorrow if I find out anything more."

But the next day, Peter Baumann was dead.

* * *

Baumann was found at the bottom of that dark, uneven flight of stairs that led to the fourth floor of the building on Norfolk Street, his neck broken. Apparently, he had been on his way home. I read about it in a small article in the *Journal-American* that Lucy brought to my attention. We found something in the *World* as well but apparently, the *New York Times* did not consider Peter Baumann's death among "All the News That's Fit to Print." Although he hadn't been a good husband, without his income or the windfall of the teacup sale, Margarethe Baumann was going to have difficulty supporting herself and her children.

According to the papers, the police were called in by the building's janitor, who lived in a basement apartment. After a cursory examination, the officers determined that there was no evidence of foul play and moved on to more pressing matters. The newspapers did likewise, as an accident wasn't really news unless someone was launching a crusade for tenement reform. Peter Baumann wasn't an appealing figurehead.

Ulysses Blake did the rounds of Baumann's favorite Bowery haunts. Witnesses at The Blue Swan, O'Malley's, and The Brown Bear Tavern told him that Baumann had been drinking for days. He'd even bought a few rounds for the house at The Blue Swan.

I waited a day or two, wondering if I would be intruding. It wasn't as if Margarethe Baumann and I were friends. Then I went around to the Norfolk Street flat to see if there was anything I could do for the widow and her children. I'd brought a lantern with me, not wanting to trust the darkened stairs myself. When my foot slipped slightly, I checked, and it seemed as though the step had been waxed recently.

When I got to the Baumanns' door, I knocked, but there was no answer. Perhaps a neighbor could tell me where the family had gone. Two of the other flats on the floor stood empty, their doors ajar. A ladder and some brushes suggested they were being repainted for new tenants. When I knocked on the fourth, there was no answer.

The janitor knew nothing about the departure. He hadn't been given any notice. We went back up to the apartment together, and it was completely empty, the toy wagon I'd seen on my first visit now broken and the only thing left behind.

"Sometimes when they can't pay their rent, they just slip out like that. They don't usually take all their furniture with them though, not without being seen," he said.

I handed him a couple of my business cards. "If you hear from them, please let me know. And here's a spare for the neighbor on the floor. Was he or she friendly with the Baumanns?"

"She's a widow who lives alone. Her children are grown now, and she's working somewhere during the days," he said.

I remembered what Margarethe had said about not having someone who could watch the children anymore since her neighbor had taken a factory job. The janitor said he knew nothing about the landlord sending anyone to collect the rent, fix the stove, or anything of the sort, and was certain he would have been notified.

I thanked him for the information.

A few days later, Blake and I met in my office again. After Lucy's third interruption, I sent her home for the evening, assuring her that I had matters well in hand. The look she gave me was not that of a cheerful employee.

"She's rather taken with you, I'm afraid," I said.

He shook his head. "You need to find her a nice young man, then. And find one for yourself, Em. I worry about you here in the office alone every evening."

"*You* worry about *me*? With the company you keep these days? But, to the matter at hand, have you heard anything more about Peter Baumann? Or the mysterious Russian who worked for the landlord? The one the janitor knew nothing about?"

"Nothing." He paused as the outer door slammed shut behind the departing Lucy. "Have you considered that there may not be a Russian? That

28

Margarethe had a friend or neighbor in for tea who told her she might have something valuable?"

"She looked into it, and sold the cups on her own? Handed her husband just enough to go on a drinking bout, giving her and the children enough time to get away?" Suddenly things became clearer. "And the tea set was probably hidden somewhere in the apartment when I was last there. Margarethe was going on about the theft—I wasn't sure whether Peter was responsible, or if she was afraid of the beating he would give her."

"Not a bad actress, then. You're not easily fooled."

"I thought that, too. Until just now." I met his eyes, then looked away.

"Dinner?" he asked.

"That would be lovely."

But there were things I didn't tell him, not that night, not ever. I've dedicated my life to the law. No one should get away with murder. But what about a woman like Margarethe Baumann, tied to a man who made her life miserable? Who saw a chance at something better, and then feared it slipping away again? What might she do? And, wrong as her actions were, could I understand them?

There was no proof, of course, just a series of possibilities. The recently waxed step on the ill-kept staircase. The broken toy cart, its missing wheel perhaps left at the top of the stairs accidentally…or not. And, carrying my lantern up the staircase, near the top I'd seen a small fragment of string which could have been broken off something which Margarethe Baumann, or perhaps her sympathetic neighbor, had carefully collected. The police weren't looking for clues, not when a drunken man plunged down a dark and uneven staircase.

And Margarethe Baumann was long gone.

* * *

I got the letter a month later. I found it in a pile that Lucy left on my desk when I was out at court, and I opened it between a request that we excuse a client his fee for another month, and an invitation to some ridiculous charity event. The handwriting was unfamiliar, in precise German script. But I knew the author's identity before I'd even begun to read.

Dear Miss Lockwood:

I expect you are surprised to hear from me. You have probably figured out by now that I already knew about the teacups. When Mrs. Thompson gave them to me, she told me they were precious. "If I give you money, Margarethe, your husband might find it and spend it. But no one will know that these are valuable, no one except you. Something to keep you safe and hidden right in plain sight."

Of course in those days, I was in love with Peter, and could not imagine things would go wrong the way they did. But the children came, too many, too soon, and he forgot how to love. I've often wondered how Mrs. Thompson knew I would need her gift someday.

I stayed as long as I could. He raised his hand to me, but never to the children. But when he started in on Rosie, I knew it was time.

A friend is mailing this from another town. And we've changed our names, the children and I. So, if you're thinking that maybe what I did deserves punishment, despite everything, you won't find me. But you were kind to me, and I felt badly about fooling you.

California really is a good place to start over.

MB

* * *

Catherine Siemann is an academic and writer. With a J.D. from NYU, a Ph.D. in Victorian literature from Columbia, and a stack of old family documents and photographs to spark her imagination, writing historical mysteries set in late nineteenth-century New York City felt almost inevitable. Her first novel, *Courting Anna* (2019), was published under the pseudonym Cate Simon. She is currently at work on a full-length mystery featuring pioneering woman lawyer Emma Lockwood. Catherine lives in the East Village, a few blocks from where her great-grandfather had a grocery shop in the 1890s, with her partner and perhaps too many cats.

THE ART OF PAYBACK

by Cathi Stoler

The Motive

The prestigious Michalopoulou & Jensen Gallery was packed. The glitterati of the New York art world were all in attendance, including the man I'd set my sights on, standing alone in front of a ghastly mixed media work.

I could have killed him right here, I thought, as I sidled up to him, flashing back on the vial of potassium chloride I'd almost tucked into my little black Bottega Veneta cocktail bag. *Just a few drops in his champagne and then watch as his heart stopped.* But that would've been too easy. For him. Not for me. Reducing him to ruins would be infinitely better and so much more satisfying.

"Hmmm," I muttered as I tilted my head to the side and pretended to absorb the painting in front of us. "What do you think?" I asked without turning toward him.

I could feel him glancing at me, taking in my face, then moving his beady eyes over the rest of me. You couldn't miss the dollar signs sliding into place like cherries on a slot machine as he took in my slit-up-the-front, Prabal Gurung black sheath and the diamonds dripping from my ears and circling my wrists. "Dressed to kill" fell well short of the mark.

"Well, Ms...." He let his words trail off.

It was time to meet the devil head on. I extended my hand. "Carstairs. Cameron Carstairs." I paused for a moment and curved my lips into a small smile. "And you are?" I asked seductively.

He held on to my hand as he replied. "Frederick Bartholome. Enchanted to meet you."

Frederick didn't recognize me. Why would he? The last time he'd seen me, I was dressed in ripped jeans, an oversized sweatshirt, and a bandana covering my then-blond hair. I looked like a drudge. One he wouldn't even deign to acknowledge.

It was a long time ago, right before he stole the Picasso from my mother's gallery. Right before he ruined her reputation and she killed herself.

"You never answered my question." I gestured with my champagne flute toward the painting in a slightly impatient manner. I knew how much he loved giving his opinion. Frederick Bartholome was a dealer in art masterworks. Think van Gogh, Vermeer, Monet, Picasso. And, as he liked to say, he was "conversant in art." His métier included brokering the works of the most famous artists in the world. Well, the dead ones.

I could count my mother's Picasso among them. He'd certainly applied his professional skills to making her and the painting his project, pretending to cosset and protect them both. But she was a mere small gallery owner who had the misfortune to meet evil face-to-face and fall under its spell.

Now it was my turn. "Frederick," I said, drawing out the word. "Your name sounds so familiar."

Of course, he preened. "You may have heard of me. I have a small reputation in the art world. I am a dealer. Art is my life."

"Oh." I made myself look impressed, eyes widening as though I'd recalled him.

"Cameron, would you like to continue our conversation over dinner?" he asked. There's a lovely French bistro just around the corner."

I was sure he meant Pourquoi, the most pretentious place in SoHo that served some of the worst food.

I smiled sweetly. "I'd be delighted. I've recently returned from several years living in Europe and it's unbelievably fortunate our paths have crossed." I laid my hand on his. "I just inherited a painting and I'm sure I could benefit from your advice. While I appreciate art, I'm used to seeing it in my friends' apartments or hanging in museums. This is my first gallery opening." I paused and looked around the room at the monstrosities on the wall. "I'm no connoisseur and really, it's a bit overwhelming." Well, they were ugly.

"Not to worry, my dear. I'd be glad to guide you."

I bet you would. I took the arm he offered and allowed him to lead me out of the gallery.

The line was cast. Now, all that remained was to reel him in.

* * *

The Means

Over dinner I discussed my inheritance, trying to emphasize my supposed lack of knowledge. "The painting was left to me by a distant second cousin in Scotland, Alistair McPherson, who, as my lawyer explained, was an under-the-radar collector."

"You mean this cousin obtained the painting illegally?" he asked.

"Oh…I…no…" I replied, avoiding his gaze, a telltale sign of lying. "Not really. Just…quietly, shall we say. I believe it's very valuable, but I'm not sure of the worth, or how to…manage it."

I'd made my point. If he suspected I thought my painting was illegally obtained, he'd be certain he could manipulate me and persuade me to sell it.

"Has your painting been evaluated by a professional?"

I couldn't miss the skepticism in his voice. He'd assumed I was talking about some minor piece of art and inflating its value. I couldn't wait to see his reaction when I told him the artist's name.

"Cousin Alistair hired a very discreet person who authenticated the painting and explained that the provenance was irreproachable, but I'm uncertain what to do with it. My attorney thought it might be wise to keep it for a while, then sell it when I'm ready." I sighed in frustration. "I understand the tax bill would be astronomical, and I prefer to spend my money on other things." I fingered my diamond bracelet to make my point.

I could see he was wavering, beginning to think my painting might actually be worth something. "Who is the artist?" he asked as he refilled my wine glass.

The question I'd been waiting for. "Picasso."

He could hardly keep his hand from shaking as he set down the wine bottle.

"Cameron, are you sure? A Picasso…. It could be quite valuable. You need to be certain."

Really? I watched those dollar signs slide back into his eyes.

He steepled his hands and brought his fingers to his lips. "There is a way to sell it legally and avoid the taxes, that is if you're prepared to part with it."

"How?" I made myself sound doubtful. "Is that even possible? What would I have to do?"

"Have you ever heard of Free Ports?" he asked. "That might be the perfect solution for your situation."

He'd gotten there faster than I thought he would. I know he kept my mother's stolen Picasso at a Free Port in Nassau, The Bahamas. It was the perfect place for it, he'd told her. Safe and secure from everyone…but him.

"Free Ports? What are those?" I asked, pulling the line tighter.

* * *

My mother's gallery had been in SoHo long before it became a hot spot for the art scene. The inventory was reflective of her spirit—colorful works bursting with vibrancy from talented painters. I was her unpaid assistant, cataloguing the art, doing the books, and helping with whatever needed doing.

Then, on a buying trip to Paris, she happened to venture into what was little more than a secondhand shop and spotted the Picasso behind a pile of paintings collecting dust. She couldn't believe what she was seeing. The technique, colors, and composition—everything shouted it was an original, even though it wasn't signed, with just a scrawled PP on the back. She thought it was a precursor to his *Les Femmes d'Alger* series, most likely a small study of a figure for one of his earlier paintings. She knew the paintings in the series were now selling for astronomical prices.

How had this painting not been discovered before, she'd wondered? She purchased it and brought it back to New York. It would have to be authenticated. If it were real, and the provenance could be searched, it would be a tremendous windfall. If it were just a good copy, well, she hadn't paid that much for it.

A friend recommended Frederick Bartholome, who was known for his knowledge of Picasso. He examined the painting, then brought it around to several other experts who declared it an original.

My mother was stunned. She had hoped for the best but never expected it to happen. Christie's said they would feature it in their next auction. They promoted it in the trade papers and magazines and my mom's gallery became a new destination for collectors. Frederick told her it was too risky to leave the painting in the gallery and that he would make sure it was safe and secure where no one could get to it. He would store it in his Free Port space in Nassau.

Right before the auction, Frederick brought the painting back to my mother's gallery for a press party and publicity photos. A few days later, he and she delivered it to Christie's, where to her horror, it was reexamined and declared a fake.

Frederick denied any knowledge of how that could have happened. He insinuated my mother had tricked him; that he would never have his name associated with such deceit.

Of course, people believed him. He was an art superstar, my mother a wannabe.

She was never the same after that. She fell into a deep depression and ultimately, unable to live with the disgrace, she took her own life.

I knew the truth. Frederick had switched my mother's real Picasso for a good copy, and I'd bet my life, the original was still in his Free Port in Nassau. I'd led him to believe the painting I'd invented was genuine and the idea of getting his hands on it was too tempting for him to pass up.

* * *

The Opportunity

Frederick invited me to the Bahamas to see how a Free Port worked. "Do you have the painting stored here in New York? I would love to examine it, and perhaps we could bring it with us."

"Unfortunately, it's still in Scotland, waiting for me to decide what to do. But please explain how this works."

Of course, I already knew. Free Ports were warehouses in certain free-trade zones where wealthy people store their valuable assets—art, precious gems, antiques, gold, and wine collections—while deferring taxes. There were conference rooms and private offices where people could do business. Buy. Sell. Make boatloads of money without the bother of paying tariffs. That is, if the goods never left the premises. It was all very hush-hush, and best of all, for my purposes, anyone could bring in goods for an owner.

Our day trip to Nassau was quick. Frederick gave me a tour of the facility and showed me the well-appointed space he rented. Recessed lighting added a soft glow over a waist-high burl cabinet topped with marble, with slots underneath for crated paintings. Each crate had initials stenciled on the side, so it would be easy to recognize the artist and access the work. I found the one with the double "PP" and knew it was my mother's.

I acted as though he were a genius to discover this Free Port and said I would have my painting shipped over in a day or two as soon as the paperwork was arranged. That is, if he were willing to keep it for me.

He couldn't say yes fast enough.

When we landed back in New York, I told Frederick I would be away for a few days and therefore, out of touch. He seemed relieved. Probably because he was going to spend the time planning how to steal my 'Picasso.'

* * *

The Payback

A day later I headed back to Nassau on a private jet. I breezed through customs—just another rich tourist in dark glasses and expensive clothes, carrying a very large designer tote bag.

I arranged for the pilot to wait for me at the airport and be ready to depart for New York as soon as I returned. Then, I took a taxi to the Free Port.

There, anonymity was assured, and no one challenged me. I swiped in using the key card I'd slipped from Frederick's jacket on the flight home and entered Room 2207.

Six of the slots held crates. The initials on the outside of each were a key to the paintings they contained. I opened each crate and carefully removed the paintings and lined them up on top of the cabinet. Each was a masterpiece by an artist ranging from Cezanne to Vermeer to Degas.

When I was there earlier with Frederick, I'd noticed a small tool kit on a cabinet at the back of the room. He mentioned it was filled with art restoration supplies and several tools he occasionally used for his work. I smiled as I opened it and found exactly what I would use to do mine.

I gently removed the paintings from their frames then used a small plier to pull out the staples holding the canvases to their stretchers. When this was complete, I rolled the canvases and transferred them to the false bottom in my bag. Their value was extraordinary. Hundreds of millions of dollars which would soon be *my* millions.

When I finished, I returned the stretchers, frames, and crates to their slots. Except for the one that had held my Picasso. There was one more thing to do before I left for home.

Next time Frederick visited the Free Port, he'd find the shelves bare and the note I left for him next to the empty frame on top of the counter. And search though he might, he'd never find me.

Frederick, you took everything from me. Now, it's my turn. Payback is a bitch, isn't it?

—*Cameron*

* * *

Cathi Stoler's Murder on the Rocks Series features The Corner Lounge owner, Jude Dillane, and includes *Bar None, Last Call* and *Straight Up*, published by Level Best Books. She's also written the suspense novels *Nick of Time* and *Out of Time* and the Laurel and Helen New York Mysteries. She is a board member of Sisters in Crime New York/Tri-State, MWA and ITW. You can reach her at www.cathistoler.com.

THE NEW GUY

by Anne-Marie Sutton

L aura Pearson hurried up the stairs of the subway exit, skillfully avoiding the half-eaten pizza slice on the top step, and walked down Twenty-eighth Street to the coffee shop where she always got her breakfast.

At the corner newsstand, she looked at the front page of the *New York Times*. There was a picture of President Richard Nixon having an audience with Pope Paul VI in the Vatican. The President of Egypt, dead of a heart attack. Laura wasn't sure if Nasser was one of the good guys in the Middle East or a baddie. They had studied the Middle East situation in her current events class when she was in high school. Nothing seemed to change.

The Saber Coffee Shop, with its Technicolor logo of a large curved-blade sword, was run by two brothers, Sol and Bernie. Laura never had to give her order; it was always ready by the time she stepped to the front of the line. Coffee with cream, two sugars, and a buttered roll. Once she saw another customer order a croissant, and she wavered. But when her turn came, her bag was ready to go, and she thanked Bernie with a smile. She couldn't hurt his feelings by changing her order.

* * *

The New York & Gotham Insurance Company was located in an imposing building with gray stone facing. Laura pushed the revolving door and heard a familiar male voice behind her.

"Wait for me."

Laura turned to see her colleague Rick Angelini squeeze in behind her. As usual, he looked bright-eyed and full of energy. It must be the air on Staten Island, she thought. She'd never been in the borough in her life but had a picture in her mind of lots of green space and water.

In the elevator, Rick pushed the button for the fourteenth floor. It was actually the thirteenth, but the building had been designed by turn-of-the-century people who thought the number thirteen was unlucky, so the thirteenth floor had been eliminated.

The communications department was a small one. A vice president, George Rayburn, oversaw two sections: advertising and public relations. Charley Krauser, assisted by Rick, took care of advertising. Chris Laurier managed the PR duties by himself. He enjoyed working alone.

Laura wrote and edited the company's monthly employee magazine, *The Beacon*. It was an important communications tool for the company, but it was 'internal' communications. Always less regarded than the 'external' communications, which the men in the department oversaw.

That fact didn't bother Laura as much as one might think. She was a young woman with other ambitions…and a trust fund. Her goal was to write novels, and she was accumulating the life experience she would use to create her stories.

* * *

On Tuesdays, the communications department held the weekly staff meeting. George, looking like the handsome, dark-haired ad man he once was, sat at the head of the table. His secretary Maggie O'Sullivan, a gray-haired, twenty-five-year employee of the company, was at his elbow to take notes. Charley, Rick, Chris, and Laura filled out the table.

George called for updates, and each staff member talked about the status of their projects. Rarely did anything arise out of the ordinary. Charley always had lunch with the ad agency on Fridays, and at this particular meeting, he showed proofs of the new print ads set to run in October. Rick nodded agreement with everything Charley said. Advertising was George's favorite part of the operation, often tagging along for the Friday expense-account-paid lunches at fashionable midtown restaurants so he could hear the latest industry gossip.

Chris, in his usual laconic voice, updated everyone on the Good Health campaign instituted by the company's CEO. This new series of canned features focused on sexually transmitted diseases, a topic Laura thought daring. But CEO Jim Bradford was a forward-thinking top executive who took his social responsibilities seriously.

Laura ended with the status of the coming month's *Beacon*. She had interviewed the Employee of the Month and was now planning the next story in the Get to Know a Department series. This month she was highlighting the actuarial department.

Normally, at this point in the meeting, George would thank everyone for their efforts and dismiss them. But today he sat solemnly, his fingers outstretched in a steeple. The staff waited expectantly.

"Is there something else, George?" Charley asked impatiently. There was no smoking at these meetings, and it was hard for Charley to go very long without a cigarette.

"Yes," George said. "I have an announcement." He paused as everyone waited.

"As you probably know, the company instituted a diversity program in the spring. New York & Gotham has a number of government contracts to provide group insurance to several federal departments. And as such, we are subject to the government's guidelines for equal opportunity in employment."

Equal opportunity for men only, Laura thought. *If we have equal opportunity, send me to those Friday lunches.*

"The company's management trainee program has been designed to offer qualified minorities a chance to work for a large company such as ours. Each man interns in various departments of the company on a two-month rotation."

Each man.

"Beginning next week, it is the communications department's turn to welcome one of these trainees. He's just finished a stint with Legal, and Dave Larson assures me he's a highly intelligent fellow. I trust you will make him feel at home here in Communications."

"One of *them* is coming here?" Charley's voice cracked with rage.

"Them?" a frowning George asked.

"You heard me," Charley yelled. "Well, I for one, have no intention of working with one of them!"

* * *

"Well, that was interesting," Rick said as he and Laura walked back to their offices at the rear of the department.

"I can't believe Charley is that prejudiced," Laura said. "I mean, this is 1970. We have civil rights and equal opportunity laws. He has to get over it."

"Guys like Charley never get over it."

"If I ever had any respect for him—which come to think of it I probably haven't—I'm still surprised. Do you think he means it? That he won't work with this new guy because he's Black?"

"When does that drunk ever do any work around here? I'm the one who carries the load in advertising. That's not coffee in that cup he's always drinking from."

* * *

The following Monday, Laura looked up from her desk to see George Rayburn standing with a young man in the doorway.

"Hi, George. What can I do for you?"

George stepped into the room and motioned for his companion to follow.

"Laura, I want you to meet Nathaniel Spencer. He's the trainee who will be working with us for two months."

Laura came around her desk to shake the young man's outstretched hand.

"Pleased to meet you, Nathaniel," Laura said. "I hope you'll like working with us. We are a small department, but we have lots of interesting responsibilities." She hoped she sounded welcoming. Nathaniel looked a bit nervous.

"Thank you, Laura," Nathaniel replied in a soft voice. "I'm looking forward to it."

"Nathaniel, Laura here edits the employees' magazine," George said. "It comes out once a month, and she is just beginning the issue for October. I thought you could start by working with her. It's a good way to get to know what's going on inside the company."

Laura hesitated before answering. She had completed planning the issue and wanted to move ahead with the interviews and then writing the stories. She didn't have time to coach someone who might not be able to work quickly enough to meet a deadline. But before she had time to finish her sentence, George was gone.

"Okay," she said, smiling at the new trainee. "Have you done much writing, Nathaniel? Take any journalism classes in school?"

"You can call me 'Nat'."

"Why don't you sit down, Nat?"

Nat sat in the only other chair in the room. Laura went back behind her desk.

"I think I'm a decent writer," he said. "I've always liked writing my papers in school."

"Where did you go to college?"

"I live in Flatbush. I went to Brooklyn College and majored in business administration."

"And you enjoyed that?"

"I figured that was the major I would need to get a job in business."

"I'm sure you're right. This training program is made for you."

Nat laughed. "As a Black man, I take whatever opportunities I can get. You probably don't understand how that is."

"You think? Try being a woman in this testosterone zone. What job opportunities are there for women in business?"

"I think that's changing."

"Not around here. I'm strictly confined to covering 'so you want to know how to process an insurance claim in ten minutes or less' stories."

"Well, I'm here to learn," Nat said.

* * *

George Rayburn didn't enjoy his monthly meetings with the company's CEO. Jim Bradford usually overwhelmed him with ideas and suggestions on how the communications department should function. George generally found himself taking voluminous notes and afterwards wondering what he should do with them.

"So, I'm anxious to hear how your new trainee is doing, George," Jim said.

"He's been working with Laura Pearson on this month's issue of the *Beacon*. She tells me he's a fast learner."

Jim frowned. "I thought you would have him working on something more important than the employee magazine."

"Did I mention Laura said that he's a good writer?"

"I have high hopes for Nathaniel. We've taken on several of these trainees.

Most will fit into the claims departments and other aspects of our internal operations. But I see Nathaniel capable of doing bigger things."

"Ah, yes," George said weakly. "What exactly did you have in mind for him, Jim?"

"Certainly more important work than writing for the employees."

"Right. Well, seeing as we know he's a good writer, I thought I'd be moving him on to work with Chris Laurier on the PR side of things. Nathaniel can write some press releases," George said cheerily, as if this had been his plan all along.

"What kind of PR do we need around here? We're an insurance company. Everybody knows what we do."

"There's the Good Health campaign."

Jim shrugged. "We have to do community public service like that. It's not challenging."

"Maybe Nathaniel could suggest some topics to appeal to the Black community."

"I won't have you embarrass Nathaniel by categorizing him as the guy who works on Black issues."

"No, no," George sputtered. "That's the last thing I would suggest."

"Good. Because I want you to put him to work on our advertising campaigns. I feel they need a jump start in a new direction."

"But Charley Krauser handles that," George protested. "He's done it for years."

"Exactly. And that's why we need the input of a young person, not some middle-aged hack like Krauser who's past it."

"But Nathaniel would have to work with Charley."

"Naturally. He'll go with him to the advertising agency and discuss some new ideas. I bet Adams and Danzinger have a whole staff of bright young copywriters and account execs who would love the chance to offer us a new media approach. What do you think, George? Am I on to something here?"

George couldn't talk. His right knee had started shaking.

He would have to tell Charley to work with Nathaniel.

"Yes," Jim continued, a pleased look on his face. "This Nathaniel Spencer's a smart one. I see a bright future for him at New York & Gotham. And getting him involved in the company's advertising is the right way to start him off."

* * *

"Table for three," Rick told the hostess at Olson's, a popular restaurant a few blocks from the office. She grabbed menus, and the trio followed her across the noisy room.

"I need a beer," Laura said as she sank into a chair. "It's been a busy week, and it's not even Friday yet. How about you, Nat? What's your poison?"

"Beer's fine."

The waitress came and took their order. Three Sam Adams on draft.

"So how are things working out, Nat?" Rick asked, chewing on a breadstick. "Is Laura here a good boss?"

Nat looked embarrassed, and Laura gave Rick a poke in the arm. "Leave the kid alone, he's doing fine." She turned to Nat. "That story on the new computer operating system was very readable for people who don't understand computers."

"Thanks, Laura."

Their beer came, and they each took a grateful swig.

"I'm going to miss having Nat's help when he rotates to another area of the department." Laura smiled at Rick. "Maybe advertising is next?"

"Oh, I don't know," Nat said uneasily. It was obvious to all that, back at the office, a certain person was pointedly ignoring Nat's presence.

"Has Charley talked to you since you've been here?" Laura asked Nat.

"No," he answered. "And I stay out of his way. It's obvious the man hates me."

"That's not right," Laura said vehemently. "George has got to do something about that."

"Yeah, and the Buffalo Bills are going to win the next Super Bowl." Rick laughed.

"It's all right," Nat said. "I'm used to it. I don't like it, but I'm used to it."

"That doesn't make it right. I *am* going to talk to George." The beer was fueling her anger.

"I wish you wouldn't," Nat said. "I can take care of myself."

"Oh, my man," Rick said. "I guess you don't know about Laura's past. You're looking at the woman who led the desegregation of lunch counters in Bronxville, New York. She even got arrested, didn't you, Lar?"

Laura's face reddened.

"Really?" Nat was interested. "Tell me about it."

"It was in college," Laura explained. "I went to college in Bronxville. At Sarah Lawrence. In the sixties, all the students wanted to protest segregation and do their part to support civil rights. The restaurants in Bronxville didn't serve Blacks. A group of students decided to do something about it."

"And you got arrested?"

"Our girl was faced with jail, Nat. Blonde, blue-eyed Laura Pearson."

"I was ready to go. I wasn't afraid."

"Jail in Bronxville? What's to be scared of?" Rick said, shaking his head. "They probably order the prisoners' food from those restaurants you were protesting."

"My dad is a lawyer up in Connecticut, Nat. He came down and talked to the judge in the case. We all got off with a warning."

The conversation stopped when the waitress arrived. They all ordered cheeseburgers.

"Another round?" the waitress asked, and Rick answered 'yes' for everyone.

* * *

As the threesome returned from lunch, they were greeted with loud shouting in the communications department.

Bobbie Howard, Charley's secretary, explained. "Charley and Mr. Rayburn are having a terrible argument."

"About what?" Rick asked.

Bobbie hesitated, looking directly at Nat.

"Me?"

Bobbie nodded. "I'm afraid so. I've never seen Mr. Rayburn so angry."

Rick pushed past her and headed for Charley's office. He found the two men glaring at each other.

"I told you what you have to do," George said. "Work with Nathaniel. That's it, Charley. Do it or resign."

"I'm not resigning," Charley said, his words slurred. "I got over twenty years in this company, and I want my pension. I'm staying right here."

Rick waited for George's answer. If ever there was an opportunity to fire his lazy alcoholic head of advertising, it was now.

"Well, George," Charley prodded. "What are you going to do? Nothing. Why don't you take the easy way out and send him over to work with Chris in PR?"

"I can't do that, Charley," George said slowly. "He's got to be in advertising."

"I can work with him, George," Rick said. "Let me and Nat work together. What about it, Charley?"

"Keep him away from me, Rick. And don't even think of taking him to the Friday lunches with Adams and Danzinger."

Outside Charley's office, the staff listened intently. Nat's face was grim as he followed the turmoil caused by his arrival. Next to him, Chris Laurier's cheeks were flaming with anger.

"I wish George would find his backbone and get rid of him once and for all," Chris said.

"Oh, I agree," Laura said, impressed that Chris was so supportive of Nat's situation. "But I don't think he will. As you say, he's got no backbone."

"You know Charley felt the same about me when I first came to the department in '63," Chris said.

"Really?"

"He told everyone I was gay. And to keep away from me."

"Oh, I'm so sorry." Laura had never considered Chris's private life.

"At first I didn't know why the others were so awkward around me."

"I wonder what he says about me behind my back," said Laura.

"That you're nothing but a spoiled rich kid," Chris said.

"That's contemptible."

"Not as much as being gay."

"Or being Black," Nat said, finally joining the conversation.

"Then it seems that we all have a reason for wanting Charley to go," Laura said.

* * *

The next day, the office had a funereal atmosphere. Both Charley and Chris stayed in their offices behind closed doors. Rick, far from being his usual gregarious self, worked quietly in his office. George's door was ajar; he could be seen reading reports.

Laura and Nat sat in her office proofreading the galleys for *The Beacon*.

"I'm sorry this is my last day working with you," Nat said.

"I am, too," Laura said. "I wasn't sure in the beginning how I would feel about having another person help write the magazine. But you have real talent. Have you ever considered a career that uses your writing skills?"

"It's funny you would ask that. No offense to you, Laura, but I really enjoyed my time in the legal department. It got me thinking about going to law school. You need to be a good writer to be a lawyer."

"I'll have to get you to meet my father. He can give you the skinny on law school. He's on some big alumni committee up at Yale. Maybe he could sponsor your application."

"Yale? I don't think I'll be going to Yale Law School. My family could never afford it."

"You got in the equal opportunity program here. I'm sure Yale has got all kinds of programs to help minorities like yourself." She shook her head. "I hear they've even started encouraging more women to apply."

"Why don't you? You've got better writing skills than I do."

"No, one of these days I'm going to write novels."

* * *

When Charley and Rick left for their Friday lunch with the ad agency, George didn't accompany them.

After Rick returned from lunch, he stopped by Laura's office where she and Nat were finishing up on the galleys. She asked him how things had gone.

"Rough," he said in a tired voice. "Charley drank even more than usual, and I might have, too. In fact, I think I'll be drinking all next week if this madness continues."

"Did Charley talk any more about working with Nat?"

Rick eyed Nat who was staring up at him.

"I don't see this going smoothly, Nat. You're in for a rough couple of weeks."

"I can handle it."

"No, don't handle it. I'll back you up on any complaint you make to Management about Charley's treatment of you."

"We both will," Laura said.

* * *

Laura stayed later than usual that night to make sure everything was ready to go back to the printer on Monday. The office was quiet. She thought that she was the only one left working.

But, as she passed George's office, she saw the light was on.

"George?" she called. "Are you still here?"

She walked to his doorway. He was sitting at his desk.

"Working on a Friday night?"

"My wife and I are going to the theater tonight. I'm waiting until she calls and tells me that she's arrived at Penn Station."

"What are you seeing?"

"*No, No Nanette.* Wendy's been dying to see it."

"I heard it's good." She paused. "George, I'd like this opportunity to tell you that I've enjoyed working with Nathaniel. He has a bright future. Charley shouldn't get away with what he's doing to him. It's not right."

"What do you suggest I do, Laura?"

"Anybody else would be fired."

When George didn't answer, Laura added, "You know that's true. The whole staff knows it as well."

* * *

Maggie O'Sullivan got to her desk on Monday in a less than happy mood. The man sitting next to her on the subway train had spilled his coffee on her yellow coat sleeve. The cream had left an oily mark, and she needed to remove the stain. She always kept a bottle of carbon tetrachloride in the bottom drawer of her desk, and she looked for it as soon as she arrived.

"That's odd," Maggie said, pushing past old lipsticks and Band-Aids. "It's always here."

Everyone in the office borrowed it when they needed a quick cleanup for their soiled clothes, but they always returned the bottle afterward. Maggie insisted upon it.

Perhaps someone had put it in the wrong drawer, she thought, searching the entire desk carefully. But the carbon tet was nowhere to be found.

* * *

The first day of Nat's rotation in advertising found him in Rick's office, getting a tutorial on the media budget. Rick had wanted to show him more exciting aspects of the department, but that was Charley's territory, and he was isolating himself in his office. Rick had no desire to make the first move and bring him and Nat together.

Lunch hour came, and the office staff ate at their regular times, noon to one, or one to two. All but Charley. His office door remained closed.

When his secretary Bobbie came back at two, she asked the other secretaries if Charley had come out of his office while she was gone. *No, he hadn't.*

Bobbie started on her typing. all the while glancing at the closed door. This wasn't like Charley to miss his usual bar lunch.

51

At three o'clock she could stand it no longer. She really had to check on him. Perhaps he was sick.

Knocking first, she opened the door and looked in. "Charley, are you all right? Don't you feel well?"

Charley's head lay down on the desk blotter. His half-empty coffee cup sat next to the scotch bottle.

"Come on, Charley, it's time to get up. You have to go home soon. I think you've slept it off by now."

Bobbie tried to wake him. But when there was no response from his limp body, she became frightened and ran to get help.

"Maggie," she said. "Can you call the company doctor down in the health suite? I think something's wrong with Charley."

* * *

Once again, the staff crowded around Charley's door. The white-coated doctor was inside, and they could see him working on their colleague.

Finally, the doctor motioned for George to join him. They spoke in a low whisper.

George shook his head and turned to his staff.

"I'm afraid Charley's died."

Was it a heart attack? A stroke?

It was Chris who said happily, "I guess he's finally drunk himself to death."

But the doctor clearly wasn't interested in diagnoses by amateurs. He picked up the phone and dialed 911.

He could read the signs. The demise of Charley Krauser was no natural death.

* * *

As soon as the police and their team arrived, the staff was sequestered in an empty conference room under the watchful eye of two uniformed officers. Everyone sat with their own thoughts.

It didn't take Maggie long to connect the missing bottle of carbon tetrachloride with Charley's death. Before the staff had been escorted from the department, she had seen the coffee cup and scotch bottle on Charley's desk. Someone must have poisoned his whiskey using the cleaning fluid to do the job.

Taking a deep breath, she stood up and approached one of the officers, asking to speak to whoever was in charge of the investigation.

Detective Dugan listened with a great deal of interest.

"So, I'm right," Maggie said. "Charley was poisoned, wasn't he?"

"I'm afraid that's what it looks like, Mrs. O'Sullivan. Can you describe this bottle that's missing?"

"Small. Clear glass. Usually, you only need a dab or two to deal with a stain on clothes."

"Usually," the detective repeated.

But how much to kill a man, Maggie wondered?

A thorough search for the missing bottle commenced.

Meanwhile, each staff member was questioned. It didn't take long for Dugan to learn about Charley's belligerent personality and the hatred he had expressed toward Nathaniel.

Nathaniel was called back for a second interview with Dugan.

"Where is the bottle of carbon tet you stole from Maggie O'Sullivan's desk?"

"Carbon tet?' Nat asked. "I'm not sure what that is."

"Don't play dumb with me, boy," Dugan said in a harsh voice. "You used it to poison Charley Krauser who hated you, wouldn't work with you, was out to ruin your big opportunity in this company."

"Yes, he hated me because I'm Black," Nat said. "A lot of people do, and I haven't killed any of them yet."

"Let's see what the others can tell me about your movements today."

But no one could say that they had seen Nat going into Charley's office.

"The door stayed closed," Bobbie said. "Charley was in there all day. That's why I finally checked on him at three o'clock."

Dugan turned to Nat. "I know you did it. No one else has a motive."

"Are you sure?" Laura asked. "Charley was an odious man. We all disliked him."

"But who hated him enough to kill him? My money's on this Black guy, and I'm taking him down to the station."

"Don't be ridiculous," Rick shouted angrily "Where's your evidence? You haven't found that bottle."

"I can break him," Dugan said. "I've dealt with his kind before."

While one of the officers was handcuffing Nat, George Rayburn started mumbling to himself. Everyone turned to see him put his head in his hands.

"I did it, I did it," George repeated in a trembling voice. "I had to."

"You poisoned Charley's scotch?" Chris asked incredulously.

"Friday night," Laura said suddenly. "I left George here alone in the office. That's when no one could see him take the bottle of carbon tet from Maggie's desk and put some in Charley's scotch bottle. He knew Charley's habits, that he would start his drinking early in the day on Monday."

"Is this true, Mr. Rayburn?" Dugan asked George. "Are you confessing?"

"You have to understand," George said bleakly. "Jim Bradford told me Charley had to work with Nathaniel in advertising, and Charley refused to do what I wanted." He looked up. "I would get fired if I didn't follow Jim's directive."

"Why didn't you just fire Charley?" Rick asked. "He gave you enough reason to do it."

"I've never been able to fire anybody in my life." He shook his head. "Never could."

"So, you're saying that it was easier for you to kill Charley than to fire him?" Chris asked.

George looked calm now.

"Yes," he said. "Yes, it was."

* * *

Anne-Marie Sutton is the author of a mystery series set in Newport, Rhode Island, which includes *Murder Stalks a Mansion, Gilded Death, Keep My Secret* and *Invest in Death*. Her short mystery stories have appeared in the Sisters in Crime Murder New York Style anthology series and in collections from Darkhouse Books, also online at *Mysterical-E*. Two stories have been included in the *Best New England Crime Stories of 2015* and more recently in 2020. Her first ghost story was in the Association of Rhode Island Authors 2019 anthology, *Past, Present, and Future.*

A TRIAL FOR THE BOOKS

by D. M. Barr

T he courtroom set looked as realistic as I'd hoped it would. What luck, receiving this mock trial invite, coinciding perfectly with our visit to New York City. So unfortunate that the offer hadn't included Evelyn and the kids, but troopers that they were, they insisted I attend, suggesting that an in-person account of a reality show would be great fodder for my next blog entry. I'd pay for the indulgence though, the credit card charges from Bloomingdale's would be an expensive reminder of their "sacrifice."

I'd never ventured so far west. The Twelfth Avenue building looked abandoned, but maybe that's what Manhattan was all about, saving money by filming in odd locations one eviction notice short of foreclosure. Still, the cameramen were in place and the producers had promised me a video of the entire proceedings, something wonderful to post on my "Crime Fiction Today" blog. The post would, no doubt, persuade some of my subscribers to book an appearance themselves, priceless exposure that was exactly why I was certain "You Be the Defendant" had chosen me.

"Are you comfortable, Mr. Elias? Can I get you some water, or coffee, perhaps, before we begin?" asked the showrunner, stopping by the Defense table where I sat with my lawyer for the day, a twenty-something Cardozo law student who'd introduced herself as "Miss Stepp." A pseudonym, I assumed; everyone involved must be actors, like at the murder mystery dinner theater I'd attended back in Tulsa.

"I'm good, thank you. This is all so…realistic. I appreciate the effort involved."

"Well, if you appreciate this, you'll really love what's coming. Enjoy the trial. Not everyone gets convicted, you know!" She flitted past the judge's bench and then behind the curtains.

"Well, that's reassuring," I told Miss Stepp with a smirk. If I'd been traveling on my own, I might have attempted to flirt her up; once I'd reached my sixties, fewer young, attractive women crossed my path. "You won't let them convict me, will you?" I asked, tongue-in-cheek.

Donning a serious expression, she stood and straightened her jacket, furthering the illusion of professionalism. "If you're innocent, you have nothing to worry about."

You had to admire how committed these actors were. I hoped they were paying her enough to make it worth her while. College credit or perhaps an acting notch on her resume? I'd ask when it was all over; the intel would make the whole story richer for my readers.

The bailiff opened the door and a group of twelve solemn-faced individuals shuffled to their seats in the jury box. With a deep furrow in his brow and an unceasing scowl, the foreperson looked especially intimidating. Good thing it's only a mock trial, I thought. I wouldn't want to attempt to convince someone of my innocence who was already so clearly predisposed.

I noted there was only one person at the prosecution table to my right, a librarian-type in her fifties, wearing a knit suit, her hair swept up in a tight bun. She wore a name tag that read "Ruth Less." Another pun. Beside her lay a pile of books, but no plaintiff. Unusual, at least based on the legal dramas I'd read.

The courtroom soon filled with what I assumed were the actors playing witnesses and onlookers. A mousy court reporter took his seat, and the silver-haired deputy cleared his throat. My chest tightened; the moment I'd been waiting for since I'd received the surprise invitation was finally at hand. Soon I'd learn of my supposed crime, confer with my attorney, and improvise my defense.

"All rise. The Court of Common Decency is now in session," said the deputy. "The Honorable Justice Noah Lott is presiding."

Judge Lott, if that were truly his name, was a paunchy, bookish, older gentleman whose round eyeglasses, bald crown, and gray mullet reminded me a little of Benjamin Franklin.

"Ladies and Gentlemen, please understand that being an independent court, we do not necessarily follow textbook courtroom procedure. For that reason, we will forego the swearing in of the jury and proceed directly to our first and only case today," Judge Lott looked down and consulted a piece of paper on his podium, "Aggrieved Authors Against Ezekiel Elias."

Authors, huh? They'd done their homework; I'd give them that.

"I'll hear opening arguments, please, starting with the prosecution," said the judge.

Ruth Less stood and approached the bench and then turned to address the jury. "Ladies and Gentlemen, Mr. Elias is accused of negligent literary criticism. Specifically, leaving one- and two-star reviews for books without justifiable cause. We plan to show the carelessness of his reviews and the aftermath of his criticism, namely, the plummeting sales of the novels involved."

My stomach jumped; the specificity was giving me the creeps. Who were these people and how did they know me and my work? It dawned on me why I couldn't find this "reality experience" in any of the guidebooks, or the show itself on cable television or the internet. A sense of foreboding suddenly overtook me. I'd been scammed.

"I think I've heard enough," I said, swiveling my head toward the exit and standing to leave.

Miss Stepp grabbed at my suit jacket and pulled me down. "You will sit, and you will listen," she snarled. "Otherwise, I will have no choice but to get

58

the bailiff involved."

"Really?" I asked, calling her bluff. "What's he going to do, refuse to validate my parking ticket?"

I'd made no attempt to lower my voice, prompting the bailiff to reach under his desk and pull out a Remington 760 rifle, which he now openly displayed and patted twice before laying it across his desk. Was it real or a prop? I couldn't tell, and I couldn't afford to take any chances. Gulping, I took my seat, hoping that my bladder wouldn't soon sully both the chair and my best suit.

"Miss Stepp, your opening statement, please?"

My counsel rose to address the judge and jury. "I'm sure Mr. Elias believes he's innocent, Your Honor." The comment dripped with sarcasm.

"That's my defense?" I whispered as she sat back down. "That's the best you can do?"

She looked me square in the eye. "Is it untrue? Do you *not* believe you're innocent?"

I shook my head. "No, I am, I am."

"Then no problem, correct?"

Who were these people, this mock court? If the rifle were real, did they intend to use it? My blood chilled while drops of perspiration dotted my forehead.

"Ms. Less, call your first witness please."

Ruth called Danica Vannoy. A heavy-set brunette plodded to the stand where the deputy swore her in.

"Ms. Vannoy, what is your profession?" Ruth asked.

"I am an author."

"Do you recognize this?" Ruth held up a book. I strained to read the title and then swallowed hard.

"Yes, it's my book, *Hope Swells*."

"How was the book received by readers, Ms. Vannoy?"

"It was doing great until one reviewer panned it with a one-star review."

And that's what it deserved, I thought. Thank goodness for those instances when I could trash a book. Those posts always triggered the most comments from readers.

"Do you see that reviewer in the courtroom?"

Danica nodded and pointed directly at me.

"Let the record reflect that Ms. Vannoy identified Mr. Elias as the reviewer. Now Ms. Vannoy, how long did you work on that book?"

"Five years, plus a year of revision."

"And what did Mr. Elias's review explain as the reason for the low rating?"

"He complained I used foul language, that I offended his Christian sensibilities."

"And did you, in fact, use foul language?" asked Less.

I leaned back in my chair, relieved. Here, I knew I was in the right.

"I included two expletives in times of distress. They were true to the character and not gratuitously used."

"Did you ever label the book as a 'clean read' or market it specifically to a Christian audience?"

"I did not."

The jury hummed its surprise.

The prosecutor addressed the judge. "No further questions, Your Honor."

"Your witness," Judge Lott said to my counsel.

"No questions, Your Honor."

"What do you mean, no questions? You're supposed to be defending me!" I growled.

"Did she lie in her testimony?"

"Well no, but there were two curse words in her book, and they destroyed the story for me."

"Was the plot good?"

"Yes, quite good, as I recall."

"The characterizations? The settings? The dialogue? All up to par?"

"Except for those two words, they were all excellent."

"So, out of what, 80,000 words, are you telling me you're such a snowflake, you couldn't tolerate two expletives?"

"It wasn't Christian."

"Hmm, I know quite a few Christians who curse. Television stations have even bleeped out a few of the president's comments. Voicing your objection would get me laughed out of the courtroom."

Again, I eyed the door and then the rifle. I harrumphed and threw my head back.

After Danica Vannoy retook her seat in the gallery, Ms. Less called her next witness, a slim, young, red-headed woman named Colleen Purser. Again, the prosecutor held up a book, but this one I didn't recognize. Thank goodness for that, I'd have a defense that perhaps my own lawyer could get behind.

"Ms. Purser, do you recognize this?"

"It's *Life at Cranwell*, the first edition of my only novel." Tears brimmed in her eyes.

"Why your only one?"

The witness pointed at me, and I winced. I never read the damn, I mean darn, book.

"I killed myself to write it, and he gave it a one-star review. After that, I almost quit writing. I never wanted to go through that kind of frustration and embarrassment again."

"I'm so sorry to cause you further stress, but just one question—what was the reason for his one-star review?"

"Amazon delivered it late and when they did, the packaging was bent."

"Was that all?"

"No. my critique group convinced me to try again. So, I changed the title, swapped out the cover, and re-released a new version."

"This one?" Less reached over and held up a different book, titled, "*Ghosted by the RAF*."

Well, that explained why I didn't recognize the original version.

Once Purser nodded, the prosecutor continued. "And then what happened?"

"Oh, this one he read. And in his online reviews, both on his blog and on the sales sites, he gave away the ending. It's a mystery, and somehow, he felt justified in divulging the name of the killer."

"Did you write and ask to have that part stricken from the review? Explain that it could impede sales?" asked Less.

"Yes, of course. Mr. Elias never returned my email. The sales site wrote back and bluntly explained that they don't edit reviews, even if they contain spoilers."

"No further questions, Your Honor."

"Your witness, Ms. Stepp."

My lawyer leaned toward me. "Should I bother?"

"Of course. Reviewers have the right to free speech, just like everyone else. I'm entitled to write what I like. She clearly hates reviewers."

Miss Stepp stood. "Ms. Purser, did you receive additional reviews for your book?"

"I did."

"Were they all negative?"

"No, just his. The rest ranged from three- to five-stars."

"Did you complain about any of the other reviews to the authors or the sales sites?"

"I did not. Some had negative things to say, but I get that. I'm a new author. I understand that there's room to improve. But I shouldn't get dinged for things beyond my control."

"So, you wouldn't consider yourself 'anti-reviewer'?"

"No," she sneered. "Just anti-Elias."

Miss Stepp sat down and turned my way. "Happy now?"

I shook my head. Fine. I'd figure out how to explain it away when it was my turn to address the jury.

She addressed Judge Lott. "No further questions, Your Honor."

"For my last witness, I call Henrietta Simpkins," said Ruth Less. A rotund Black woman lumbered to the stand.

Less held up a thick tome. "Do you recognize this book, Ms. Simpkins?"

"I do, indeed. *Death While Abroad*. It's a timely and heart-wrenching story of a woman murdered for making the difficult choice of changing her gender from male to female."

"Thank you for the synopsis, Ms. Simpkins. Could you tell us if you received any poor reviews for the book?"

"Only one. From him." She steered her gaze my way. Big surprise.

"Let the record show Ms. Simpkins has identified Mr. Elias. Tell us, Ms. Simpkins, did that one bad review affect your sales?"

"Killed them. My publisher wasn't particularly adept at marketing, and Mr. Elias's cruel words were all it took. No one bought or reviewed the book after that."

"I'm sorry to hear that. What was his reasoning?"

"He said it wasn't his preferred genre," said Simpkins.

"So, why did he read the book?"

"That's the thing. He didn't read it. He gave it one star and said that he put it down after the first page because transgender stories weren't his thing."

"Giving him the benefit of the doubt, was it clear from the cover that it was a story about the transgender community?" asked Less.

"Crystal, both from the cover art and the subtitle."

"No further questions, Your Honor."

"Your Witness, Miss Stepp."

"No questions."

I just slumped in my chair, waiting for my opportunity to get onto the stand.

"The prosecution rests, Your Honor."

"Miss Stepp? Would you like to proceed with defense?"

"The defense rests, Your Honor."

I leapt to my feet, incensed. "What do you mean, the defense rests? I want my moment in court. I demand to tell my side of the story."

Miss Stepp stood so she could address me face to face. "You will get as much of a chance as these authors did. Numerous sources warned them never to engage online critics, that if they did, all the other reviewers would turn on them. So, you'll get as much of a chance to dispute their claims as they got to argue your reviews."

Oh yeah? No one silences or victimizes Ezekiel Elias. If my lawyer wouldn't call me to the stand, I'd argue from my seat.

"Who are you people and what the hell do you want from me, anyway? I'm not a professional critic. I do the best I can. If you didn't realize that before, now you do. My readers like what I write. If you don't, you can all go suck my dick!"

"Very Christian," the judge mused.

I collapsed back in my seat, realizing I was out of options. I had no choice but to endure the rest of this kangaroo court and hopefully hop out of here alive, with my *joey* still safely in its pouch.

Judge Lott turned to the jury. "Do you need time to deliberate?"

The foreperson rose. "No, Your Honor. As twelve publishers, we can confidently render a verdict without discussion. We find the defendant, Ezekiel Elias, guilty of criminal critique."

"Thank you for your service, ladies and gentlemen of the jury. You are dismissed."

The jury slowly shuffled out, throwing nasty looks my way as they exited the courtroom.

The judge cleared his throat. "Will the defendant please rise so we can proceed with sentencing?"

I stood, one wary eye on the shotgun, still within the bailiff's reach.

"Okay, you've had your fun and made your point. What are you going to do, shoot me through the head?"

He stifled a laugh. "Nothing that painless, I assure you."

The lighting dimmed, and a video appeared on a screen above the judge's head. My face loomed, large as the screen itself, screaming, "I'm not a professional critic. If...my readers...don't...like what I write, you can all go suck my dick!" The editing was shoddy, that was clear to me, but to anyone else, who knows? I pressed my palms down on the defense table to keep my balance, willing my knees not to buckle.

Judge Lott gave me a hard look. "Mr. Elias, does your blog mean much to you?"

"I'm retired, it means everything to me. It's all I have. Five thousand subscribers read me every day." A frisson of pride caught in my throat. I'd worked hard to build up my audience. I had no intention of losing them.

"Well, we are not a heartless court. If you don't want this video emailed to every one of them, we have an alternative to offer."

"What's that?" I asked weakly.

"Write a book of your own. You have six months to submit it to each of these publishers. On the day one agrees to publish it, under your name and not a pseudonym, we will destroy the video."

"But I'm not a professional. I've never taken a writing class."

"Exactly."

"I don't know everything that goes into preparing a novel for publishing."

"Clearly."

"Six months isn't enough."

"It will have to be. Your blog will go on temporary hiatus while you work on it, so you won't have any interruptions."

"But what if it isn't any good? What will my followers say?"

"I wouldn't worry too much about it," said the judge with finality. "After all, what's the worst thing that can happen? A bad review?"

* * *

Hailing from New York's Hudson Valley, **D.M. Barr** writes tales of suspense, satire, and sweet romance. Previous novels include *Expired Listings* (Punctuated Publishing, 2016); *Slashing Mona Lisa* (Beachwalk Press, 2018—rereleased as *Murder Worth the Weight* by Punctuated Publishing in 2021); *Saving Grace—A Psychological Thriller* (2020, Black Rose Writing); and the sweet romance, *The Queen of Second Chances* (Champagne Books, 2021). When she isn't co-editing anthologies, rescuing shelter dogs, or playing competitive trivia, D.M. serves as the President of the Hudson Valley RWA, the Programming Chair of Sisters in Crime New York/Tri-State, and an active member of both MWA and ITW. Learn more at www.dmbarr.com.

DAVID AND THE GARMENTO

by Roz Siegel

I shot him twice in the head to make sure he was dead. My husband David was not a person you could trust. I would have hardly been surprised if he had suddenly jumped up and tried to grab the gun. But as I watched the blood slowly oozing down his neck, his body still, and his vacant eyes staring upward, I felt a little sorry that I had killed him so quickly. It would have been better to make him suffer for a while. But I did the best I could under the circumstances. After all, it was his idea to meet me. He wanted something only I could deliver. He got more than he bargained for.

* * *

"Daavid is here." My son Michael pronounced my husband's name with a long aaa, the Hebrew way. "He wants to see me."

"If your father wants to see you so badly, why has he stolen your inheritance and fled to India to live with a psychopathic guru?"

"Mom!"

We had been through this many times before. Since Michael was six. Now he was twelve.

I had hoped that David would die of one of those terrible diseases they have in India. Leprosy, for example. First, his nose would fall off. Then his fingers. Then his cock and balls. Or maybe he would get a tapeworm that would devour his internal organs one by one until he collapsed like a pile of turds into the mud. But so far, no such luck.

"He wants to take me with him."

Yeah right. "Over my dead body!"

I hadn't seen David since he absconded in the middle of the night after emptying our safety deposit box. My dad's company in the Garment District practically had a monopoly on manufacturing bridesmaid dresses. It wasn't glamorous but he'd made a lot of money and the safety deposit box had been filled with jewelry I had inherited. We both had keys to it, and I didn't even realize it was gone for days after David left.

It wasn't the kind of jewelry I would ever actually wear on the Upper West Side of Manhattan where we lived. Emerald earrings and a ring with a sapphire as large as the pull on my dresser drawer had never been my style. But once or twice a year, when I'd open the box, it was like a visit to my childhood. There was my mom's two-carat diamond ring that she never took off and the gold bracelet with hand-hammered links she'd worn to my wedding. There was a three-strand necklace of pearls, iridescent like the wings of a butterfly that she'd worn to her twenty-fifth-anniversary party. There was the locket with its delicate gold chain my parents had bought me for my tenth birthday and the small gold watch they had given me for my sixteenth. There was my grandfather's gold pocket watch with its heavy gold chain. And there was the antique diamond bracelet that had belonged to my grandmother. It wasn't worth much, set with old mine cut diamonds, small and insignificant, but the art deco design of the bracelet had always delighted me. All of it was gone, including our passports that I had unfortunately decided to store there for safekeeping.

Oh yes—and David had convinced me to hide all these things in the safety deposit box to escape the estate tax we would have had to pay, so everything was uninsured, and in the eyes of the law, didn't actually exist.

"You're just jealous that he has another wife!"

"It's not jealousy, it's bigamy—we are not divorced."

This particular guru, the Rajneesh, had been outed in an article in the *New York Times* in which they said he was a leader of "a crazy sex cult." Among other activities, he specialized in wholesale marriages in which the men can take multiple "wives." One, at least, was wearing my diamond bracelet.

"You are so, so bourgeois!"

"And a garmento, besides!" I reminded him.

Two names David had bestowed upon me. Michael's father might be in India, but he had a long reach.

We were not divorced, but I got a lawyer smart enough to convince a judge David was an unfit father and to award me full custody. After all, he had deserted his wife and son, never gave us a dime for food or rent, and joined a sect in India that practiced bigamy.

Earning money was never David's strong suit. When we were first married, David used to sing at the local temple. He also sang at the local church. He had some fantasy about becoming an opera singer. Office jobs were beneath him. Particularly one in the garment center working for my father.

In my dad's time, the garment center was filled with immigrant Jewish workers from Russia and Eastern Europe. Since they couldn't own land, many became tailors and eventually made a good living in the needle trades. Their children became doctors, lawyers, and teachers. The people who were left were called "garmentos," a derogatory name often used by their own children.

I had worked for my dad all my life, even during summers while I went to college, and thought the whole garmento stigma was funny. After he died and the business was sold, I went to work in the design department for a friend of his. As time went by, the workers became much more diverse: Chinese, Korean, Italian, and Indian. It was really a bit like working in the United Nations. To David, any work in a factory was an embarrassment. He felt it was beneath him and anyone associated with him, especially his wife, to work in the garment center. He was too proud to work at a job he considered below him, but not too proud to accept—and live off—the paycheck I earned there.

He disliked all religions equally until he met a guru whose way of life seemed to satisfy his every desire. This great spiritual leader preached that God rewarded the righteous with sex and money. He himself had twelve Rolls-Royces and at least a dozen wives.

"This time I'm going with him and you can't stop me!" Michael got up from the bed and stood next to me. Over me might have been a better description. He had suddenly grown quite tall. In a year, he would be Bar Mitzvahed.

When David first went to India, about three years ago, he made a couple of attempts to kidnap Michael. The first time, when I saw my son pack his knapsack with underwear and his soccer trophy, I locked him in his room. When David knocked at the door, I called the police.

The second time, I found David in the apartment when I came back from my morning jog around the Reservoir in Central Park. He tried to push past me, and I kicked him in the balls and started screaming. My neighbor called the police, and my lawyer got a writ of protection that forbade him from coming within a mile of the apartment.

This time would be more difficult.

* * *

"I don't think we can really do much to stop them. If your son wants to go…"

"Of course, my son wants to go. David told him high school is a waste of time. They can read the Kama Sutra together and hang out!"

"Asshole," my lawyer Sherry muttered. "As a minor, Michael can travel by himself if he has parental consent, but the document has to be signed by both parents, so there's that."

"Forging my name will not be a problem for David. He has done it before."

"Well then, as long as he has a ticket, a passport, and parental consent, he is good to go. We can send out an alert to Kennedy, but unfortunately, we can't watch every airport." She put her arm around my shoulder. "Do yourself a favor and stop worrying. If Michael goes, he'll come back as soon as he sees through all the bullshit. He's a sensible kid."

"Was. Did I mention David is the chief of police in the town they've taken over? He's a celebrity—irresistible to all, especially his son."

Sherry stopped me at the door. "How come David allows Michael to call him by his first name instead of Daddy like ordinary people?"

"Just one more way to show how liberal-minded and unique he is. So, your advice is to do nothing and hope for the best?"

She nodded. I had a better plan.

* * *

It would be more accurate to say I had a goal—to murder David. That would be the easy part. There was really no other way to prevent him from accomplishing *his* goal of taking Michael to India. If I managed to thwart him this time, there would always be a next time, and since Michael was now too old for me to lock in his room for days at a time—that would be considered child abuse—there was no solution to the problem except murder. How I was going to accomplish that was the hard part; I needed a plan that had thus far eluded me.

I lay in bed staring at the ceiling for hours.

My first inclination was to strangle him with the sash of one of my garmento father's bridesmaid dresses that I had saved in the bottom drawer of my dresser. The firm had been out of business for fifteen years and it was unlikely that anyone would be able to trace the sash to me. But there was the problem of my being able to overpower him and get rid of the body.

Poison? I knew I could get my hands on something that would work. I had a box of rat poison under the sink in the kitchen. That plan had the advantage of a certain irony that made me smile. But how could I get close enough to David to poison him? How could I get close enough to him to injure him at all? Had I outsmarted myself by signing all these warrants against him?

And then there was the problem of getting away with killing him. I had read enough mysteries to know the police always suspected the husband or wife of the murdered party.

I could cut up the body and put the parts in various garbage cans along Upper Broadway. David's parents were dead; it was unlikely that the Rajneesh would file a missing person's report for his Chief of Police—and if there were no body, it would be difficult to establish his identity.

I shivered. The idea of touching David, of sullying my hands with his blood, was repugnant. Also, much too much trouble. I would need a saw, knives…definitely out.

As the clock near my bed registered 3:00 a.m., I suddenly realized that the weapon was not the problem. I already had the weapon. A gun stashed happily right under that very bed.

For fifteen years we'd owned a little cottage in the woods in a small town in upstate New York. It was a town where everyone hunted deer, turkey, ducks. Anything that moved and didn't have a first and last name. Our house was in the middle of ten acres of woods. We bought it because we wanted privacy.

The first week we were there we were terrified. The darkness. The rattling garbage cans. The creaks and the squeaks of a house in the country. David and I, who didn't even look out the window when we heard sirens cross in front of our building on Broadway and Ninetieth Street, turned pale and shaky on a moonless night in the woods.

It was David who insisted we buy a gun to keep under the bed. It was David who insisted we go to a local range and learn to shoot. There was never any license issued for that gun. We bought it off one of the locals who needed cash. In those days, in that town, nobody asked too many questions. The gun was loaded, and I knew how to shoot.

There was some poetic justice in that.

But the larger questions remained. How could I get close enough to David to shoot him? And where could I do it without getting noticed?

I volunteered on Saturdays at the Museum of Natural History a few blocks away. The building had some storerooms people rarely visited; closets that hadn't been opened in years. It was a possibility, but I would need to get copies of keys made, then wait until closing time.

It was complicated.

And then, as the morning light seeped through the Venetian blinds of my bedroom window, it came to me. Central Park! As a mother living on upper Broadway, Central Park was my backyard. I took Michael to different playgrounds every couple of weeks when he was little. When he was older, we went to Little League games on the Sheep Meadow; we had both learned to play tennis on the public courts near the Ninetieth Street entrance. And I had been jogging around the Reservoir daily for years. I knew Central Park like the back of my hand. Yes, it was busy at 6:30 a.m. when most people took in their fresh air and exercise before sitting at a desk inside a stuffy office all day. But there were other times, like after dark, when visitors were rare. Many believed it was dangerous to go to Central Park after dark. There were homeless people, drug dealers, desperados of all types, and plenty of bushes and places to hide.

But my plan still lacked one essential element: how to coax David to meet me there after dark.

Maybe there really is a righteous God or spirit of justice or something up there to balance the universe because about an hour after I returned from my jog in Central Park and Michael had gone off to school, my phone rang.

"It's David. I'm in New York and I want to talk to you."

"So, talk."

"You have something I want, and I have something you want, and I think we can make a trade."

"If you think you can give me something in exchange for Michael, forget about it!"

"I'm not stupid. It concerns the safety deposit box."

"The one you stole. You already have everything in it."

"Not quite. There was a watch of mine we kept there. A very special watch."

"Your father's Rolex watch. The one with his initials on the back."

"It wasn't in the safety deposit box."

It should have been there. And then I remembered: it had stopped working and I'd brought it to that repair shop near the garment center. When I picked it up, I'd put it in my underwear drawer and forgotten all about it.

"I know you have it. And I want it."

"So, you need money so bad? What about the watch my mother gave me? My mother's two-carat engagement ring? Did you give them to one of your wives?"

"My wives have no interest in those baubles, such materialistic treasures of a decadent society. I want that watch because it is the only thing about my father I ever admired. His congregation gave it to him on the twenty-fifth year of his being their rabbi."

This was total bullshit. Just like the guru's supposed rejection of materialism. David hated his father. He wanted to sell the watch for whatever he could get for it.

"And what do you have to trade for it?"

"The diamond bracelet with the old mine cut diamonds you liked so much. Do you know a place where we can meet in private?"

My heart was beating so loudly I could hardly think.

"Central Park. Across from the tennis courts. There's a bridge over a small tunnel. We can meet in the tunnel."

"Yes. Yes. I know the place."

"Come at midnight. We'll have the whole park to ourselves."

"No police."

We knew there was a police station in the middle of the park near the Eighty-first Street transverse, but it was too far away to worry either of us.

"No police," I agreed.

"No need to mention this to Michael. He still has fantasies that we will get back together."

"No need."

I hung up the phone and looked at the clock. It was only a little after 9:00 a.m. It was going to be a long day.

I called in sick and walked into the bedroom, where I rummaged through my underwear drawer until I found David's father's Rolex watch. On the back, there were some Hebrew letters engraved which, according to David, said something like "God loves the Just," and the initials, MP, for Myron Perlmutter.

They were Michael's initials too and David had promised the watch to Michael.

A ray of sun lit up the pink gold face and bathed it in a special glow. The leather band was cracked and discolored by sweat. I held the watch up to my ear. It was a wind-up watch and had stopped ticking.

Perhaps Michael would still receive his grandfather's watch. I hoped Myron had been a good man but judging from how David turned out, I figured he probably wasn't. I would decide what to do with the watch… afterwards.

The hours dragged on. Michael stayed in his room and did his homework. Did he plan to escape the next morning and was even now receiving texts on his iPhone? I had no idea.

At 10:30 I knocked on the door of Michael's room. He was in bed, staring at his phone. "I made you a cup of cocoa. A new blend I bought at Zabar's."

I put a marshmallow on top which I knew he couldn't refuse. I added half an Ambien as well. I couldn't risk Michael waking up, realizing I wasn't home, and wandering around the neighborhood searching for me.

He fell asleep quickly. Donning my dark blue hoodie and a pair of rubber gloves I used to touch up my hair, I placed the gun in a small pouch around my waist and tucked the watch into the pocket of my jogging pants. I took the back stairs out of our building so not even the doorman would notice me. I kept my head down just in case there were security cameras overhead.

I walked up Broadway, which was pretty deserted at 11:30 on a weekday, and crossed over to Central Park. There was a red rubber pylon blocking the entrance with a sign that said CLOSED. I moved it aside and walked in.

I didn't realize how creepy Central Park really was at midnight.

It would be just my luck that I had come so close to murdering the man who wanted to kidnap my son and some perfect stranger murdered me instead.

I walked quickly past the dark tennis courts. Were those shadows or people crouching in the corner near the bushes? I walked more quickly.

I had been jogging in Central Park for fifteen years and had only encountered a policeman once—he'd accosted a Black man after some white woman yelled that she had just been robbed. So, I figured there wasn't much chance I would be stopped by a cop, but I didn't have a good excuse prepared if I were. The best I could come up with was that I was from out of town and didn't know the rules.

There were lights here and there as I walked through the park. There were probably cameras as well, but I doubted anyone was watching now. They would only look through the footage after they discovered the body—and they would have a hard time tracking down a middle-sized person wearing a five-year-old Gap hoodie and sweatpants.

A block from the underpass, I could see a stocky figure standing as far away from the lights as possible. As I drew closer, I could tell it was David with a bushy beard. He was wearing jeans and a baseball cap. But a few yards before reaching his side, I saw somebody stretched out on the ground. Another murder victim? Or a possible witness who would awaken when I shot my gun?

When I backed away, David called out: "Don't worry about him—he's totally wasted on drugs. Did you bring the watch?"

"Did you bring the bracelet?"

He drew it from his pocket and held it under the lamplight for me to see.

The man on the ground rolled onto his side and snored. That was when I took out the gun.

David stared at me for a minute in disbelief "You can't be serious!" He drew two steps closer.

"Not so bourgeois after all," I said. "Let's just say it is the revenge of the garmentos." And I shot him in the head.

The explosion was much louder than I had anticipated. I had forgotten that sound bounced off walls like an echo chamber. The man on the ground grunted and twitched but did not open his eyes.

David fell backwards onto the ground and groaned in pain. The bracelet rolled away from him. I moved closer and shot him again.

He was quiet then. A pool of red blood slowly seeped from his head.

I bent down quickly and put the bracelet in my sack. Then I reached into his pants pocket and took out his wallet, iPhone, hankie, a pen, and receipt for something. In his back pocket, I found his passport, Michael's passport, and two one-way tickets to Delhi, India.

Then I headed back through the park the way I had come. When I reached Broadway and Ninetieth Street, I walked to Riverside Park. It was darker and as dangerous at night as Central Park but that was of less concern than being caught with a murder weapon. I climbed through a few bushes and threw the gun into the Hudson River below.

Then I hurried back to my apartment building, used the back entrance, and climbed the eight floors to my apartment.

Michael was fast asleep, his iPhone next to his head on the pillow.

I washed off my rubber gloves and put them back in the bathroom in my hair dye kit. I took off my hoodie and pants and sneakers and put them in the washing machine.

I took out David's driver's license, the plane tickets and the two passports, the handkerchief, receipt, pen—everything I had found in his pockets, except for two ten-dollar bills—cut them all up into small pieces and flushed them down the toilet. If somehow his identity is discovered his murder would be blamed on a simple mugging, a result of a stupid man who didn't realize how dangerous it was to venture into Central Park after dark.

Then I poured myself a shot of vodka, set the alarm for 6:30 as usual, and went to sleep.

* * *

When I walked into Michael's room the next morning he was fully dressed, his backpack stuffed full.

"I'm leaving. You can't stop me."

I guess I was more distraught than I realized. Holding myself together last night was taking its toll. I sat down on his bed and started to cry. This surprised Michael as much as it surprised me. I was not the crying type.

He sat down next to me and put his arms around me. "It will only be for a little while. A visit. I will come back, I promise."

I kissed him and took out a wad of cash from the kitchen drawer. "I suppose you will need some money. Your father is usually short."

He kissed me and I walked him to the door.

"Where are you meeting him?"

"I can't tell you. Somewhere on Broadway." And then he opened the door, handed me the *New York Times,* and rang for the elevator.

I made myself a bagel with lox and a cup of hot cocoa. And as I ate and glanced through the *Times*, I pictured Michael, full of love and trust, sitting on a bench somewhere on Broadway hour after hour, waiting for his father. Yes, I felt a little sad robbing him of his innocence at such a young age. But mostly I felt as if a great weight had been lifted off my shoulders. I decided to tell Michael his father left a message that he had been called away for an emergency and had to return to India without him. He would contact him again soon.

The man was a terrible son of a bitch, but he must have loved his son. Why else try to kidnap him so many times? I reached into my pocket and took out David's father's watch. If the Hebrew really said, "God loves the Just," I would give it to him next year at his Bar Mitzvah.

* * *

Roslyn Siegel, PhD., has been a writer/editor for more than thirty years. She has held senior positions at Book of the Month Club, Simon & Schuster, Crown, and MJF Books. Her articles and book reviews have appeared in *The New York Times, Cosmopolitan Magazine, Publisher's Weekly* and many other publications. She is the author of the mystery novels *Goodie One Shoes*

(2018) and *Well-Heeled* (2015) set on New York City's colorful Upper West Side and recipient of a starred review in *Publisher's Weekly.* Her short story "Sylvia" appeared in the anthology, *Family Matters,* Vol. 3, Sisters in Crime New York/Tri-State (2014) and "Levitas" in *Where Crime Never Sleeps*, Vol. 4, Sisters in Crime New York/Tri-State (2017).

THE THANKSGIVING RAGAMUFFIN

by Kathleen Marple Karb

New York City, Thanksgiving Morning, 1899

"Anything for Thanksgiving?"

The cry from the children pounding on our door would be a shocking start to the holiday anywhere else. But, unlike the other dramatic events that came before our feast, that early commotion at our Washington Square townhouse was no surprise. Even though we lived in one of the nicer areas of the city, we still saw the occasional Thanksgiving Ragamuffins. It was a relatively new tradition in New York: kids wandering the streets in the morning, begging for treats or pennies for the holiday.

Neither my cousin Tommy Hurley nor I minded the children at all. We grew up poor on the Lower East Side, and we knew how lucky we were. It wouldn't have surprised me in the least if word had spread among the neighborhood children that they could expect generous compensation from that strange lady singer and the Champ. Especially since our cook, Mrs. Grazich, never let a visitor—even a delivery boy or newsboy—leave without a sweet.

"Want me to get it?" Tommy asked, putting the marker in his book, a new edition of Mr. Lincoln's letters, as he walked into the foyer.

I came down the stairs from the studio, still in my rehearsal clothes of breeches and an old white shirt. Of course, I would never expect anyone from our opera company to work on Thanksgiving morning, but I had finally figured out the change I wanted to make in a sword fight scene for the next tour and had tried it out myself in front of the mirror upstairs.

"You get the basket; I'll open the door." I pushed back a strawberry-blonde curl that had come loose from my knot.

Tommy picked up the basket of penuche fudge. Mrs. G had neatly wrapped the pieces in waxed paper, and I'd slipped a shiny penny into the top layer of the wrapping of each before tying them with red string. It wasn't fussy, but it looked festive. Why not?

At the door, four little faces, carefully smudged to appear unkempt, lit up at the sight of us.

"Miss Ella! Champ!"

I recognized them as boys from our street, the children of two prosperous and happy families—like us, Irish folk who'd done well. "Happy Thanksgiving, fellows!"

"Been behaving yourselves?" Tommy asked, the gleam in his greenish-blue eyes softening his stern tone.

"Of course, Champ."

The boys knew Tommy from Holy Innocents Church. He and his best friend, Father Michael Riley, played checkers with them, taught them to box a little, encouraged them to do their homework, whatever was needed to keep the fellows on the right path.

Running footsteps, and a howl. "Jimmy, you rat! You were supposed to wait for me!"

The fifth member of the ragged band blasted to the top of our stairs, a few red curls straggling free of someone's old cap.

"I haven't given out the candy yet, Daisy," I assured her. Jimmy's little sister tagged along with the boys whenever she could, but they were much less kind and tolerant than Tommy had been with me.

"Good." She stuck her tongue out at Jimmy and then turned to me with a sweet smile. "Thank you very much, Miss Ella."

Tommy and I did our best to hide our laughter as we handed out treats and sent the ragamuffins on their way. We'd barely closed the door before a second knock.

"Anything for Thanksgiving?"

These voices were a bit rougher, and so were the kids. Newsboys, unless I missed my guess. Their faces were thinner, and the grime was real. And the worn clothes weren't hand-me-downs roughed up for the occasion. They were all they had.

Some newsboys came from poor families, "doing their part in the house," the way I'd once done with piecework, and Tommy had done with odd jobs in the old neighborhood. Others had no one. The boys all knew the stories, but they'd never tell them to us. Over time and hot cocoa in the Holy Innocents rectory, Father Michael would find out and help where he could.

I didn't feel the least bit guilty sending these fellows on their way with two pieces of penuche each instead of one. Honestly, I'd have given them the whole batch if they could have carried it.

"Did you recognize any of them?" I asked Tommy as I closed the door.

He shrugged. "I've seen a couple of them around Holy Innocents. The little one, with the dark hair and eyes, he's new."

Tommy's gaze lingered on my face. He knew what I was thinking. The world saw opera diva Ella Shane, internationally acclaimed, or at least paid in several different currencies, for my performances in "trouser roles," heroic men's parts played by women. But inside was Ellen O'Shaughnessy, Irish-Jewish orphan who'd made good, with more than a few scars from my childhood. Tommy knew better than most; we'd been looking out for each other since my mother died and his family took me in. Just eight, sad and scared, I'd attached myself to twelve-year-old Toms, even helping him fight the bullies who called him a "sissy."

"I'm fine, Toms." I took the basket from him and put it back on the small table by the door. "C'mon. Mrs. G left us some penuche."

"That's an excellent idea, Heller." He rarely called me by anything but the nickname I'd earned during our street-fighting years, before he grew half a foot and became the star of his boxing gym, and I found my mentor and voice teacher, Madame Lentini.

We had just turned for the stairs when the shouting came from the street.

"He's dead! He's dead and that rotten little newsboy killed him!"

"Let go of me, lady! I didn't do anything!"

Tommy and I stepped outside to see the small dark-haired boy struggling with a sturdy woman, next to the body of the apparent victim. From across the street on a cloudy morning, though, the remains looked like nothing but an indistinct rounded shape lying near the entrance to Washington Square Park.

"I didn't hurt anyone! Let me go!"

The child let out a shockingly loud howl, his face contorted with fear.

Even the officious, overdressed woman who'd accosted him looked stunned, dropping his collar, and backing off in confusion.

I didn't think about it. I just walked over to the little fellow and put a hand on his shoulder. He looked up at me with tear-filled, bottomless dark eyes.

"Come here, sweetheart. You're safe now." I pulled him to me, and he burrowed into my arms as my friends' children sometimes did. As I rubbed his back, I noticed that his clothes, while grubby, were of good quality and relatively new. Maybe one of the luckier ones. "Call Father Michael, Toms."

"And Cousin Andrew the detective, too, I think," Tommy added. Andrew Riley was actually Father Michael's cousin, not ours, but everyone called him that, and there was no doubt that we–and that poor boy–would need a friendly police detective.

* * *

Within fifteen minutes, everyone involved was safe and warm inside. Since the admirable Mrs. G was celebrating the holiday with her family, I was in charge of coffee, cocoa, and cookies, fortunately well within my limited skills.

Cousin Andrew had arrived at the same time as the uniformed coppers from his precinct. He was quite willing to move the investigation, such as it was, into the comfort of the parlor. I'd taken a moment to slip away and put on a simple purple merino house dress, not for the detective, but because I did not want the unpleasant Mrs. Morton Winch staring at my masculine attire.

The neighborhood busybody had quite proudly informed Cousin Andrew that she was a witness and followed him toward our townhouse after Tommy suggested we adjourn to a more pleasant venue for conversation. But that, of course, was not all.

Despite inviting herself, the matron, whom I knew only slightly—mostly from her disapproving scowls at my velocipede rides in the park—had stiffened at the door and sneered at Tommy and me. "I'm not sure I wish to enter such a house…"

Such a house indeed. All but the most narrow-minded now recognized opera singers as perfectly respectable artists. And if that were some sort of veiled comment on the fact that Tommy was not the marrying kind, Mrs. Winch was setting herself up for a good right cross. From me.

Fortunately for all, the detective gave her a hard look, and me a quick side-eye.

By the time I appeared with the coffee tray, transformed into my proper ladylike self, the little boy was on the settee with Tommy, with space left for me. Father Michael had arrived and taken Tommy's chair, and Cousin Andrew was just settling into the other, slightly smaller, wing chair. Our witness, Mrs. Winch, was sitting sidewise on my chaise. Of course, she was.

The child took his cup of cocoa carefully, but with an eagerness in his eyes that gave him away. I put the cookie plate within easy reach and shot Tommy a glance. He nodded.

Though it was a serious situation indeed, I swallowed a smile at the sight of the men. Tommy and Father Michael were both well north of six feet and sturdy: with sharp Celtic features, the priest blond, my cousin auburn-haired. The detective, though, was most of a foot shorter, with flame-red hair and a rounded face. He looked like their lunch.

Cousin Andrew, however, had long since made his peace with being the runt of the litter, and he accepted his coffee with a smile. "Sorry to start your Thanksgiving this way, Miss Ella."

"And yours." I gave him a careful nod and left it at that.

"It's not quite as serious as it looks, though. Mrs…Winch, is it?" the little detective asked as he neatly placed his cup in the saucer.

"Mrs. *Morton* Winch, thank you. When are you going to arrest that boy?"

"Well, he may be many unpleasant things, Mrs. Winch, including badly washed at the moment, but he's not a killer."

"I'm sorry?"

"That poor man is ice cold," Cousin Andrew said patiently. "He's been dead for hours and not a mark on him. Looks like he just collapsed and died on the sidewalk. It's sad, but probably not criminal."

"Well, I'm sure that wretch robbed him, anyway!"

"I'd never!" the child snapped around a mouthful of snickerdoodle. "I told you, lady, those other boys—"

"Good boys like that would never—"

Cousin Andrew silenced Mrs. Winch with a glance. She huffed but held her tongue.

"Why don't you tell me what happened, son? Let's start with your name."

He swallowed the last of his cookie. "Moishe."

"Moishe what?"

The boy shook his head.

Cousin Andrew's hard look got him nothing this time. He sighed. "All right, we'll go back to that later. What happened?"

"We newsboys were out knocking on doors for Ragamuffin Day. The other fellows ran on ahead and I saw the man on the ground. Three boys were standing over him. They looked like rich boys just playing poor—"

"How would you know that, you little street urchin?" Mrs. Winch's silence apparently only endured for so long.

"Because they were fat. Newsboys...ain't fat. The rich boys took the man's wallet and ran off laughing."

Something was off with this boy; the 'ain't' didn't sound right coming from him, as if he had to think for an instant to use bad grammar. And really, I thought, it should be fairly easy to prove his story; there were a lot of kids running around this morning, and one should have seen something.

"How dare you accuse good boys—"

"Ma'am," Cousin Andrew cut in, his voice brittle with exasperation. But he turned to Moishe with a carefully grim face. "Now, son, if you *did* take anything from the man..."

Just then, there was a frantic knock on the door.

I'd barely opened it when young Daisy Neill flew in like a whirlwind, followed by her parents, my neighbors Grace and Joe Neill, and their son Jimmy, walking as if he were on his way to the scaffold.

"Don't arrest that little fella!" Daisy Neill cried. "He didn't do anything wrong!"

Cousin Andrew walked into the foyer, followed by everyone else. Mrs. Winch hung back in the parlor doorway, her scowl deepening to make her face look like an unpleasant marionette's.

The Neill parents, a nice Irish couple we often saw at Mass at Holy Innocents, were at least as upset as their girl, if hiding it better. Joe Neill reached behind him and pulled Jimmy to the front.

"Tell 'em, Jim. Be a man."

"All right, Da." Jimmy, a plump, slightly older version of his redheaded sister, squirmed a bit, but then took a breath and turned to face Cousin Andrew.

The detective waited.

"The Smith boys came out before we did, and after we stopped here at Miss Ella's, they asked me if I wanted to see a dead man. So, I sent Daisy on ahead to look for houses with the curtains open—"

"You got rid of me again, you rat!" the young lady in question snapped.

"Mary Daisy Neill."

It was the only time we would hear Grace Neill's voice that day, but it was quite enough. Her daughter clammed right up, though she continued to convey her upset by folding her arms and glaring at her brother.

"So, we went over, and sure enough, there it was."

"Do you know who it was?"

Jimmy swallowed hard and nodded. "Mr. Hawley from over on MacDougal Street. He was really old and mean...but he didn't deserve to lie dead in the street."

"And..." Joe Neill said, pushing his son.

"He didn't deserve to have the Smith boys take his wallet, either." A tear oozed out of Jimmy's right eye. "But they did. I told Daisy, and she made me tell Da."

"And right she was." Cousin Andrew gave the young lady a scowl as she opened her mouth to gloat. "You're going to have to give me a statement, son. And then we'll go ruin the Smith boys' Thanksgiving."

But Mrs. Winch wasn't ready to accept defeat.

"There is simply no way those nice Smith boys did that. And I saw that dirty little Jewish boy—"

Brisk footsteps announced another visitor. Everyone turned to see Dr. Edith Silver walk through the still-open door, upright and elegant in a black wool overcoat and simple hat. The faint shadows under her eyes, and slight loosening of her snug knot of curly dark hair, were the only hint that she might have come from a long night's work.

I hadn't expected to see her until dinner time, but doctors, and especially the babies they deliver, didn't always keep to precise schedules.

Whatever sharp response Dr. Silver might have had to Mrs. Winch's vile slur vanished when she saw the boy.

"Moishe Kanter!" the doctor exclaimed. "Your mother has been worried sick."

"No, she's not. She and Papa finally got a new baby girl, and they don't want me. So, I ran off. Don't worry, I'm fine, Doc."

Dr. Silver, who normally moved with deliberate grace, sprang across the floor to the boy and grabbed his arm in a grip just shy of painful. "She certainly *does* want you. She's been haunting the police station for the last three days!"

Cousin Andrew looked sharply at him, clearly remembering his reluctance to give his full name. "You're the Kanter kid? My pal in the next house over told me about you."

"He did?"

"Said your ma comes to the station morning and night, begging the sergeant for any word. He feels real bad for her. Says she's a sweet lady and it's just breaking her heart."

Moishe Kanter burst into tears again, just as he had outside. Only this time, both Dr. Silver and I surrounded him, comforting him, and stroking his hair.

I glimpsed the menfolk exchanging amused glances and had no doubt there would be some smart-alecky comment later about modern women and the same old adorable children.

Behind us, Mrs. Morton Winch let out a sniff. "Disgraceful."

Dr. Silver stiffened and wheeled on her. "Do you know what's truly disgraceful?"

The matron shrank back, stunned silent by the sight of mild-mannered Dr. Silver's metamorphosis into an avenging goddess. The physician's hazel eyes blazed with fury, and her voice was calm and steely as she continued. "It's shameful that you think it's perfectly fine to speak of that innocent child in such terms…and that you assume he must be up to no good."

"Indeed! I don't have to stay here and be insulted."

"No, as a matter of fact," Tommy began, looking to Cousin Andrew for confirmation, "you do not need to spend one more minute in this house. Your presence offends us."

"Well, I never!" She swept toward the door and turned to deliver a parting shot. "What do any of you feeble-minded Irish know about how real Americans behave, anyway?"

One of Dr. Silver's brows quirked, and I suspected she was tempted to point out that we aren't *all* Irish, and that it was more than a little feeble-minded to confuse the Irish and the Jews.

"We're as American as you," I said quietly. "Maybe more, because we don't try to close the door after us."

Another sniff, and Mrs. Winch flounced out.

I turned to Dr. Silver. "I thought you weren't coming over until later."

"I was just stopping to tell you I was up all night with a new mother and would not be coming by for pie after all. Thank heavens I did."

"The Lord works in mysterious ways," Father Michael said. "However you talk to Him."

"Isn't that the truth?" Physician and priest exchanged a smile of ecumenical understanding.

Cousin Andrew cleared his throat. "I'd like to stay and discuss the ways of God, but at the moment, there are three boys whom I need to acquaint with man's justice."

Jimmy Neill swallowed hard and nodded.

I opened the door for the detective. As Joe Neill guided his son out the door, I saw him pat his back with an encouraging smile.

"You did the right thing, my boy."

Daisy beamed. I didn't doubt that she was going to hold the incident over her brother for the rest of his life. But that was only fair. At least from my point of view after a lifetime as Tommy's junior partner.

Once I closed the door, I turned back to our remaining guests in the foyer.

"Come along, little one," Dr. Silver said, taking Moishe's hand. "Your family has missed you something awful."

Moishe smiled, turning from ragamuffin to cherub.

Over the curly dark head, Tommy and I gave the doctor a sharper gaze.

"Yes, you two, it really is all right." Her serious professional mien gave way to a girlish grin. "His parents will be so glad to have him back."

"All right, then." Tommy nodded and gave Moishe a very dignified handshake.

"Goodbye, sweetheart." I smoothed his hair, and he leaned into my hand for a moment, gazing up at me with the wonderful trusting expression that only children have.

"Thanks, Miss Ella."

If I were a florid romance novelist, I might have said my heart melted a bit. I'll just leave it that I had a wave of unfamiliar and not entirely unpleasant emotions.

"Not too late for a wee one of your own, you know," Dr. Silver said with a knowing smile. "You should think about it."

I bit back a sharp reply and bid her a cordial farewell, glaring at the fellows, daring them to say something.

Neither was so foolish.

Dr. Silver nodded to us and guided the boy out the door. For a moment, Tommy, Father Michael, and I stood quietly in the foyer.

"That Mrs. Winch is pretty horrid," Tommy said finally.

"An awful lot of prejudice in this world," I agreed.

"But at least we pushed it back today," Father Michael reminded us. "For that, we should definitely give thanks."

"Well, that's true," Tommy spoke, but we both nodded reluctantly.

"The Lord does His work if we help Him along," said the priest. "Sometimes that's all we can do."

"And sometimes, we deserve a slice of pumpkin pie for our efforts." I nodded to the kitchen stairs. "Mrs. G has left us well provided for."

"It's a bit early for pie, don't you think?" Tommy asked.

"Pie was a breakfast item in the Colonial Period," I said. "The Pilgrims often had it."

"Good enough for me," replied the priest.

"I'm always willing to do my part for Pilgrim heritage," agreed Tommy.

Not to mention the grand old American tradition of making sure everyone ended up where they belonged, I thought, reflecting on pie and providence. And, at least on that Thanksgiving Day, all got their *just desserts*.

* * *

Kathleen Marple Kalb, a proud member of Sisters in Crime New York/Tri-State, is the author of the Ella Shane historical mystery series for Kensington Books, most recently *A Fatal First Night*. She grew up in front of a microphone and a keyboard and is now a weekend morning anchor at 1010 WINS Radio in New York City, capping a career begun as a teenage DJ in Brookville, Pennsylvania. She, her husband the Professor, and their son the Imp, live in a Connecticut house owned by their cat.

RISKY ASSUMPTIONS

by Ellen Quint

"**H**IDE."

That's all the text message from an unknown number said. So that's what Michael did. Truth was, since he heard on the news that Simon Priestly had been found dead, he'd been terrified that the police would come for him. He may have been the last person to see Priestly alive. His fingerprints would be in the apartment. He turned off his phone, threw some clothes into his backpack, ran down the eight flights of stairs, out the back door of his apartment building, and through the alley.

* * *

It wasn't until the next day that his lawyer, Harriet Baum, became really concerned because she couldn't reach him. So, she called her private investigator, Babs Ward.

Babs didn't answer on the first three tries. Harriet didn't leave messages. She knew better. She just kept calling. Finally, on the fourth attempt, Babs picked up.

"Why didn't you answer? Where were you?" Harriet asked.

"Where do you think I was?" Babs replied. "I was in the bathroom, of course."

"What have I been telling you? You have to learn to hold it. Investigators don't pee. Does Harry Bosch ever pee? No. Does Jack Reacher pee? No. And he drinks lots of coffee. And Gabriel Allon, does he ever pee? No. And these guys are all old now like us."

"Yeah, but they're all men," said Babs.

"Okay, how about Kinsey Millhone? No, never pees."

"Hate to break it to you, Harriet, but those folks are all fictional characters. Me, I am very real, and I have to pee often. So, get over it and tell me why you're calling."

"I have an urgent job for you. My client is missing, and we have to find him before the police do," Harriet said. "Can you come to my office now?"

"Yeah, I'll be right up."

* * *

Babs packed her laptop in her messenger bag and headed up one flight to Harriet's office. She could have taken the elevator, but at sixty-six years old, Babs viewed climbing stairs as her confirmation that she still had it, whatever it was.

Babs was breathing a little hard when she walked through the law offices of Baum & Sisters. Harriet didn't have any real sisters. She just had formed her law firm with brilliant female lawyers who had a reputation for winning big time in divorce and sexual harassment cases.

She walked past the receptionist, who gave her a wave, and right to Harriet's office at the end of the hall. She opened the door to see Harriet in her wheelchair parked next to the printer. Harriet suffered from a debilitating neuromuscular disease. Maybe "suffered" was the wrong word as she seemed to conquer every attack, every challenge that was foisted upon her. Babs watched as Harriet pulled the pages from the tray and handed them to her.

"As I said on the phone, I need your assistance. My client has disappeared. I'm worried. We had a conference scheduled for later this week—a sexual harassment case. But the defendant was found dead yesterday. Police aren't saying the cause yet, but it seems likely he was murdered. Did you see the news—Simon Priestly? Now the police are looking for my client, Michael Harmon. They called here to see if I had heard from him. But I haven't been able to contact him at all. I don't know what to think. Can you see if you can find him?" Harriet said.

"If the police are already tracking him down, why do you need me?"

"I need to find him before they do. He's a young Black male and frankly, he would be terrified by a confrontation with the police. And I know you can do it—you are the best at it, and you do it without anyone noticing—which is why you are the CEO of PIs—the 'I' in my book standing for 'invisible and ignored.'"

Babs looked at the picture on top of the papers that Harriet had handed her. "Wow, good-looking kid. Tell me about him."

"Michael has been a model since he was sixteen. Now he's twenty-three. Priestly has been representing him for the last three years. He came to me about two months ago and told me Priestly had been demanding sexual favors in return for sending him on the premier assignments. Michael just had enough. He said he was inspired by the #MeToo movement and even though he knew this kind of sexual harassment was rampant in the business, he was ready to sacrifice his career to bring this situation to light. Brave kid," Harriet said.

"Why hasn't the media picked up on this suit? It seems like something they would be all over," Babs said.

"We hadn't officially filed the papers yet. We were in discussions with Priestly's lawyers who were offering a settlement if Michael agreed not to file a lawsuit and instead, sign an ironclad non-disclosure agreement."

Babs pulled her laptop from her bag, set it up on Harriet's small conference table, and googled Simon Priestly. Stories popped up about his death. The latest newsflash indicated Priestly was found dead in his apartment by his assistant, who stopped by after she was unable to reach him by phone or text. She said she used her own key, which Simon had given her as she often helped with social events held in the apartment. The story also stated that the police had not ruled out foul play and were searching for a person of interest.

"Where would Michael go?" Babs asked. "Whom does he trust?"

"Well, his only family is his mother who lives in Atlanta. I don't think he would go there. He wouldn't want to get her involved."

"How did he come to be your client? Was it your sterling reputation?" Babs asked, channeling her best Columbo.

"As a matter of fact, it was through another client, Shana Smith. Although she doesn't work with Priestly, Shana is also a model and we brought a similar case against her agent. She actually came with Michael to our first meeting. She was like his cheerleading squad, encouraging and supporting him. I should have thought of that first thing. Let me call her."

Harriet reached for her phone and stopped to stare at the news notification that popped up on the screen. "Breaking news—Police are treating Priestly's death as a homicide. Cause of death, poison. No specifics."

"We better find Michael quickly. I'll call Shana," she said.

The call went to voicemail, so she left a vague message about urgently needing to speak, with no mention of Michael.

Meanwhile, Babs continued to research Priestly.

"You probably know all this," she said but read aloud from the information she had found in her Google search. "Mr. Priestly, fifty-eight years old, President, Priestly Talent Management, offices on West Forty-Eighth Street.

Divorced from his first wife, Cynthia, with whom he shares two college-age daughters. Now remarried and living in Scarsdale with his second wife, Tiffany, age thirty, one of his former models who is now also a partner in the agency. Keeps a *pied-a-terre* on West Seventieth Street where he was found murdered."

Babs turned her laptop screen to Harriet to show her a picture of Simon Priestly with a stunning young woman on his arm. She was a couple of inches taller than Simon and had long blonde straight hair parted in the middle that hung like curtains on either side of her large blue eyes. "That's Simon with Tiffany," Babs said.

She continued clicking through items on her screen. "The agency seems to have a good reputation. They represent magazine, runway, and advertising talent. If he has been doing nasty things, he has been managing to keep it under the radar. What did you find when you did your initial research on lawsuits against Priestly?"

Harriet turned to her computer and opened the case file. "Let's see, over the last five years he has been named in six lawsuits—five of them in the last two years. Looks like #MeToo has paved the way for victims to finally take a stand. None of the lawsuits resulted in court appearances, so they all must have been settled out of court. What this tells me is that Michael wasn't the first. But this is interesting. It looks like he is the only male. And he may be the first to refuse to accept a settlement."

Harriet's phone rang. She held a finger up to Babs to be quiet and put the call on speaker.

"Hi, Shana. Thanks for getting back to me quickly. How have you been?"

"Hi, Harriet. I'm okay. I was surprised—but you know what, I am actually glad to hear from you. I have a complicated situation here."

"What's going on?"

"Are you still my lawyer? Can I talk to you in confidence?"

"Yes, I am still your lawyer. And by the way, I am Michael's too," Harriet said.

There was a long pause before Shana continued. "You hit it. It's Michael. He might have been the last person to see Simon Priestly alive. He's afraid the police are after him and frankly, he's really scared. I finally convinced him that you're cool."

"Would it be possible for you to bring him to my office?" Harriet asked.

There was some arguing in the background and then Shana came back on. "Michael is just afraid they are watching our building and he will be recognized. But we'll figure something out. We can be down there in an hour." Shana disconnected the call.

"Okay," Babs said. "While you are working on that end, let's see if we can dig into the murder, so we can get Michael off the suspect list. Let's start with the crime scene—Priestly's apartment. Police will have finished processing it by now, leaving it taped up, and maybe an officer stationed out front." Babs, having worked for thirty years for the NYPD in several administrative capacities including computer specialist, knew all the routines.

The investigator went to her laptop and pulled up Priestly's address and then used Google Earth to hone in on the street scene—a surprisingly old brick apartment building on West Seventieth Street. Then she researched the building's past real estate transactions. This was a typical older Upper West Side, rent-stabilized building, whose tenants had been there a very long time, she shared with Harriet.

"That's odd," Harriet said. "Considering his image and his profession, you would think Priestly would want a flashy East Side *pied-a-terre*."

"Well, it looks like the deed is actually under his mother's name—Samantha Priestly, who has owned the apartment for thirty-five years." Babs did a search for Samantha Priestly. Her New York Times obituary topped the results. "She passed away five years ago. Simon must be holding on to the apartment. Typical New York real estate story," Babs said.

"So, how are you going to get inside?"

"I'll show you. Give me five minutes." Babs packed up her things and hustled out of Harriet's office and back to her own where she retrieved a floral print dress and shapeless trench coat from her closet. She slipped the dress over her T-shirt and took off her jeans replacing them with heavy skin-colored leggings. Then she strapped her customized tool belt underneath the dress. The tool belt held all the items she would need to get entry and process the apartment.

Next, she studied the collection of shoes in the bottom of the closet. She replaced her Nike's with black, round-toed orthopedic-looking shoes. They were comfortable and would allow her to move fast if need be. Checking out her reflection in the full-length mirror, she took a comb and flattened her curly gray hair, then placed a scarf around her head, purposely allowing a few strands to stick out from underneath. A metal cane completed the ensemble.

Babs packed her phone and wallet into a pocketbook she had picked up at the Salvation Army, certain she had seen Queen Elizabeth wearing the same one. Then she ran back up the stairs to Harriet's office.

She slowed down as she walked into the law offices. The receptionist looked up and said, "How can I help you?"

"Jenn, it's just me," Babs said with a wink. She could hear Jenn laughing as she headed down the hall to Harriet's office. "So, how do I look?"

"Like a harmless, little old lady. In other words, perfect," Harriet said. "Call me when you get inside."

Babs grabbed the Two train heading uptown. As soon as she stepped into the car, a young woman jumped up to offer her a seat, which she graciously accepted.

At Seventy-second Street, she climbed the subway steps using her cane to assist. Busy New Yorkers bustled past her. She walked unhurriedly to the apartment building, keeping her head down to avoid any cameras. She surveyed the building from across the street to get an idea of the police coverage and the doorman situation.

As she suspected, there was a police cruiser parked in front of the building. One officer was standing out in front, staring down at his phone. No sign of a doorman, which was not unusual for a rent-stabilized building. That was both good news and bad news. She wouldn't be stopped by anyone, but she could only get through the locked front door if she followed some other folks in.

She crossed the street and positioned herself in front of the store adjacent to Priestly's apartment building. The store's bins of fruits and vegetables jutted well into the street. She stood in the aisle between the tomatoes and the apples and watched as two chatty older women headed to Priestly's building. She cozied in behind them.

The police officer smiled, held open the door, and didn't ask any questions. He seemed to take no notice of the little old lady who toddled in behind them. The trio headed directly to the elevator.

When they got in and hit the button for the fourth floor, one of the women finally noticed Babs and asked politely about her destination. Babs told her the eleventh floor, although her target was on the tenth.

Babs exited the elevator on the eleventh floor and headed for the stairwell on the end of the hall near the G-line of apartments. Then she walked down the steps at her normal pace and stood on her toes to peer out the small window of the fire door. Priestly's apartment, 10G, was made obvious by the yellow crime scene tape barring the doorway.

Before leaving the stairwell, Babs unbuttoned her coat, lifted her dress, and took out the lock pick tools secured in her utility belt. Picking locks was her specialty, practicing the art in her spare time, a Zen-like experience. She donned a pair of latex gloves and slowly inched her way through the empty hallway to the front of Priestly's door. There was a regular lock over the knob and an old deadbolt further up the door. Babs was betting that the police only secured the bottom lock when they left.

She quickly reached over the crime scene tape, worked her magic and sure enough, the knob turned in her hand, and the door swung open. She bent down and maneuvered through the crime scene tape, then closed and locked the door behind her.

Babs leaned her cane against the doorframe and took a moment to take in her surroundings. In contrast to the building's traditional Upper West Side exterior, this apartment had been refurbished in sleek, high-end modern. The furniture was cream-colored leather, the floor, polished oak. Striking, enlarged photographs of models covered the walls. Babs gazed up at the sculpture-like metal light fixtures. She didn't turn on any lights. The sunlight coming through the windows filled the room with a warm glow.

She reached for her phone and Facetimed Harriet. "I'm in. Are your clients there yet?"

"Shana just texted from downstairs. They're on their way up. Let's just keep the line open."

Babs then pulled out a thin, black video camera from her tool belt. Her newest spy toy. She hit record and turned the camera to film the room, something to review with Harriet later. There was no chalk body outline on the floor but there were several cushions missing from the couch. Too bad, nice couch. There was black fingerprint dust on all the surfaces.

Babs continued her surveillance, recording every inch of the apartment. She noticed a small wet bar behind the couch. All the bottles and glasses had been removed. The NYPD must think the poison was in a drink, she concluded.

Babs glanced at her phone and saw that two tall and strikingly beautiful black women had just walked into Harriet's office. She put her tour of the crime site on hold and watched as the scene played out.

Harriet asked, "So did Michael chicken out?"

Shana and the other woman broke into big smiles. "Harriet, don't you recognize Michael?" The other woman stepped forward and offered his large hand to Harriet.

Harriet stared openly at Michael and then she broke into a laugh. "Wow, that's some disguise. Oh, is it a disguise? I am cool no matter what."

"Yes, it's totally a disguise and a great one too," Shana said. "People were eyeballing us up and down, but no one suspected. Including the cop who was standing in front of my building."

"Brilliant," Harriet said. "Goes to show you that people make all kinds of assumptions based on what they see. That's my life story. People assume I'm helpless because I use a wheelchair and therefore, they don't take me seriously. Big mistake on their part!"

Harriet invited Shana and Michael to sit at the small, round conference table, then maneuvered her wheelchair to join them. She noticed through the table's glass top that Michael had slipped off his fashionable heels.

Michael noticed her noticing. "Oh, sorry," he said. "Hope you don't mind. These shoes are killing my feet. Don't know how you guys wear these things."

Harriet laughed. "No problem. Make yourself comfortable." She pointed through the glass at her own black Christian Louboutins. "No way I could wear these if I actually had to walk in them."

She gestured toward her iPad and asked if anyone objected to her private investigator, Babs Ward, listening in on their conversation. "Just so you know Babs Ward, as the firm's contracted investigator, is covered under our confidentiality agreement," Harriet added. She didn't mention that Babs was in Priestly's apartment.

"Michael, tell me what happened the night you saw Priestly," Harriet started.

Michael shifted uncomfortably in the chair and looked to Shana who gave him a nod. "Priestly called me yesterday morning and suggested I come by. He said that we should talk and settle things amicably—just between the two of us. That we didn't need lawyers. When I got there, I could tell he had been drinking, He was already a little tipsy and slurring his words. I actually recorded the whole thing on my phone."

Babs' voice came over the iPad. "Hi Michael, can you tell me what he was drinking?"

Michael searched for the source of the question, and then stopped breathing. "Is she in Simon's apartment?" he asked with shock in his voice.

"Yes," Harriet admitted. "She just dropped in there to see if she could find anything that might support your story."

"It's not a story," Michael said quietly. "It's what really happened." Then he answered Babs' question. "He was drinking scotch from his private reserve. Everyone knew that Macallan was Simon's poison. Oh, I didn't mean that. It's just that everyone who knew Simon knew that was his drink.

"I know it was a mistake to go there. That's why I didn't ask you first," Michael said, looking sheepishly at Harriet. "You told me not to speak to anyone without your being there. But I thought maybe I could get Priestly to acknowledge his advances and that would strengthen my case. He said he assumed I would play the game like everyone else. There must be boundaries and I told him so. He yelled 'What makes you so special?' and that's when I got out of there. He was definitely alive when I left. Drunk and stumbling, but alive. I thought he was going to follow me out of the apartment, but he slammed the door after I ran out. I heard him lock it.

"I've had it with this business," Michael added. "Besides, I'm aging out."

Shana reached over and put her hand over his.

Still listening to the conversation in Harriet's office, Babs resumed her tour of the apartment. She found the master bedroom dominated by a king-size bed with a black furry bedspread. Then she noticed the mirror on the ceiling. *Kinky.*

"Michael," she heard Harriet say in her most consoling voice. "You are very brave to take a stand. It takes people like you who are willing to go public and make personal sacrifices to protect others. Again, I need to ask you not to speak with anyone unless I or someone from our firm is with you. We are here to protect you. I'll make the arrangements for you to meet with the police, and we will be by your side. I also want to make a copy of your recording of the meeting with Simon."

"Okay," Michael said, sounding both resigned and resolved. "I know that's the right thing to do."

Watching from Priestly's master bedroom, Babs was so absorbed by Michael's story that she didn't hear the front door opening. She jumped when she heard two women murmuring in the next room. Desperate, she scanned the bedroom for a place to hide, hoping there might be a tub and shower curtain in the master bath but alas, there was only a fancy, glass-doored shower stall as big as Babs's bedroom. Then she spotted the cabinet below the vanity. Her only option. She fumbled the video recorder back into its holder on her tool belt. She opened the louvered doors and saw that the cabinet was empty save for a couple of rolls of toilet paper.

Babs squatted down and crawled in backwards. If she stayed squished in a fetal position, she could close the doors behind her and peer through the slats. With phone in hand, she whispered Harriet's name until she got her attention. "I'm not alone. Hiding now. Quiet." She saw Harriet and her guests stare at the screen in shock. She turned the volume down so no sound would give her away and placed the phone face down so no light would show through the slats.

"I don't understand why you just didn't take the stuff when you were here last week when you took care of the scotch," said one of the women.

"What? And take a chance that the bastard would realize it was gone?" the other woman said.

Babs heard the voices grow louder as they entered the bedroom.

"This is so creepy. Why can't you wait till they release the apartment? It will be all yours. Right?"

"Well, Liz, I am not sure about that. Simon was threatening to change his will. I would bet anything that his bitchy daughters get everything except the agency. I made sure that would be mine when we got married. And to think he would have destroyed it all because he couldn't control his disgusting dick. It was bad enough that he kept forcing himself on those young girls—now he had to try it with a guy. And with a decent guy who wouldn't be bought off. There have to be boundaries. Enough is enough! If the media had gotten hold of that information, it would destroy the agency. I couldn't let that happen."

Babs heard the women opening and closing doors and drawers.

"Tiffany, do you want these?" Liz asked.

"Yeah," Tiffany said. "I can wear them to the funeral. Just throw them into the suitcase."

She heard more shuffling around. Then Liz said, "Just wish you hadn't thrown Michael under the bus. He's such a sweet guy. Why did you have to drag him into this?"

"He dragged himself into this with that lawsuit. I knew Simon was meeting with Michael that night. So, this morning, I just texted him to hide. He was just a convenient distraction to buy me some time. Don't worry about him. He has a good lawyer. He'll be fine."

Then Babs heard a mechanical sound.

"Wow, that's cool," Liz said.

"Yeah, Simon had it built in a couple of years ago. This is where he kept the real valuables. Bring that backpack over here."

"How much do you think is in there?"

"Last time I counted, about $20,000. It's not a lot. But I feel like I earned it.

And the jewelry and coins are worth much more. Okay, let's go."

"Wait," said Liz. "I have to use the bathroom."

Babs held her breath. She heard the woman flush the toilet and then saw her thin, jeans-clad legs linger in front of the cabinet, apparently taking a minute to look at herself in the mirror.

"Come on, Liz. Let's get out of here," Tiffany called.

"*Go, go, Liz.*" Babs thought to herself, and imagined everyone in Harriet's office thinking the same thought as they listened in. Thanks to the power of suggestion, now Babs really had to pee. As per Harriet's earlier comment, she tried channeling Jack Reacher. Of course, Reacher was a giant, and Babs would probably come up to his…. The thought made Babs want to laugh which only made her need to pee more.

Babs could see Liz turn and walk out of the bathroom. Thank goodness.

She heard the two women head for the door. Then she remembered the cane she had left leaning against the door frame. Would they notice?

Babs quietly opened the vanity cabinet door.

She heard Liz say, "What's that?"

Tiffany responded, "Don't know, don't care. Let's get out of here."

Babs heard the front door open, close, and the lock tumble into place. That's when she exploded out of the vanity on her hands and knees. She held onto the vanity to stand, ignoring the phone as it fell from the cabinet. She pulled down her leggings and let out a big sigh as she peed. Then her gaze turned to her phone, which she now realized was lying face-up on the bathroom floor.

Oh, shit, she thought as she saw Harriet, Shana, and Michael with their hands covering their eyes. She finished her business, grabbed the phone, hit the mute button, and placed it on the vanity, screen side down, before flushing. Then she turned the phone over, turned the volume back up, and hit the speaker button.

"Sorry about that," Babs said. "Did you catch that whole thing?"

"Yes, of course, we did," Harriet said.

"No, I mean the conversation between Tiffany and Liz?"

"So that solves the locked-door murder," said Harriet. "Tiffany poisoned

Simon's private scotch when she was there last week. No dumb blonde here. Another good reason to never make assumptions. Michael, what's all this about a text telling you to hide?"

Michael pulled out his phone and showed her the text message.

Babs collected her cane at the front door and walked right over the crime scene tape that the two women had pulled down when they came through.

She walked briskly down the hall, but before ringing for the elevator, she studied herself in the mirror opposite and adjusted her scarf and coat. Then she pushed the button and leaned heavily on her cane as the doors opened. She walked through the lobby. The officer still standing outside held the door open and smiled down at her.

* * *

Ellen Quint is a mystery writer, an audiobook reviewer, and a judge for the Audies, the annual awards for audiobooks. Ellen brings a love of mysteries and a deep knowledge of the genre to her regular column on audiobook mysteries for *Audiofile Magazine*. Her own crime short stories can be found in *Family Matters: A Mystery Anthology* ("Crossing the Line"), and *Where Crime Never Sleeps: Murder New York Style* Vol. 4 ("Taking the Brooklyn Bridge Back"). Ellen is a Board Member of the New York/Tri-State chapter of Sisters in Crime.

FAMILY MATTERS

by Mary Jo Robertiello

Young and old, gay and straight, Black, brown, and white streamed through Smith Memorial's doors. It was a perfect fall day.

Standing at the church door, Tom Reed, Smith Memorial's senior minister, held Malcolm, his new husband, with one arm and shook hands with the other. Tom had a shaved head and an open and welcoming facial expression. Malcolm was about five foot, eight inches, trim, black hair with a part on the left as straight as U.S. Route Twenty.

As part of the wedding celebration, blue and yellow balloons were tied along the fence surrounding the Greenwich Village church. A yellow one came loose and floated upwards.

Across Washington Square South a man crouched behind a plane tree. He watched the ascending balloon and raised his right arm, cocked an imaginary shotgun, and shot. Underneath his Mets cap, his face was lit up with fury. Hank Simpson, husband of Wendy Reed, turned back to the lively scene at the church entrance. He watched his wife kiss her son before she joined another group. She wants AIDS? Divorce? No can do, he said under his breath.

A neighborhood dachshund woofed up at Hank. Hank tore his eyes away from the happy mother, son, and his husband, glared at the dog, put his navy running shoe on the dog's right front paw, and rammed it into the sidewalk. The dachshund yelped and sunk his sharp little teeth into Hank's slightly soiled khakis until he reached hairy skin. Hank's yelp was much louder than the dog's, drawing attention from across the street.

Malcolm glanced over Tom's shoulder. "Holy shit," he muttered. "Sorry."

Tom laughed. "Fed up already?"

Malcolm jerked his head toward the street. Tom looked across at the angry man bouncing on one leg and holding onto the tree trunk. "Holy shit is right."

The newly married couple's youth and good looks added to the charm of their well-cut, flashy suits. Even so, they both realized that their approaching guest's outfit cost more than the two of theirs together. The extremely tall man and his extremely short wife mirrored the general happiness.

"That guy across the street?" Lorenzo smothered them with his sexy Italian-English accent.

"The one who's attacking a dog?" asked Tom.

"I know him," said Lorenzo.

"You know him?" asked Tom.

"He saw me at a fundraiser. He stalked us, waited outside our place.

Remember, darling?"

Monique, his wife, laughed knowingly. "Brrr." Her sculpted shoulders shuddered theatrically. "He hustled us down Seventieth Street."

They all laughed, keeping an eye on the scene across the street.

Hank hid behind the tree and shook his baseball cap at the yapping dog. A woman in pajama bottoms and a Disney Princess T-shirt yelled in chorus with her dog.

"He's my father-in-law." One of Tom's unusual traits was revealing what most people would keep secret.

Malcolm blurted, "He hates gays. Wouldn't come to the wedding."

The laughter stopped. Embarrassed, Lorenzo and Monique gave Tom and Malcolm a quick hug and melted into a nearby group.

"Be right back," Tom said. Malcolm gave him a look. Tom held up his hands in surrender before heading through the loving crowd and down the stairs to the all-gender restrooms. He was following his mother. They had to talk.

All-gender in theory. In practice, the older members followed childhood rules: boys in one, girls in another. Tom wondered for the millionth time why women took so long.

The minute she came out of one of the restrooms, Tom said, "Mom, Hank's across the street."

Wendy Reed was in her early sixties. She was plump with reddish-brown and white hair, giving her the look of a pretty fox. She said quietly, "I saw him."

"Why did you marry him, Mom?" asked Tom.

"The usual. Lonely. Alone."

A few days ago was the first time Tom had seen her in months. He and Malcolm had driven out to Benson Avenue to introduce Malcolm to Mom. But today, under the happy, hopeful atmosphere of Tom's wedding, Wendy's lips drooped when they weren't propped up in a smile.

"Tom, you've got a life. I do too. I'm divorcing him."

"He knows?"

"But isn't accepting it. It's our elephant in the bedroom."

"Mom, we have to talk."

The restroom door opened. Hank Simpson stepped out.

The three of them stood and stared for a few seconds that seemed like hours.

Wendy said in a feeble, cordial attempt, "You're joining us?"

"I'm using the men's room. Not against the law, right?" Hank growled and headed up the back stairs to an open door.

Son and mother kept their mouths shut until Hank was out of sight. Even then, they whispered. Tom pulled his mom into a deserted corner. He studied her wounded face, in contrast to her meticulous appearance. She adjusted his shirt collar.

"Just so," he teased her as he placed his hands on hers.

She blurted, "I was a fool. I fell for his line. He had a good one, especially if you're lonely."

"You've been married two years?"

"Two hundred years, it seems like."

"He's giving you a hard time?"

"That's putting it mildly."

"We're discussing this tomorrow." Very much the minister in charge, Tom tapped on his cell and checked his busy schedule. He read on his iPhone calendar: 10/31: Halloween - Stonewall.

"Make that the day after tomorrow, November 1st. Okay, Mom?"

Wendy stared at her son's phone. She saw the ubiquitous sexy girl image on Tom's cell, the logo of an Atlantic City gambling casino. "Tom?"

Tom caught her glance. "Just checking, Mom. They're always advertising."

"Promise me you're over that."

"I promise," he said gently if not truthfully. "So, dear Mom, I'll see you the day after Halloween."

"I made a batch of pumpernickel. I'll wrap some up for you and Malcolm."

Tom raised his mom's hand and kissed it.

* * *

November 1st, four p.m. Tom pulled up to the curb at Benson Avenue, relieved his eight-year-old clunker made it. *I'll get it fixed as soon as I'm paid off...right now, I've got to find out what's going on with Mom.*

Tom swept bagel crumbs off Mom's birthday present, a black and tan plaid shirt. He was back in the Brooklyn neighborhood, light-years from his Manhattan life. He inhaled deeply the ocean breezes from nearby Coney Island. The neighborhood looked sleepy, worn out from Halloween. He studied his childhood home, a single-family house built in the 1930s. Mom and Dad bought it for peanuts about thirty years ago. He thought it looked good with its fresh coat of white paint and royal blue trimmed shutters. There was the large Halloween bowl still near the front door at the top of the steps. Mom forgot about it, he figured.

He gripped the steering wheel. He had to ask her point-blank; did she tell Hank before they married that she had a gay son?

"Mom?" Tom called as he lugged the bowl through the living room and parked it in the eat-in kitchen. On the sill of the east window, he saw the purple African violets they'd brought Mom a few days before. Her kitchen was so spacious. So tidy compared to their West Village nest.

Tom's inner nine-year-old pawed through the bowl's remaining candy on a Snickers search. Out of habit, he opened the refrigerator. He smiled at his mom's meticulousness: clean jam jars, ketchup containers, salad dressing bottles lined up according to brand. On the top shelf was a loaf of homemade pumpernickel wrapped in Saran Wrap. His name and Malcolm's were written across it.

When he had passed through the living room, he'd noticed a drawer in the TV bureau was pulled out. Concerned, he circled back and poked around in the drawer. He assumed Mom had found his old gambling receipts. That was in the past, for the most part. He looked around the darkened, familiar room. The silk drapes were closed. The room was a study in books, cozy armchairs, and oriental rugs. A fireplace, once welcoming with a warming glow, was swept clean. Where was the MacBook Air? Four days ago, it was on a desk near the fifty-inch TV.

Tom was flooded with memories. Ten years ago, Dad had a heart attack and died in his favorite armchair. This was where he told Mom he was gay.

"Please be careful. I love you," were the first words out of her mouth.

Tom shook himself out of his thoughts. "Mom?"

No sound. He headed for the backyard recalling she often took an afternoon nap. Where's Hank? he wondered.

Tom saw his mom's curly ginger hair peeking over the top of an Adirondack chair. He walked around to the front of the chair, not wanting to startle her. Her eyes were closed. Her face was red as if lit from within. She was still. Too still. Tom noticed her wedding band was missing. He touched her left hand. It was cold. He grabbed the chair for support.

"Mom," he said softly, then louder. The tears rolled down his cheeks. He yanked out a handkerchief and wiped his face. He lightly touched her bruised neck. The first call was to 911. The second call was to Malcolm. Tom folded himself into the cell, sobbing. "She's dead. She's dead."

Malcolm said he'd be with Tom within the hour. "I love you," were his last words.

Within thirty minutes, the Emergency Medical Services, cops—including an inspector—and lastly, the coroner arrived. Officers had Tom sit in the living room. They wandered in and out asking him questions. When was the last time you saw your mother? What time did you get here today? Have you talked to anyone in the neighborhood this afternoon? She lived alone? Was she married? Was she in good health?

Tom had often faced death. Many a midnight call from a parishioner begging him for help. Why were they keeping him away from his mom's body? She'd had a minor stroke a few years ago but the bruises told another story. The EMS crew treated him like a kid or a moron.

"Where's Hank?" he asked an officer.

"On his way," was the noncommittal answer. After a half hour, Tom stood up and walked briskly into the backyard. A young cop stopped him. Tom wished he'd worn his collar. He curled his fingers, noticing the cop staring at his purple nail polish.

An older official joined them. "I'll take care of this."

Tom glanced at the woman's ID on her lapel. "You're a detective?"

"Detective Judy Yelvington and the inspector assigned to this…" The detective gestured to the Adirondack chair, surrounded by her team. "You're the Smith Memorial minister, Reverend Reed?"

"That's right. What's going on?" He eyed the older woman whose face had spent too much time on the beach but whose hazel eyes were large and clear.

"Your mother didn't die a natural death," Detective Yelvington said.

Tom put one foot behind him, steadying himself, waiting for the next words. Things were about to get worse.

"There is evidence she was strangled."

Tom covered his face with his hands.

Detective Yelvington led him to a picnic table and some chairs. After questioning him about his relationship with his mother, she said, "Do you have access to your mother's legal documents?"

Tom nodded.

"I'm gay. She was completely supportive." He sensed the detective was ill at ease, so the words spilled out of his mouth. "Loves, loved my husband." The detective flinched but remained steady. "We were married two days ago. She was there."

Was he a suspect? Suspected of killing Mom? Tom's innards did push-ups. He slouched over from the thought. First person to find the victim.

"What's your husband's name?"

"Malcolm Babian. He should be here by now…" He looked across the lawn at the young man running toward him.

"At last," Tom cried. After a tight embrace, he introduced Malcolm to the detective. "Mom made us pumpernickel," Tom whispered. "Strangled."

"What?" Malcolm yelled and jumped back from Tom. A look of confusion spread across his face.

Tom looked down at his empty, outstretched hands. He glared at his husband. *Does he suspect me too?*

Malcolm grabbed Tom's hands. "Sorry, sorry, sorry."

The detective studied the two men. "Reverend Reed, don't leave the neighborhood."

"I'm not going anywhere." Tom still glared at Malcolm. "I have to call the church." He opened the kitchen door.

"Those legal papers, Reverend," Yelvington called after Tom.

Tom ducked into the house.

When Malcolm started to follow him, Detective Yelvington blocked his way. "Take a seat, Mr. Babian." She pointed at the nearby chairs.

Malcolm sat. "Tom's a wonderful man. He's loved, admired at the church." He put his head in his hands.

"Take your time. I need your assistance," Yelvington said in a calming tone. "Tell me about Reverend Reed. Where did you and Tom meet?"

Malcolm's lawyerly instincts snapped to attention. He figured he'd tell the truth but not the whole truth.

"Atlantic City. We were both into weekend gambling. Not seriously," he added.

"What's your profession?"

"I'm a lawyer."

"You were married a few days ago?"

Malcolm nodded.

"Was Mrs. Reed at the wedding?'

"Of course. She and Tom were close."

"What about Tom's father?"

"He died about ten years ago."

"She's remarried?"

"Yeah. A guy who hates gays."

"Was he at the wedding?"

"Hank Simpson stood across the street and gawked at us. You know the Village? The church is on Thompson and Washington Square."

Detective Yelvington nodded. "Beautiful."

Is this lady playing sensitive or being truthful, Malcolm wondered?

"Tom and I were here a few days ago before the wedding."

"Why?"

"Tom hadn't seen his mother very much. Combination of guilt trip and introducing me to Wendy."

"Here's the hard part." Yelvington studied Malcolm who was clamping his shaking hands together. "Any reason why Tom would kill his mom?"

Malcolm held on to his outrage. She was doing her job. "He loved and respected her. I wish I had a mom like Wendy."

Yelvington looked up from tapping on her cell. "Financial problems?"

"No, of course not."

"You met in Atlantic City?"

"So?"

The detective stood up. "Show me the house."

"Okay. I've been in it once four days ago," Malcolm said.

They walked up the back steps and into the kitchen.

Sitting at the round table, Tom had his ear to his cell and papers in front of him. He pointed to some documents. "I dug these out."

Yelvington sat down and examined the power of attorney, health care proxy, and a two-year-old will. Malcolm peered over the detective's shoulder.

"She told me about the will, but this is the first time I've seen it," Tom said.

"What about you?" Yelvington turned her head toward Malcolm.

"Same goes for me," Malcolm said as he noticed that Wendy Reed had left her estate equally divided to her husband and her son.

"She married him on August 10th two years ago and the will was drawn up August 15th," Tom said.

Yelvington read a name from the will. "Her lawyer?"

Tom sent the lawyer's cell number to Yelvington. "She told me that she was divorcing him."

"Did she say his reaction?"

Tom thought a minute. "She said it was the elephant in the bedroom."

"Meaning?"

"Hank is usually on the verge of a temper tantrum," Tom said. "Where is he?"

"He's talking to my team downtown."

Tom figured she meant the police station.

"Tom, let's walk through your home."

He hoped being called by his first name was a plus. He shoved papers into his briefcase and locked it in the pantry.

Yelvington watched but didn't say anything.

"How many floors?" she said.

"Two and there's an attic."

"We'll start at the top." At the second floor, Yelvington pulled in air.

Tom and Malcolm looked out the window, giving Yelvington time to breathe easy. Tom texted Malcolm: Tell everything? Malcolm texted back: Wait.

Yelvington's eyes roamed over the clean, quiet space. Three doors were open. "What have we got?"

"My mom and her husband's room," Tom pointed to the room closest to the backyard. "That second door leads to my dad's office. Now, it's a junk room." Tom pointed to the door nearest the stairs. "That's my old room. Now, our room." He smiled at Malcolm.

"Let's hit the attic." The detective pulled the hatch in the ceiling.

"We didn't go there the other day," Malcolm said.

Yelvington had already started a slow climb up the steep stairs. Shades were pulled down on the four windows. She yanked on the light. It cast a dull glow.

"Welcome to my childhood." Tom's hearty tone didn't hide his anxiety. He stared at the shady heap of bikes, trikes, wagons, and scooters. Puzzled, he walked closer and ran his hand over a cut bike tire. He eyed the mangled mass of wheels.

"How does your attic usually look?" Detective Yelvington said, thinking of her own jumble heap. "I never assume a neat attic."

"Mom was a neat freak." Tom fingered the bikes' tires. "They've been slashed."

Yelvington tripped over a cloth. She yanked away the shredded remnants of a Boy Scout uniform. "When was the last time you were up here?"

"A few years ago."

The detective pulled out a compact flashlight, then got on her phone, telling the team to send some guys to the attic. She ran the strongest lighting mode over the labels adorning the jumbled boxes, many ripped open. Boy Scout uniforms, Camping stuff, Hot Wheels.

"Your stuff?" she asked.

"Yeah. I was a spoiled kid."

"Hot Wheels?" Malcolm said in a tone of wonder.

Yelvington directed her light at the guys' feet so she didn't blind them. "Where's the stuff?"

In double shock, Tom shook his head, his mom's murder, and now this, his childhood destroyed and missing.

They heard stomping up the stairs. "My team's going over this." Yelvington yanked open the attic's stuck door. "We're looking at your room now."

Down on the second floor, Tom swung open the door. Dated posters of David Bowie and Brad Pitt faced the single bed. On the wooden floor was smashed glass and a man's portrait ripped in two.

Tom banged his fist on the nearby bureau. He bent over to pick up the torn pieces.

Yelvington blocked him. "Don't touch it."

Tom gave her a dirty look but stepped back while Malcolm videoed the ripped photo, using his phone.

"Who's he?" Yelvington looked down at the destroyed photo.

"Dag Hammarskjöld. A gay social rights activist." Tom propped his arms on the bureau and hid his face.

Malcolm slid behind him and put one arm around his waist. With his right hand, he showed Yelvington a recent selfie. "Taken four days ago."

The guys, smiling deliriously, were holding Hammarskjöld's photo between them.

"Send me that photo." She contacted her attic team. "Second floor, Tom's bedroom."

"We're out of here." She pointed her thumb toward the corridor. "Your mom's bedroom."

Tom remembered his parents' bedroom as being comfy and lavish. His mom had splurged on cashmere spreads, linen sheets, and creamy pillowcases piled on an ivory canopied bed. His dad had teased her about their royal suite, but Tom had figured Dad liked it too.

The bed now resembled a neglected orphan. Rough white sheets and pillows squirming out of too-tight covers. Tom hadn't been in the room in a few years, ever since Hank and Wendy married. He and Malcolm looked out the window down at the backyard.

Yelvington circled the room, yanking open bureau drawers, examining a desk's contents, exploring the bedside tables. At the back of a drawer in Wendy's bedside table, she found a container labeled Xanax. She looked up to see Tom staring at her.

"Your mom took tranquilizers?"

Tom shook his head. "I can't say. She was anxious at our wedding."

Yelvington slipped the Xanax into an evidence bag. She opened the mahogany closet. One side had dresses, slacks, nightgowns. The other side had only a dirty T-shirt on the floor.

The bathroom medicine cabinet was empty except for a toothbrush. After calling the team, she joined the guys at the window, staring down at Hank being escorted by an officer into the backyard. At that moment, Hank saw them. He clenched his fists.

"We're going downstairs."

When they reached the kitchen, Yelvington gestured at the large table. "Sit here."

The back door opened, and a young officer came in. He nodded at Detective Yelvington, Tom, and Malcolm.

"Reverend Reed, Mr. Babian, this is Detective Brinkly," said Yelvington. She studied the two men. "Reverend Reed, I'm requesting you not leave the neighborhood in case you need to be questioned further."

"I'm not going anywhere. I want to be close to Mom."

"We need a few days to collect information. Mr. Babian, you're free to go."

"I'm staying," Malcolm said.

"Today is the first of the month. We'll meet on the third."

"What about Hank?" Tom asked.

"Mr. Simpson is not staying on the premises."

"So, where's he staying?"

"I'm not at liberty to say. I'll see you in two days." Detective Yelvington opened the back door and was gone.

"You're a lawyer, Mr. Babian?" Detective Brinkly asked.

"Yes. Call me Malcolm."

"Here's my cell number and email address," the detective added.

Malcolm reached into his hip pocket for his.

"Already got it," Detective Brinkly said. "We've sealed off the second floor, the attic, the cellar, and the backyard. The rest of your house is yours. We'll be coming in and out. Ignore us." Detective Brinkly looked at Tom. "Reverend Reed, someone needs to identify your mother."

Tom knew this was coming but it was still nerve-wracking.

"Of course, I'll do it."

"I'll pick you up tomorrow around three."

"I'm coming," Malcolm said.

"Mr. Babian, that won't be necessary," Brinkly said with finality.

Tom clutched his cell. "I need my laptop and iPad."

Malcolm held up his hand like the teacher's pet. "They're in the car."

"Thank God," Tom said quietly.

Two hours later, most of the take-out pepperoni pizza eaten and a few beers drunk, Tom said, "One hell of a honeymoon." The brave tone slipped away, and tears started rolling down his cheeks. Malcolm got up and folded Tom in his arms. They pulled out the living room's sofa bed.

The next morning, they toasted Wendy's pumpernickel and heated up coffee. Neither had slept well.

Tom turned the kitchen into his makeshift workspace while Malcolm chose a living room corner. Unlike Tom who was used to lots of parish activity and wouldn't be bothered by the law enforcement walkthroughs, he liked working in privacy.

Around nine, the back door opened. Detective Brinkly escorted an older woman into the kitchen. She glanced at Tom and Malcolm before following the detective.

Tom addressed his church's daily meditation group on Zoom. Malcolm heard the congregants offering their condolences. Detective Brinkly had told Tom not to go into details about Wendy's death.

For lunch, they had their choice of Kraft cheese, more pumpernickel, and leftover pizza. Malcolm ate his sandwich with one hand and held his cell with the other as he argued about licensing. Tom had no appetite.

Working on his laptop, Tom heard the law's footsteps on the second floor. He checked his cell: 2:50. "Porch?" he texted Malcolm.

On the porch steps, they whispered about the house being wired. Had Tom's car been wiretapped? Or Malcolm's rental car?

"I didn't recognize that woman," Tom said.

"Then she probably didn't recognize you," Malcolm said with more love than logic.

Detective Brinkly poked his head out the front door. "Hi, you ready to head downtown?"

"Sure." Tom stood up, all business.

Brinkly drove into town. He stopped at the one traffic light. "Tom, you want to talk about anything?"

Everything. "I'm okay," he said. "Who was that woman you brought through the house?"

"A neighbor." Brinkly kept his eyes on the traffic light.

"You wanted her to identify me? I didn't recognize her."

"We're here." Brinkly opened the main door of a nondescript three-story building. He showed the desk officer his ID and led Tom down a corridor, stopping outside a metal door.

Once inside, the smell reminded Tom of other morgues where he had accompanied parishioners. He stared at the rows of drawers. An attendant pulled out a refrigerated drawer with a covered body on it.

Tom and Brinkly stood on one side and the attendant on the other. Brinkly nodded and the attendant lifted the gray-green covering, Only the head showed.

Tom looked at his mom's still face. "That's my mom, Wendy Reed."

"I'll wait outside," the detective said.

Pulling into the Reed driveway, Brinkly said, "Detective Yelvington will call to set up our Wednesday appointment."

"Thanks, Detective. These tasks must be hard on you too."

"You said it." Brinkly drove away.

* * *

November 3rd, eight a.m. Tom's cell phone rang. He held it so Malcolm could hear. "We'll be at your place in an hour. Meet us at the kitchen table. Any questions?"

Aside from asking if you'll be arresting me for murdering my mom? he thought. "I'll save my questions for later."

Yelvington clicked off.

At nine, Detective Yelvington opened the back door. She was accompanied by two younger associates. Their biceps and hands clasped behind their backs beamed ex-military.

"Tom and Malcolm, let's sit down." Yelvington pulled out a folder. Ignoring Tom's and Malcolm's stares, she sorted the contents like solitaire cards. Her two associates stood behind her.

Tom's and Malcolm's eyes were glued to the stacks of gambling debts.

"Tell me about the gambling."

Tom took a deep breath. "I had a problem but that's almost in the past."

Tom recalled the open drawer in the living room. "Hank have anything to do with this?"

"He's claiming you killed your mom for her money."

Tom gritted his teeth. "My poor mom." His voice broke.

Lawyer Malcolm countered, "Hank gets half her money."

Yelvington placed a document in front of Tom and Malcolm. "This is a copy of a new will signed and sealed a week ago."

Everything was left to Tom. Nothing to Hank.

"Your church knows about the gambling?"

"Not yet." Tom took a deep breath.

"My call. My fault." Malcolm held up his right hand to stop Tom from objecting.

"No, God damn it. I was wrong." Tom sat very straight. "I was out to get hired. A man of God who hid his faults and lied to get the job."

Yelvington studied Malcolm's expression of protectiveness, surprised by her own reaction to the normalcy of their closeness.

119

"Stop. Your problem with your church is your problem. Whether or not you killed your mother is my problem."

"Do I need a lawyer?" Tom asked.

"You've got one," Malcolm answered.

"We're taking Hank Simpson on a walk through the house." Yelvington put a recorder and the new will on the table, the latter placed so it could be easily spotted by anyone who might pass by.

Someone knocked on the back door before swinging it open and a moment later, Hank shuffled in. To each side was an officer. They were replaced by the two officers behind Yelvington. A sickening scent, a mixture of booze and unwashed body parts, filled the kitchen. Scratches lined Hank's face. He stumbled and placed his large right hand flat on the table for balance.

Tom's insides turned to water as he studied his dead mother's husband. To redeem any past failings, he asked, "Can I help you, Hank? Maybe we got off to a bad start."

Malcolm mouthed: Are you fucking crazy?

Hank held on to the table. He ran his eyes over the new will. "They forced her. She told me."

"What did Wendy Reed tell you?"

"He hates me. Lots of times," Hank mumbled and glared at Tom.

"Recently?"

"Yeah, the afternoon they killed her. She told me her son wanted everything." He shook his head, agreeing with himself.

"Did anyone overhear you?" Detective Yelvington said. She expected a demand for a lawyer.

Instead, she got, "Bullshit."

She tapped on the recorder. The first sound was Hank screaming, "You bitch!"

"Get out. I'm divorcing…" Wendy Reed cried. No more words. Grunting sounds. Silence.

"That's a neighbor's recording," Yelvington said.

"The woman Detective Brinkly escorted through the kitchen the other day?" Tom interrupted.

Yelvington nodded and continued, "Mr. Simpson ran into the house at 2:58. The neighbor remembered because she checked her watch. Then she approached Mrs. Reed, who was shaking and crying. She told the neighbor she was expecting her son."

The detective looked at Hank. "Where were you, Hank?"

His blood-shot eyes focused on Tom. "He's a minister who gambles with the church's money," he ranted. "Question him. Ask him why he scavenged through his old belongings so he could hawk the contents for cash. When that didn't cover the debts, he killed her."

"Were you in the house that day?"

"So, it's still my house."

"On the landline, there's a 3:05 call to the family lawyer. Why?"

No answer.

"Checking on the will!" Tom yelled. His voice rose an octave as he stood up and moved toward a sweating and cringing Hank, who was shielded by the officers.

"Sit down, Tom," Yelvington ordered.

Tom sat down.

Yelvington gave a signal to the officers. One of them showed a photo of Hank in a Thompson Street pawn shop.

The cop swiped to the next photos. In each one Hank was selling attic toys and using an old Tom Reed license for ID.

"What's the date on that photo, Officer?" Yelvington said.

"October 30th."

"Our wedding," Malcolm said. "Using a false ID and pawning stolen stuff to frame us for a murder we never committed."

Tom jumped out of his seat.

"You strangled my mom?" He grabbed Hank's arm as the officers moved in.

"Don't touch me," Hank screamed.

"Mrs. Reed recorded her own death on her cell," Yelvington switched on the recorder.

Tom froze, hearing mom's voice.

Wendy Reed panted. Hank cursed. For five long minutes, Wendy fought to live, gasping slower and slower.

"Take your final breath, Mom." Tears and sweat poured down Tom's face.

* * *

Mary Jo Robertiello says: Being a mystery writer, I'm in love with the unfathomable. What's more unfathomable than death and how people meet it? I live in the love of my life and my hometown, New York City. I'm fascinated by its essential DNA and its constant change: its ethnic, age, sexual orientation, capitalist, socialist mix, its architecture, its skyline, its buzz, its food. Should I go on? It's all in my police procedural, *The Lemrow Mystery,* my short stories, as well as my website where I write a weekly blog, NYMysteries.com.

WHEN THE CAGED BIRD FLIES

by Catherine Maiorisi

T he knock on the door shattered the safe silence of her home, sending Dana Saunders flying from her chair, gun in hand. In her haste, she dropped her book and knocked over her glass of wine. Keeping her eyes on the door, she dabbed at the wine with a tissue and considered whether to ignore the knock. She couldn't remember the last time she'd had a visitor. Other than her best friend, Margo, her family and friends didn't know how to deal with her after the...the thing and had backed off except for an occasional perfunctory call. She grasped the gun in both hands. It would be better to know than not to know and worry about who was out there, wouldn't it?

She crept to the door and peered at the displays from the three cameras installed at various points outside. It looked like Margo and that white detective, Detective Fielder, on the screens, but Margo always called to alert her when she arrived outside. Maybe it was an imposter. After all, the bastard had tricked her the first time. "W-w-ho is it?" She cringed hearing her voice so weak and shaky.

"It's Margo, Dana. Detective Fielder is with me. I tried to call, but I think your phone is turned off. Can we come in?" Margo pulled on her ear, the safe signal they'd agreed on, and said something to the woman standing with her. "Detective Fielder is going to hold up her badge and ID so you can verify them."

"All right, Dana, here's my identification." Detective Ellie Fielder's compassionate voice always triggered the memories and reignited the anxiety and terror that had plagued Dana since the night they'd met. So, unless Margo was with her, Dana refused to let the detective in. Even with Margo smiling at the camera, Dana's heart was racing and the gun was shaking in her hands. In the seemingly endless silence, she struggled to breathe, to find her voice. She blinked, forced herself to examine the picture on the ID, then put the gun in a drawer in the table next to the door before disarming the alarm, undoing the two chains, turning the two deadbolts, and opening the door. "Come in." She stepped back.

The two women moved quickly into the apartment. After Dana closed and re-locked the door, Margo opened her arms offering a hug. She was the only one Dana allowed to touch her. She stepped into Margo's arms and breathed in the familiarity of her, feeling the caring and deep friendship they'd shared since nursery school and enjoying the human contact she'd once taken for granted. She reminded herself that the few times Fielder had visited since the...assault she'd only wanted to review her story and ask questions, hoping something new would pop up. And actually, a couple of months ago, Dana had remembered the tattoo. After a few seconds, she turned to the detective. "How can I help you?"

"I'm so sorry, Dana, I know this is out of the blue, but the good news is we think we have your attacker."

It was a gut punch. Dana doubled over and for a minute thought she'd pass out, but Margo wrapped herself around her from behind, grounding her. "You're safe, Dana, you're safe. Take a deep breath."

After breathing deeply for a minute, she straightened. "Sorry, I just didn't expect there would be a real investigation, that you'd ever arrest him." She hoped she hadn't insulted the detective, but she knew the higher-ups decided which cases were important.

Detective Fielder nodded. Her caring gaze and gentle manner were always comforting. "Believe it or not, we investigate every rape regardless of the color of those involved. We're pretty sure it's him and he's behind bars, so maybe you'll be able to relax a little."

"What's the bad news?"

Detective Fielder glanced at Margo before answering. "You need to come downtown to pick him out of a lineup tomorrow. Margo has agreed to come with you."

She swayed. She hadn't been out of her apartment since she was released from the hospital, almost seven months ago. "I—"

"Margo and I will pick you up. My partner will drive us to the station, and I promise we'll stay with you the whole time."

"Listen, sweetie, you haven't left your house in what seven, eight months? You're only thirty-one. You can't live like a caged bird the rest of your life. This is the perfect opportunity for you to fly out of your cage, breathe fresh air, and test how you feel in the world. You'll have two armed guards and me at your side and, if it is him, maybe you can begin to heal. C'mon, give it a shot, Dana." Margo squeezed her hand. "You can do this. I know you can."

Dana eyed the drawer where she'd stashed the gun. She'd have to go unarmed, but the two detectives would have guns. It would be a toe in the water. Besides, she'd heard what happens to rapists in jail and she really wanted the bastard to suffer. "Okay," she locked eyes with Detective Fielder, "as long as you and Detective Green stay close to me."

"Great. We'll pick you up at eleven tomorrow morning." Fielder walked to the door. "You're staying, Margo?"

"Yes. I left my overnight bag and our takeout dinner in your car. You promised to bring them in before you left."

"I did and I will."

*   *   *

At eleven sharp there was a knock on the door. Dana checked the display, and Margo confirmed it was Fielder. Dana glanced at the drawer again. She really wanted to bring the gun with her, but it might be a problem at the police station.

Only her dad knew she had the Glock. He'd taken her hunting from the time she could hold a small rifle, and she was barely a teenager the first time he took her to the gun range and taught her to shoot. She was a good shot but had never felt the need to have a gun around the house. Until now.

Before she was released from the hospital, she'd asked him to have an alarm system installed at her house and to get her a handgun. He wasn't happy about her going back to her own house alone, but he did as she requested. When he and her mom had driven her home, he'd walked her through the alarm system and slipped her the gun, holster, and ammunition while her mother was cooking in the kitchen. "With all them cops shooting Blacks these days, protect yourself. But only shoot to kill if you have no choice."

It wasn't the police she worried about; she was afraid her rapist would come back to finish the job. What her dad didn't know, and what she hadn't told anyone—even her therapist—was how many hours each day she fantasized about torturing the rapist, slowly cutting away his genitals, running the knife over his body, and seeing the red blood stripe his pale white skin. The fantasy ended with her slicing his carotid arteries and watching him panic as he slowly bled to death. She wanted him dead. She wanted him to suffer then die. When he was dead, she would call the police and happily spend the rest of her life in jail. Actually, her life wouldn't be much different since she was already living in a cage of her own creation.

As she stepped out of the house, the first blast of fresh air caressed her face. It felt delicious. And it petrified her. She felt exposed, vulnerable. Her heart sped up and she gulped, trying to get enough air. Margo murmured quietly, trying to calm her. Dana clutched her friend's arm. Fielder moved to her side. "Will you be okay if I draw my weapon, Dana?"

Dana nodded. She would feel safer seeing the gun.

She felt even safer when she noticed Detective Green standing by the car with her gun at her side. Dana slid into the middle of the rear seat. Margo sat on one side and Fielder on the other. Fielder kept her weapon out, facing down next to her knee, and never stopped scanning the traffic on either side of them as Green drove downtown. "Everything looks good, Dana."

They entered through the back of the station and moved quickly to a small room with two rows of chairs facing a mirrored wall. The police chief, a huge white man, followed them in and loomed over her. Dana flinched. Margo and Green moved closer as if to protect her. The chief seemed unaware of his effect on her, or maybe he didn't care. Fielder noticed, though, and said something to draw his attention away from Dana. After a brief discussion, the chief tipped his head at Margo and Green, thanked Dana for agreeing to view the lineup, and wished her luck, as if she were in a contest or something.

Dana nodded but didn't look at him. She'd never been frightened of white men before, had even dated a couple. Now, with her rapist's crude words about Black women echoing in her head, she felt like prey. Her therapist said it was post-traumatic stress from the attack, but maybe it also had something to do with the very visible recent murders of Black men and women by police officers.

Fielder explained they would view the men through a one-way mirror, so the men couldn't see them. Each man would have a number, and Dana should take her time before deciding. If she needed the men to move or turn any way, she should let Fielder know. "We can start whenever you're ready."

She closed her eyes and did some relaxation breathing she'd learned from listening to the CDs Margo had given her, then turned to Fielder. "I'm as ready as I'll ever be."

"You're doing great, Dana. I know this is hard." She pressed a button on the wall and instructed someone to bring in the lineup.

Her anxiety vanished as seven men slowly filed in and turned to face the mirror. All tall, slender blue-eyed blonds with the build and pale coloring she'd reported after the rape. "How did you find him?"

Fielder smiled. "A partial bloody fingerprint on your wall and a member of our team spotted the tattoo you remembered on a Facebook posting."

Dana's gaze went back to the window. She studied each man but kept coming back to number four. "Ask them to smile."

Fielder transmitted the request.

"Ask them to put their hands out so I can see their fingers."

Fielder transmitted that request.

Dana felt in control for the first time in almost a year, and her voice communicated that. She felt Margo relax. Number four had the long fingers she remembered. She studied him. He seemed to be avoiding looking at the mirror. "Ask them to look directly in the mirror."

Those eyes. And the almost smirk. "It's number four." She had no doubt it was him. Her gaze went to his hands again and an image of the tattoo flashed in her mind. She'd forgotten it initially but remembered it a few months ago. She'd noticed the unusual design through the tears and blood flooding her eyes when trying to ward off the blows that had broken her nose and arm. "Ask them to roll up both sleeves."

There it was. "Definitely number four."

She sensed Fielder's excitement. "You're absolutely sure?"

"I'm positive. I recognize his eyes and his long fingers and the smirk. And I remember seeing that tattoo on his right arm as he punched me over and over."

Fielder spoke into the microphone. "Number four."

The mirror went dark, and the four of them were silent for a few seconds, absorbing what had happened. Fielder stood. "We've got him, Dana. Two women he assaulted in bars picked him out of the lineup yesterday. We're sure his DNA will match the scrapings taken from under your fingernails and the traces of semen found on the floor near you. He's going to trial, and he's going down for rape and assault. He'll be held in jail from now until the trial is over."

Dana burst into tears. But she wasn't sure whether it was relief or disappointment. She'd been afraid he would come for her again, so she felt safer. But if he went to prison, she wouldn't be able to kill him. "What's his name?" She knew that naming the fear lessened it.

Fielder hesitated then took a deep breath before responding. "Chuck Donner the third, our newly elected representative to Congress. And, yes, he's the son of Senator Charles Donner II."

Dana gasped. "That's why he looked so familiar."

Once she knew who he was, she wasn't surprised when he was released on bail. But now that she had identified him and he was awaiting trial, her family and friends, apart from Margo, seemed to expect her to forget the whole thing. They assumed she could go back to her life and the Dana she'd been before he invaded her apartment and brutally beat and raped her. They didn't get that though she'd mostly recovered from the black and blues and the broken arm, the real scars were internal. Donner had stolen something valuable from her, her feeling of being safe in the world. It didn't matter that he might go to jail. He had appeared randomly in her life. Who could say it wouldn't happen again? That some other sick bastard would decide she was the perfect foil for his sexual fantasies? It could happen when she was home or, she'd come to realize from reading the newspaper articles about other rapes, on the street.

Knowing who he was, knowing he spent most of his time in Washington, eased her anxiety, and she slowly emerged from her self-imposed isolation to venture out into the world. She began meeting face-to-face with her therapist, doing normal things like grocery shopping and eating in restaurants. She even started working on her half-written book again.

But as the weeks passed, she learned from the assistant district attorney assigned to her case that Donner was claiming they met on the street a few times and she invited him to her apartment. He brought the flowers to impress her, not—as he claimed—to entice her to open the door to a stranger.

He also claimed the sex had been consensual, and that her injuries were the result of the rough sex they both wanted. He'd left her, he said, thinking she'd just passed out and didn't realize how much he'd hurt her. As for the two women he'd assaulted in bars, he claimed they'd all had too much to drink, and things had gotten out of hand.

She spent hours reading about rapes and rapists, about the low rate of convictions and the relatively short sentences for those who were convicted. She read about judges who thought rapists had just had a lapse in judgment and didn't want to ruin the rapists' lives by sending them to prison, about the women who were destroyed on the witness stand. It didn't take a genius to figure out that she was the one who would be on trial, that Donner wasn't going to pay for raping her, that he would go free. It would be up to her to punish him.

She joined a gym. And being a full-time writer, she had the luxury of making her own schedule, so she spent hours exercising every day. After a month she figured out lifting weights and doing aerobic exercise wouldn't be enough to accomplish what she wanted to do. She researched martial arts and found Brazilian Jiu-Jitsu. BJJ, as it's commonly referred to, uses leverage instead of physical strength, so size doesn't matter. She learned what to do if she ended up on the ground and how to take an opponent down using throws and trips and sweeps. But she didn't want just to defend herself, she wanted to be able to attack. She rounded out her education with several other martial arts classes and learned to use elbows, knees, fists, and legs to strike an opponent while standing, to use eye-gouging, foot stamps, and kicks to the groin to ward off an attacker, to defend against weapons and to use anything handy as a weapon.

After training for six months, Dana felt confident, empowered, and prepared to take on any man. She started following Chuck Donner III whenever he was back in town, hoping to catch him in the act. But it appeared he was being a good boy while in his home district.

She took an interest in every rape case in the surrounding towns; and when rapists were released with light sentences, she followed them; and when the time was right, she punished them. She didn't kill. She just administered justice when the system failed and warned them that the next time they raped a woman, they would die.

Reading newspaper stories about freed rapists being badly beaten and terrorized gave her enormous satisfaction. She enjoyed the symmetry of two cases in particular. One was a college student headed for a professional football career who had been released with thirty-five hours of community service because the judge decided he deserved a second chance. His legs had been smashed so he'd never play football again. The arm of the other, who was headed for a career in baseball as a pitcher, was so badly damaged that he'd lost use of it. Both seemed fitting punishments since she was sure the girls involved had lost something valuable too.

Finally, Donner came to trial. But, no surprise, she was the one put on trial. The smiling blond golden boy made a grand mea culpa speech. With a hand over his heart, he confessed he was in therapy trying to change and no longer indulged in rough sex. He went on to say he thought they were having consensual sex, that he never intended to hurt her, but he might have lost control, and then—with tears in his eyes—he apologized and begged for her forgiveness. As she expected, he was found not guilty of rape and assault. He tried to look humble as the judge sentenced him to forty hours of community service and attendance at an anger management class, but he couldn't hide the look of triumph he sent in her direction. Margo, her parents, and her few friends in the courtroom for sentencing were dismayed, but she'd known it would end this way. And she knew justice would prevail in the future.

As soon as the court adjourned, she bid her parents and friends goodbye, then stood outside on the courthouse steps waiting for Margo, who had gone to use the ladies' room. Donner was among the last to leave. He stopped near her and pretended to light a cigarette. He said for her ears only, "I'm coming for you again, bitch."

An image of the trickles of blood running over his pale skin popped into her mind. She smiled and fingered the gun in her handbag. "I'm ready for a rematch whenever you are, sweetheart."

He stared at her. Puzzled. Then he smiled and ran down the steps to speak to the press. A reporter asked, "Representative Donner, would you share what you just said to Ms. Saunders?"

He looked at her. "I apologized again for hurting her, even though she asked for it."

That was it. Consequences be damned. She eased the gun from its holster and palmed it. As soon as she had a clear shot, she would kill him. It would be worth it.

Donner walked away from the reporters and huddled with his small entourage. One of them pointed to an SUV idling across the street. Donner turned to grin at her as she watched from the top of the steps. With his eyes on her, he backed into the street to cross to his black SUV and angling his body away from the press, gave her the finger. She started to pull the gun out, but the earsplitting sound of sirens jolted her, and she looked up instead. People were shouting at Donner, who was standing in the middle of the street; but he was so focused on flipping her off, so focused on showing his superiority, that he paid no attention to them or the speeding ambulance as it skidded around the corner and hit him full on at high speed. As if in slow motion, his body sailed into the sky, bounced off the windshield, then fell in front of the ambulance and was hit again. It happened so quickly, and the vehicle was going so fast it couldn't stop. It dragged him halfway down the block.

She slipped the Glock back into the holster in her bag. She was disappointed. She had been looking forward to the day she would play out her fantasies of killing him slowly and painfully. Then today he'd goaded her into shooting him in front of the world, and she decided to do that instead. And now she'd been cheated out of even that.

But there are some things you can't control. Sometimes justice works on its own. And sometimes you have to help justice along.

* * *

Catherine Maiorisi is the author of the NYPD Detective Chiara Corelli mystery series featuring Corelli and her reluctant partner, Detective P.J.

Parker. These two tough women fight each other and stand against the blue wall while solving high profile crimes. The first two books in the series, *A Matter of Blood* and *The Blood Runs Cold,* were Lambda Literary Award finalists. The third, *A Message in Blood,* was published in January 2021. "When the Caged Bird Flies" is her third short story included in a Murder New York Style anthology. Catherine has also published four romance novels and four romance short stories. She is an active member of Sisters in Crime and Mystery Writers of America. Visit Catherine at www.catherinemaiorisi.com.

WHAT MATTERS MOST

by Nancy Good

Madison Avenue may be to Manhattan what Rodeo Drive is to Beverly Hills—a symbol of luxury and excess—but to me, it's the most boring street in this otherwise exciting city. Millionaires are dull. I've had to deal with too many of them from the moment my daughter Chloe started on a scholarship at Huntley, a private school on the Upper East Side, one block off Madison. Being there nearly every day for pickup, I got my daily dose of the overprivileged.

That mild day in December, though, I was there as a chaperone. The fifth grade was attending a classical concert at a nearby church along with other classes from the best private schools.

While I waited for Chloe's class, I leaned against the rear bumper of one of the four Mercedes G-Class SUVs parked in a line outside the school, with black-suited drivers waiting to pick up their young charges. I googled the cost of these "family" cars. In total, $550,000 worth of metal and leather.

I worked as a freelance writer, usually tasked with boring stuff like corporate newsletters. But my last assignment had just been cut. My husband worked freelance too. Money was always tight.

I looked up from my phone to see Sandra Crane approaching—another Huntley mom and the wife of a partner at an investment bank. She was decked out in a red cashmere sweater festooned with snowflakes, a string of pearls, and a gray pencil skirt that fell modestly below the knee, her neat cherry blonde pageboy bouncing cheerfully. Straight out of the 1950s, a perpetual Frigidaire commercial.

"I heard you and I are chaperones today. I don't suppose you've ever been inside the Madison Avenue Episcopal Church?" she asked condescendingly. To my surprise, she pulled out a compact and began adding some eye shadow—a little heavily, I thought. She'd never struck me as the type to put on makeup on the street.

Sandra Crane was the self-designated Church Lady at Huntley—pious and proper, even though everyone knew her husband had cheated on her with a younger associate, and rumors suggested she might be cheating too.

"The church is absolutely stunning," Sandra said while applying bright red lipstick. "The windows are Tiffany. Gorgeous beyond belief. Richard and I are benefactors." My best guess was that being "benefactors" cost them $150,000 a year.

"So noble of you. Can't wait to see those windows." To my relief, the school doors opened, and Chloe's class was led outside.

"Mrs. Connor, Mrs. Crane, over here." Chloe's homeroom teacher, an earnest young Harvard grad, thrust a bag into my hands. "Can you run ahead and make sure our area is reserved? I've put everything you'll need in here.

It's going to be crowded. The conductor is Dr. Curt Lawson." Her tone suggested the name should mean something to me, but it didn't.

I took the bag and waved at Chloe, who, like a true fifth-grader, ignored me. I peered inside and saw cardboard signs, a length of heavy twine, and a large pair of scissors with impressively sharp blades.

Sandra and I walked quickly down Madison. The church was ten blocks away. Sandra's fists were clenched. A dark cloud seemed to have come over her.

"I've heard about this conductor," she said. "He's got a reputation, and it's not all about music." A flash of anger crossed her face. Just as quickly it was gone.

"Really. What did he do?" I asked.

"Oh, just the usual." Sandra's tone was back to bright and bouncy. "Nasty to female students. Cut-throat ambitious. I shouldn't gossip. I've never met the man."

I'd thought cut-throat was *de rigueur* in this part of town.

The uncomfortable moment disappeared as she chatted about her family's Christmas plans to ski in Vermont at their six-bedroom chalet. We arrived at the church, a 125-year-old neoclassical structure with formal Greek pillars across the front entrance. School buses were parked outside, and children clad in solid blue or plaid uniforms were already lined up on the steps.

"I'll take the signs and get us seats." Sandra grabbed the bag and charged through the noisy group. I followed her, dodging annoyed looks from teachers. A security guard stood in front of the door.

"Good afternoon, Mrs. Crane." He practically bowed before her.

"Hello, Fred. How's the family?"

"Very well, thank you." He ushered us in and then closed the door securely. I could almost feel the angry glares from the group still waiting outside.

Inside, the sanctuary was hushed and gleaming. The highly polished cherry wood pews and altar glowed. The sun shot beams of light through the purples, greens, and bright blues in the Tiffany windows. One window depicted an archangel whose halo glowed like a flame. Those windows were almost enough to make me a believer.

Sandra marched right to the first row of pews. She took out a sign, threaded the thick twine through the pre-punched holes, and expertly wound it around the top of the post. Then she attempted to stretch it down two rows. "This isn't enough twine. Can you go find some more?" she asked, pointing to the right of the altar. "Go out that door and make a left to the front office. Tell Mrs. Porter I sent you."

Obediently, I trotted out the back of the church. Having wandered around churches on a trip to Europe, it occurred to me how easy it would be to get lost inside. And sure enough, it took me less than a minute.

I made a left and confronted a staircase. Sandra hadn't said anything about the office being up any stairs. Circling around them brought me to a large parlor with several worn-out couches, a few empty violin cases, and doors on the far end. No windows, no sign of an office. I looked at my watch nervously; at this rate, I'd miss the concert. I retraced my steps into the sanctuary, hoping to get better directions from Sandra. There I discovered dozens of children already seated for the concert and a truncated area roped off for Huntley. But no Sandra.

I returned to the staircase and walked around it, across the parlor, and through the doors where I found myself plunged into a dimly lit chapel. The hairs went up on the back of my neck. I saw another door and scurried through it.

Man, Sandra was terrible at directions. Now I was in a hallway facing two choices: either take the stairs down to the basement or push open another door. I chose the door. It was heavy. I leaned against it. It swung open, and I found myself in the business end of the church, complete with elevators, recycling bins, and leaflets advertising future events. And still no sign of an office.

Suddenly I heard a noise that sounded wrong, a cross between a dog's howling and a low, tortured moan. A chill went up my spine. I knew there was a reason I didn't like churches. Next to the elevators were built-in bookcases with glass doors. Then there was another door, which was ajar. A library? The tortured sound came from inside.

I was definitely not going to charge in to find out what was causing that sound. I'd read too many mysteries, and this felt like one of those scenes where the snoopy bystander would either get blamed or killed. Yet the reporter in me couldn't resist a peek. I saw legs—male, based on the brown slacks and recently shined loafers—sticking out from behind a leather wing chair. The chair was at an angle to the door, so I couldn't see the rest of the person. And I didn't want to. Even from the door, I detected a dark stain on the light beige carpet.

I ran into the lobby, crowded with people milling about. I spotted a security guard standing at the top of steps that led down to exit doors. I ran over, and from the corner of my eye, I thought I caught a glimpse of a woman who, from the back, looked like Sandra. She was part of a crowd walking out the double doors. *That couldn't be.* I approached the guard—a tall, good-looking guy in a turban.

"There's something wrong—someone's moaning in the library. Can you please check on him? I saw stains on the carpet."

He shook his head. "Ma'am, I have to stay here and make sure the crowd doesn't come through this entrance. Maybe the man just needs privacy to cry. People do that here. It *is* a church, you know." He turned away. Maybe if I dressed like Sandra he'd rush to help.

Behind him, off to the side, was a glass-enclosed office. Finally. I bolted through the door. A gray-haired woman looked up, startled. On her desk was a small nameplate: Denise Porter.

"Mrs. Porter, I'm Jessica Connor, a chaperone with the children today. We have a problem in the library." *We*, meaning this was *her* problem and I was just trying to help. "Someone inside is moaning. It sounds like the person needs an ambulance. There are stains on the carpet."

She gave me a cursory glance and returned to her computer. "We have a large homeless shelter downstairs. I'm sure it's just one of the men from the shelter. They aren't supposed to be in the library, and they know it." Looking disgusted, she picked up the phone. "Jim, come on up. One of your guys is sleeping it off in the library again. He may have made a mess."

Judging from the tweed trousers and buffed loafers he'd been wearing, even Madison Avenue homeless guys dressed a lot better than we did in my neighborhood.

"I don't think that's the problem, Mrs. Porter."

Her eyes narrowed. "Have you worked in a lot of shelters? I don't remember seeing you here before." She looked at me as if I were about to rob the offering. The last thing I needed was to stir up trouble in this posh church while Chloe's class was around. Chloe was already a scholarship kid. We were outsiders among these millionaire investment bankers with their charity balls and midtown dining clubs.

So why was I barging in to save the world—*their* world? This situation was not my problem. The man in the library wasn't dead. I could just ask for the stupid string I'd been sent for in the first place. *Stay away from trouble, Jessica,* my husband's voice boomed at me.

"No, I've never been here before." I attempted a gracious, Huntley-mom smile. "Sandra Crane asked me to get more string to cordon off an area for the children from Huntley. Would you happen to have any?"

Mrs. Porter's back straightened like an invisible trainer had snapped her shoulders. "Of course. Anything for Mrs. Crane." Anything for $150,000 is what I thought. She rummaged in a drawer and drew out a ball of heavy twine. "Will this do?"

"Perfect." I took the string and gave her another smile for good measure.

At that moment, a large Black man walked quickly past, wearing an apron over a well-pressed, blue, button-down shirt and slacks. Guessing this was Jim, I followed him back to the library. He took one look at the man in the chair and rushed in. This was no homeless guy.

"Jesus, what happened to him? Call an ambulance."

I quickly took out my phone and froze.

"Jim, what do I say?"

"A man's been badly hurt and is bleeding. They should get here right away, or he may not make it." He looked at me, impatiently. "Or give me the phone."

"Sorry, I've never done this before." My hands shook, but I dialed and followed the script. An ambulance was on the way.

"Can you hear me?" Jim asked the man. No answer. "Get a towel," he ordered. But where? Then I saw blood coming from the man's abdomen. I don't do well with blood. The walls began to spin. I felt bile rise in my throat and ran out to the lobby for fresh air.

Before I could even begin to find a towel, the EMT team arrived and pushed through the crowd. The guard who'd brushed me off earlier caught my eye and looked sheepish.

Even feeling queasy, I couldn't help but watch as the EMTs worked. One put an oxygen mask over the man's nose. The other unzipped a plastic pouch and took out large gauze pads. Jim stood nearby, his frame thankfully blocking my view.

"I need a bathroom." My voice sounded like a five-year-old's. I'm sure I looked green.

"Here, I'll take you." Jim took my elbow firmly and walked me back through the parlor, now filled with musicians sitting on the couches, chatting idly, some cleaning their instruments. At the far end of the parlor was a bathroom. I darted in and locked the door, just in time to lose my breakfast. I sat for a minute with a cold paper towel on my eyes. My phone dinged.

Couldn't save you a seat. Sit in back. Sandra was in the church. Could it have been her I'd seen leaving?

Problem in church library, I replied.

I walked out of the bathroom. Jim had waited for me. "Sorry for not asking earlier. What's your name? Why are you here?"

"Jessica Connor, chaperone for a Huntley class. I was looking for the office, and I heard the man moaning."

"Good of you to report it. Most people wouldn't."

"Do you know who that man is?"

He shook his head.

"Not one of my guys, I can tell you that. More like a concertgoer, from the looks of him. And the poor bastard got stabbed."

"Are you sure?" The question got him annoyed.

"I was in the army and did security for years. I know a puncture wound when I see one. And people don't stab themselves in the stomach."

A small, slight man in a navy three-piece suit pushed past us and ran out the doors of the parlor. He reminded me of the White Rabbit in *Alice in*

Wonderland. I knew the safe place for me was sitting in the back of the church, not following him down a rabbit hole. But like Alice, I couldn't help myself. Nor, apparently, could Jim. We followed him.

Police were gathered in the library, where the EMTs had prepared a stretcher. An officer was questioning the White Rabbit. I was losing my grip.

"Do you know this man?" he asked, gesturing to the victim.

The small man's face was pale but composed.

"That's Professor Curt Lawson, the guest conductor for today's concert."

There goes the concert. A strange thought, I knew, given that a man had been stabbed. I turned to leave. Better late than never to be a good mom, like Sandra.

"Ma'am? Where are you going?" a cop called out.

"I'm a chaperone for my daughter's class for the concert. I have to get back—the kids will be leaving."

The Rabbit suddenly came to life, his smooth round face lighting up. When he spoke, his voice was far more commanding than I would have expected.

"No one is leaving. I will conduct. I'm the music director here, and I know the program. We start with the Dvorak String Quartet. It's called the *American*—lots of folk and spiritual influences. No child should miss hearing that. And the chorus will have time to take in the news before they sing Bernstein's *Chichester Psalms.* A sure crowd pleaser." He looked ecstatic for a moment, clapped his hands, and bounded out of the room.

"Well," I said to Jim. "I guess the show must go on?"

There was no great love lost, it seemed, between Professor Lawson and the music director. The EMTs now had Lawson on the stretcher. I headed for the door.

"Stick around after the concert," the cop called out again. "We'll need to get a statement from you."

"No problem. I'll be in the church." *Praying that my name won't get dragged into this, whatever this is.* Poor Chloe. She was already the new kid; now she was the new kid with a nosy mom.

Jim followed me out.

"What's the music director's name?" I asked.

"Oh, that's Dr. John Mace. Been here for years. Everyone loves him. Heads the music program, which is a big job. I've heard they were thinking of adding a new conductor to lead the music series, and have Mace just do the church music. I think this Lawson guy was here as sort of a trial run. The church is very committed to music."

But not so committed to security. A well-known conductor being stabbed on the premises wasn't a good look.

"Jim, is it possible someone from the shelter could have done this?"

His face hardened.

"That's what everyone will think, right? But I know those guys. They're not violent, not like this. They might throw a punch now and then, but nobody uses weapons. We wouldn't have them here if they did. And I've been with them all afternoon anyway, cooking lunch and cleaning up." He shook his head and looked at his watch. "I've got to get back; this is gonna be bad."

He paused and looked me in the eye. "You did the right thing, asking for help. Most ladies wouldn't. Here's my card." I took it and gave him mine.

I watched him leave, laughing to myself at being called a "lady."

The chorus was coming down the stairs into the parlor to line up, chattering loudly.

"Can you believe what a jerk Lawson was to Mindy?" one of the young women asked. "He's the worst. I don't know how she'll get through her solo."

"Steve looked like he wanted to kill him," another girl said. "Takes his boyfriend duties a little too seriously, if you ask me."

So, Lawson made enemies, as Sandra had said. Steve, the boyfriend, had apparently become enraged. But was he enraged enough to stab him?

I found the rear entrance to the sanctuary and sat in a pew about ten rows back, on the opposite side from the class. Here I could see Chloe, and also Sandra. I noticed Sandra had managed to expand the Huntley area without my help, and there was plenty of room next to her. Yet she had told me to sit in the back. Why didn't she want me beside her?

John Mace entered the church and addressed the crowd, explaining there had been an accident. The audience gasped and murmured. For an instant,

I saw Mace glance at Sandra and she at him. The look between them was a lightning bolt. Maybe her interest in this church was about more than stained-glass windows. She smiled at him encouragingly, and he reassured the audience the concert would proceed.

"Let us pray for Dr. Lawson's full recovery," he said, and Sandra bowed her head. When she glanced up, the two exchanged another look which connected them as if they were entwined. He turned to the orchestra and raised his baton.

John Mace was clearly exhilarated to conduct the concert. He didn't seem at all upset that his colleague had been nearly murdered. After the first piece, he turned to the audience to accept their applause. The orchestra stood with him, all smiling except for a cellist who looked grim. Maybe Lawson had cut her down, too. Sandra beamed and never took her eyes off Mace. I shivered, despite the warmth in the crowded sanctuary.

The chorus filed in and filled the area in front of the altar. The soprano soloist was in the front row. Her eyes were red. I looked over the section of guys. One looked tense and unsmiling.

As I listened to the chorus, I thought about Sandra's flash of anger when she'd first mentioned Lawson's name. And she'd been missing when I came back to ask directions. She'd told me to go the wrong way out of the sanctuary, even though she knew the church well. She'd deliberately gotten me out of the picture. Maybe it had nothing to do with Lawson, and she had just wanted to be alone with Mace. Those two were lovers, or at least very close. She didn't want me to see the looks between them. That's why I'd been ordered to sit in the back.

The concert ended, and the fifth- and sixth graders—sleek, well-groomed blondes, most of them—started out the door. I waved to Chloe, one of the few brunettes.

"See you back at school," I mouthed as she passed my pew. The police had asked me to check in with them, and I figured the class could head back without me. I walked toward the altar and passed the Huntley section, now abandoned, with a length of heavy twine still hanging off the end of a pew. A speck of dark red on the beige twine stopped me short. I glanced around the empty sanctuary, took out my phone, and snapped a few photos. I was no forensic expert, but it sure looked like blood. Would the police even look in here? I took down the section of thick twine and carefully placed it in a plastic bag I had in my satchel. I walked back to the library. Police tape blocked the entrance, and more cops were inside taking pictures and dusting for fingerprints.

Just as I was trying to attract the attention of one of the cops, I heard a commotion near the exit. I headed back to the lobby, where two police were escorting a disheveled Black man out the door clutching a beat-up shopping bag. A frantic Jim stood nearby.

"Stewart would never do anything like this," he protested loudly. "He's not violent. He was with me all afternoon! It couldn't have been him."

"What's going on?" I asked the nearest cop.

"There's been a murder, ma'am."

So, Lawson had died. That was news. And Jim had been right—they'd immediately suspected his "guys."

"Is that man a suspect?"

The cop nodded. "He had the victim's wallet."

But Jim had been with his group all afternoon.

Meanwhile, the officer who'd asked to talk with me was gone. No one was asking me for a statement and Jim had my number. It was time for me to get out of here. I'd had enough church to last a lifetime.

Suddenly Sandra appeared at my elbow.

"Jessica, we need you to walk the children back to school. One of the teachers has to leave and we need another adult." Suddenly she noticed the cop who was right next to her. "What's going on here?" she asked, sounding annoyed.

"There's been a murder, ma'am. A visiting professor has been killed."

Sandra looked slightly stunned, but not as upset as I would have been, had a murder been committed in my favorite house of worship. If I had a favorite house of worship.

I jumped in and asked Sandra my burning question.

"Did I see you exit this door just before the concert?" Sandra's eyes showed fear for a millisecond, but then it was gone.

"Jessica, I was in the church waiting for you. Why on earth would I leave?" Her voice was knife-blade smooth, and her eyes held a dare. As if I were a foolish child, she said, "Here, let's ask Mrs. Porter if she saw me earlier."

Mrs. Porter, naturally, had not seen a thing.

"It's important who you did see, Jessica," Sandra said as we left Mrs. Porter. "And what you tell the police. Think about this very carefully. I'm sure there were many people coming in and out." Sandra's voice was calm in a terrifying way, like a cobra slithering up to its prey. I started to reply when I saw Jim walk back into the church, his head hanging in frustration. Stewart had been taken away by the police. His cheeks were wet with either sweat or tears.

"Hello, Jim. Are you all right?" Like magic, Sandra was the kind Church Lady again. Jim was certainly not all right.

"You have such a powerful influence here in the church, Mrs. Crane," he said. "Please put in a good word for Stewart."

"Of course I will, Jim. The shelter is a vital part of what our church does for the community." She smiled and took his hand, the snake transformed into a teddy bear.

Or Jim's shelter had served as a vital part of a setup, conveniently covering up her role in a murder. Even if I had imagined a romantic connection between her and Mace, Mace was certainly not sorry that Lawson had been stabbed. He was threatened by the possibility of losing a big part of the job he loved to another conductor. A White Rabbit, with the help of a snake, could be capable of murder.

But that still didn't explain how Lawson's wallet had ended up in Stewart's possession. Or the speck of blood.

But assuming Jim had been with the guys, cleaning up from lunch, Sandra could have planted the wallet in Stewart's things while they were in the kitchen. And then walked out the door. The large pair of pointed scissors in the bag flashed in my mind. I had to say something, but I didn't want to make trouble for Chloe at school. I looked hard at Sandra.

"Sandra, do you have the bag Ms. Bingham gave us, with the scissors and signs? I walked past the pew and didn't see it. I did see some twine left

145

behind, though. I have that right here." I smiled benignly and patted my bag.

Sandra's face went white. She stared at my bag as if it had superpowers.

"I gave the rest of the things back to Ms. Bingham, of course." I could see her internally debating with herself, then in a moment, her confidence was back.

"Jessica, you and Daniel, and Chloe *must* come over for dinner one night. And maybe you can all be our guests in Vermont over the Christmas break? Sarah would be thrilled."

A tempting offer. Chloe would love Vermont. But we would never go near Sandra's house. I had a much better idea.

"Jim," I waved to my new friend, who was heading back down to the shelter. He walked over to us. "I've just been talking with Sandra. She and some of the other church supporters want to help Stewart's defense fund. Get him the best lawyer in town. Isn't that what you were just saying, Sandra?" I smiled at her brightly. She was caught. She gave me a furious look and turned her warm smile on Jim.

"Of course, Richard and I will contribute anything you need."

I kept smiling and went on. "I think $25,000 will be enough to retain a good criminal defense lawyer, don't you think? You could write a check right now, and Jim can get on the phone. And with all your connections, you and Richard could probably raise Stewart's bail money just by calling a few friends. Let's call it Stewart's Righteous Defense Fund!" I looked at her smugly. Sandra glared as if she'd like to kill me too. But the relief on Jim's face was worth it. She took out her checkbook.

Sandra knew that I knew. Yet as long as she bailed out Stewart, I'd keep my mouth shut. Money was the only thing that mattered on Madison. But this time, money could buy more than a Mercedes.

* * *

As best-selling author of the Difficult Man books, **Nancy Good** appeared on numerous TV shows including Oprah and CNN. *Killer Calories*, the first in the Melanie Deming Manhattan Mystery series, was released in

November 2019. *Kirkus* said, "Good has a knack for spinning humor into her characterizations... [the mystery] touches on themes of class and social status..." The second in the series, *Killer Condo,* to be released next year, continues with an expose of the real estate industry amongst the wealthiest segment of the Big Apple. Nancy is thrilled to have "What Matters Most," her first short story, included in this anthology among all these esteemed mystery writers. She is a lifetime NYC resident along with her Maine Coon cat. Nancy sings in choruses in New York and loves biking on trails around the gorgeous Hudson River.

WINDY WILLOWS

by Nina Mansfield

T here are worse things to throw up than a Vanilla Caffè Latte. In truth, I'm more of a black coffee kind of gal. But I was under the mistaken notion that the milk would settle my stomach. The vanilla had been the barista's mistake. I didn't complain, as I didn't want to draw any attention to myself. If I was going to get away with murder, I needed to stay as far under the radar as possible.

My stomach had been kickboxing itself since I'd woken up, which is why I skipped my morning cup of java at home. Plus, I wanted to catch an early bus into the city from Jersey—one crowded with eyes-glued-to-screens commuters. One where I wouldn't stand out—not that anyone ever paid any attention to me. I guess it's what happens to women my age. I wore one of Billy's old baseball caps low over my eyes, my graying ponytail pulled up into it. I'd put on some of his old clothes too—a big black sweatshirt and his ripped jeans. He'd been a skinny kid, but taller with a wider frame than me. Plus, I'd lost so much weight recently, I was able to fit into his clothes just fine. I hadn't been able to bring myself to get rid of any of his stuff after he died. I'd have to dispose of them after today though if I were able to go through with it.

The toilet at the Starbucks on Forty-third Street and Eighth was surprisingly clean. Still, as I heaved up the latte and the bits of bagel I'd tried to eat, I thought about how maybe I didn't have the stomach for murder, that maybe I should just forget about the whole thing. I rinsed my mouth, washed my face, grabbed my duffle bag of gear, and decided to walk back to Port Authority, where I could catch a bus and go home with no one the wiser.

But when I walked out of Starbucks, there was this kid sitting there on the sidewalk. He was holding up a sign that read, "Give a Dollar, Help Me Home." If I thought he'd actually use the money for bus fare, I'd have willingly given him five, but I knew that was unlikely. He was probably eighteen or nineteen, same age as my Billy. Skinny like him too. And he had that same look in his eyes. I wondered how long it would be before he would OD. I bet he'd been raised by a single mom—like Billy had been—one who worked two jobs, trying to do right by her kid, but wasn't around enough to catch the signs until it was too late.

"Spare some change, ma'am? Or you got something to eat?"

I handed the kid the bagel. "I just took one bite, if you don't mind."

He shrugged and ripped a piece off for himself.

"Can I ask you something?" I said.

He held out his cup. I took the hint, searched around in my duffle bag for my wallet, and reluctantly gave him a dollar.

"Your mom know you're out here?"

He shrugged and looked down.

"Your dad?"

"Fuck him."

"What'd he do?"

"Never knew him."

Yeah, that settled it. I went back into the Starbucks. I glanced briefly at the kids working behind the counter and was pleased to see they weren't paying any attention. I clutched the bathroom key one of them had handed me earlier.

When I left, I was wearing my first disguise. I had this dirty blonde wig, short, nothing showy. As I said, I didn't want to stand out. The horn-rimmed glasses were left over from some Halloween long ago when I still spoke to my girlfriends, and we went out as the Pink Ladies. I'd picked up a business suit at Goodwill. It was a little loose, but that wasn't a problem. I wasn't trying to be stylish. I'd also bought some pantyhose. I couldn't find them in those little eggs they used to sell, and the only size they had at the grocery store was Queen, which meant the excess nylon bunched up in my leg creases. I realized I forgot the heels I'd meant to bring. I looked like one of those commuter women in their suits and sneakers, and that was fine by me. The only thing that looked out of place was my duffle bag, but I didn't have a choice about that. Depending on how things went, I might need another change of clothes.

I wiped down anything I might have touched in the bathroom. I didn't want to leave a trace of me anywhere. I used a paper towel to open the door. Probably good practice anyway. Who knew what kind of toxic microbes lived in those bathrooms?

I headed east toward Times Square.

* * *

It had all begun when I'd finally dragged my ass off to Al-Anon the day after Billy's funeral. I just had to get out of the apartment. Everything reminded me of him. The last glass he drank out of was still in the sink. The baseball cap he'd flung onto a chair in the kitchen. Mud from his shoes still sullied the floor by the front door.

I hadn't gone to a meeting in over a year. They were always touting this line about how we couldn't do shit for the addicts in our lives, how we had to put ourselves first. But when it's your son's life—when had I ever put myself before him?

I'd done everything, including locking him in his bedroom, to keep him from heading out, just like the Mole, Rat, and Badger did to Mr. Toad in *The Wind in the Willows*. I used to read that book to him when he was a little kid. He called it *Windy Willows*. "Read me *Windy Willows*, Mama." I could still hear his little voice say in my head. He was my Ratty, and I was his Mama Mole. "And if I had a daddy, he'd be the Badger," he once said. I didn't have the heart to tell him that I'd never met a man like the Badger—always ready to help a friend, someone who appeared when you were in need. His real dad was more like the weasels and stoats in the Wild Wood. The chapter where Mole finally meets Badger was always Billy's favorite, but mine was the one in which Rat and Mole help find Otter's missing son, Portly. "Would you wait up all night for me, too, like Otter?" Billy used to ask. "Of course, I would," I'd say, and squeeze him closer.

The Al-Anon meeting was held in the basement of a Methodist Church across town. I got my cup of watery decaf—because I didn't need anything else keeping me up at night—and a couple of cookies—'cause I realized I hadn't eaten all day. Folding chairs were set up in a circle—only ten or twelve, like they weren't expecting a large crowd. I hated that. I started to get all sweaty and I wanted to get out of there, but this white-haired woman who seemed to oversee the coffee, and looked like everybody's grandmother, started to chat me up.

"Your first time?" she asked.

"No. It's just been a while."

"We're always glad to have you back." She gave my shoulder a squeeze, which normally I find intrusive, but it felt kinda good.

I stared into my coffee as the other seats filled up. This rumpled woman came in just as they were about to start, and grandma pulled up an extra chair. We all pushed our seats back to make room.

We went through all that stuff they do—the steps and the prayer—I never liked that bit about the higher power, but if that's what some people needed, then whatever. Then the sharing started. I skipped my turn. I kind of zoned out, wondered why I'd come at all until the rumpled woman opened her mouth. Said her name was Tess. She looked young and old at the same time, like the lines on her face had been painted on. Her blue eyes were tinged with pink, and the length of her roots showed she'd clearly given up any attempt to remain blonde. She went on and on about how she was able to get some extra hours at the restaurant where she worked, and her temp job at the office during the day was fine even if her boss was an ass, but it still wasn't enough. And how her mother was sober but dying of cirrhosis and in and out of the hospital. And how she had to get more stable daycare for her kid and how that cost a fortune. Then she started going on about the father of her kid.

"I don't know what to do. I've taken him to court, but he still won't pay. His lawyers are tying everything up. And meanwhile, daycare's putting me in debt." She started sobbing.

Heads nodded. Some people stared into their coffee.

I watched this woman's tears roll off her face like they were mine.

I thought of her kid. What would happen to him with his mother working two jobs? I'm fully aware that plenty of single moms can handle it. But some can't. And kids—yeah, sure, some are like those flowers that can sprout out of cracks in the sidewalk. But some never blossom. Some get stepped on. Some die. If he was like my Billy, he might need comfort from someone, or something found at the end of a needle. What if her kid ended up like him?

"I mean—what can they do? I know the asshole has money, plenty of it. He says I told him I was on the pill—and that's bullshit. Let's make a baby, he said. Then suddenly, six months in, he stops returning my calls."

At least Billy's dad had stuck around for a year. I couldn't imagine doing that first year alone.

But she had.

Someone needed to help Tess. It wasn't gonna be the courts, and it wasn't gonna be some higher power. If the asshole wouldn't help her while he was alive, maybe she could claim some of the cash after he was dead. I'd read that some woman over in Paramus had made out nicely when her deadbeat baby daddy got struck by a bus. I figured it could be a *Strangers on a Train* sort of thing. Except she would know nothing about it.

But first, I'd needed to figure out who the guy was. With Al-Anon being anonymous, I didn't even know Tess's last name, and even if I did, some

Family Court records were sealed. I wasn't sure how I was going to navigate all that, figure out the identity of the man I was determined to kill. It's really all I could think about during those nights I lay awake. At least it kept me from thinking about Billy.

I suppose I could have sidled up to Tess after a meeting. But what exactly would I say? "What's the name of the asshole? And then she would counter, "Oh, why do you ask?" And where would I go from there? No. It was better off if I never spoke to Tess.

Turned out, I didn't have to. Because every Tuesday night, Tess divulged some new piece of information.

The next week she let slip that the guy's name was Randall. The following week I learned he worked in the city at some small real estate investment company. I heard her mention Craig Investments to someone before the meeting started, and I figured I had enough info to start my search.

Since Billy died, I'd been trying to spend less time on the Internet. I've lost years of my life sucked into that screen, Googling stuff about addiction. Reading online testimonials for miracle cures. Researching rehabs I couldn't afford. After he died, I swore I'd stay away from my screen. It was my own addiction I needed to kick.

But I knew I could find out pretty much anything online. I didn't want to leave a trail on my home computer, so after work, I headed over to the North Bergen Library.

From its website, it looked like Craig Real Estate Investments was a one-man operation. Midtown address. There was this glossy pic of Randall Craig, sandy hair slicked back, business casual attire, full lips curled into a forced-looking half-smile, light-brown eyes set just a little too close to each other. Not my type, but then again, I hadn't had a type in nineteen years.

I swung by the mall and picked up a burner phone 'cause any idiot knows cell phone data is traceable.

First time I called, Randall Craig answered the phone. He had the kind of voice that could sell you the Brooklyn Bridge. I hung up quickly.

I called again the next day during my lunch break and a squeaky voice answered.

I called a few more times, different hours, different days, and asked a few questions. I've been a receptionist for years in various types of offices, so I pretty much knew what I should ask and how not to sound like a stalker. Figured out Randall Craig rarely got to the office before ten, but his receptionist was in by nine. She sounded about twelve years old, and clearly found saying, "Craig Real Estate Investments" to be a mouthful.

Sometimes, no one answered. And when I asked if I could get help from someone other than Mr. Craig, I was told plainly there was no one else. And that's pretty much all I needed to know.

*   *   *

I couldn't remember the last time I'd been to the city. New York always made me think of the Wild Wood—and I was Mole. Lost. Scared. On the lookout for anyone who might do me harm. I had no right to feel that way today.

There were still some patches of dirty snow on the ground; the spring sun hadn't been warm enough to melt everything yet. I crept my way through the crowds in Times Square. A group of tourists loitered outside some attraction. Suit-types pushed past. I steered clear of the giant Elmos and Olafs.

At first, I couldn't find the address and hated myself for not writing it down. Then I realized I was on Seventh Avenue instead of Broadway, and I was looking for the wrong kind of building. I expected one of those metal and glass monstrosities. What I found was a revolving door that led into a dark, cramped foyer. Black-and-white-tiled floor, shades of olive green and brass. Either the building or the security guard smelled like day-old curry.

He asked to see my ID.

I'd forgotten this might happen and had no choice but to hand him my own. He studied it for a second. Looked up at me in my blonde wig.

"Where you heading?"

I named a dental practice off the sign behind him.

Was he going to scan my license somewhere? Record my info? If so, I might as well turn around and head back home now. But he just handed it back and told me to sign in. I didn't sign my real name.

"Third floor," he said. I took the elevator to three and walked up two flights.

I found Craig Real Estate Investments at the end of the hall. Brass nameplate. I fished the burner phone out of my duffle bag and dialed. "Could I please speak to Mr. Craig?"

"I'm sorry, he's in a meeting," the kid chirped. She was lying. He was never in this early. "Can I take a message?"

"I'll call back," I said.

"Try back in an hour," she said.

So far, everything was going almost as planned. Thing is, I had gotten to the part I hadn't quite figured out, because I wasn't sure what I'd come up against when I reached the office. I'd pictured a glass door, the kind I could peek through and wait until the receptionist left her desk. This door was one of those solid, metal ones. I'd just have to wait outside and hope she came out at some point. If she never left the desk, I might have to kill Randall Craig right there in the hallway. I looked up. Didn't see any security cameras.

Someone exited an office down the hall. I placed my duffle bag on the ground right outside the door. I started taking off one of my sneakers like I was changing into dress shoes, in case they wondered why I was just standing there.

I was holding the sneaker I had just taken off when I heard the click of the doorknob behind me. I scooted back alongside the door and held my breath. The woman who came out looked as young as her voice. She wore black slacks that might have been yoga pants and a short, checked blazer that barely came to her waist. Her hair was a shade of red no one was born with. Her eyes were focused on her phone. I hoped she wouldn't spot me, but I was kinda hard to miss.

"Uh...can I help you?" she asked, thumb mid-swipe on her cell.

I dropped my sneaker. "Oh, no..." I crouched down and peered into my duffle bag, partly to shield my face, and partly to buy time as I figured out what to say. "I...uh...I just got an interview down the hall," I said.

"Good luck with that," she said.

She certainly wasn't the observant type, or she might've noticed that her office door never fully clicked shut. I'd managed to drop my sneaker in such a way as to keep the door from closing, and for a moment I believed there just might be some higher power.

Redhead's little ballet flats pitter-pattered down the hall. I heard the jingle of a key. Clearly headed for the restroom. I continued to rifle through my duffle bag in case she looked back my way. I donned the latex gloves I'd packed, the second skin that would separate me from the deed I planned to commit. Once Redhead disappeared into the bathroom, I slid into the office.

Based on the website I'd visited, and Tess's rants about this dude's supposed wealth, I expected a classier setup. Instead, it looked fly by night. It sorely needed a new coat of paint and perhaps some artwork on the walls. There was a copy machine against one wall and an unplugged fax machine stood on a crate, just behind the Ikea-style desk that I assumed belonged to the receptionist.

An open door led into a back office. Again, I expected leather chairs and bookshelves. There was a shabby wooden desk and binders stacked up on the floor, along with a couple more crates filled with file folders. A wilting plant sat sadly in a corner.

I circled around the room, keeping one eye on the front-office door. No closet. No couch to hide behind. I thought of crawling under the desk, but that seemed like something that only worked in TV sitcoms.

The walls may have been pictureless, but not his desk. Three black-framed photos revealed more about the man's life than even Tess probably knew. The first one was Randall Craig holding a baby. For a second, I thought it might have been Tess's kid until I saw the picture right behind it: Randall Craig as Dad in one of those professional family photos where everyone is wearing cream-colored sweaters. The woman looked a little like Tess but with a rounder face and blonder hair.

The third photo was a wedding picture.

Before I could contemplate the obvious, I heard the click of the door handle. There was only one place to hide—behind the open door of the back office. I slid in and held my breath. I could see Redhead through the crack where

156

the door hinges met the paneling, which meant she could potentially see me.

I slowed my breathing. Cautiously, I reached into my duffle bag for my next disguise. It was from the Halloween my gang of girlfriends decided to go as former first ladies. We drew names out of a bag, all hoping to get Jackie-O. I got Nancy Reagan. I wore a Just Say No T-shirt and one of those rubbery Nancy Reagan masks that I'm fairly sure someone used to rob a bank in some movie.

Next, I pulled out the syringe. I'd found a couple of clean ones in the back of one of Billy's dresser drawers, along with a stash of the stuff that killed him.

Amazing and terrifying what you can learn on the Internet. It was easy to find a video on how to mix the drugs with water, melt them, and suck them into the syringe. I made the solution extra strong and mixed it with bleach. Figured if the drugs didn't kill him, the bleach would. And maybe, just maybe, someone would rule the death an overdose and no one would be out looking for a killer. The guy didn't look like a junkie, but neither had my Billy. At least, not at first.

The waiting was the worst part. The mask made it hard to breathe, so I pushed it up over my nose. Redhead, thank goodness, was fully immersed in her phone. Normally, my thoughts would hop, skip, and jump over to Billy whenever there was silence. But in that moment, my mind fixated on how I would do the deed. I'd have to wait for Redhead to leave her desk again—and then what? Leap out and jab him with the syringe? Maybe wait until he was settled in his chair and sneak up behind him? If I could stick him in the neck somehow, that would be ideal. I hoped it would be quick. But what if he saw me first? I was banking on the element of surprise being on my side, and I hoped there wouldn't be a struggle.

The phone rang and I jumped.

"Craig Real Estate Investments," Redhead said in that birdlike voice. "No, Mrs. Craig, he isn't back yet. Uh, huh. Who? The FEC? Oh, okay, 's' as in Sam. SEC…uh huh." Redhead jotted something down on a Post-it. "And pick up more formula. Okay, got it."

The word formula made me wince for some reason.

The phone in the front office rang again. Redhead was evasive this time. "He's in meetings all day, I think...No, I'm sorry...uh huh...of course."

Just as she hung up, the front door clicked. Randall Craig entered. I pulled Nancy Reagan down over my face.

"Your wife called. You need to pick up formula."

I winced again.

He paused at the front desk and flipped through a pile of mail.

"And she said those people called you at home. The ones you told me to tell that you were in a meeting the other day. They called here too. Said they really needed to speak with you."

He looked up at her. For a second, I thought he might punch her. "If they call again, tell them I'm on vacation. Out of the country. And you don't know when I'm coming back." He handed her a folder. Told her to make some copies. She squeezed past him to get to the copy machine.

He took a step toward his office. Another step. But he paused and looked back at Redhead. Her back was to him.

"Still with the boyfriend?" he asked.

"Yeah," she said. She turned toward him, and I could tell she knew where his eyes were focused. She didn't seem to mind; he was her boss. Maybe she couldn't afford to mind.

He didn't shut the door when he went to his desk, which was a good thing, because if he had, I would've been immediately exposed. If he were paying any attention at all, he would have seen me hiding there. But if I've learned anything from life, it's that people don't see what they aren't expecting to see.

His desk chair creaked. I could see him eyeing Redhead, looking right past the photos of his wife and kid.

Formula. I realized why it bothered me so much. Those pictures on the desk were recent. Or maybe, there was another baby now.

My hand loosened its grip on the syringe.

If I did this thing, maybe I'd be helping out Tess. But this other kid. He'd be left without a dad. I felt like someone had carved my insides out. I wanted to kill him because men like him deserved to die. But now...

What had I been thinking? That killing a man would bring back my Billy? I couldn't do it.

"Yeah, it's me, Bob," I heard him say. He was facing away from me, holding a cell phone to his ear. He crumpled up papers and threw them into a wastebasket. Maybe I could sneak out now. So, what if Redhead saw me? I hadn't actually done anything yet.

"No, we need to talk," he said. "The Windy Willows project."

I breathed in hard. Windy Willows. Had he really said Windy Willows? For a second, it's like Billy was there in the room with me, like he was telling me to stay.

"Of course, I'm an open book. You know I don't have anything to hide." Is that the voice he'd used to ask Tess to have a baby with him? I could tell why she'd believed him. But I knew better.

And right at that moment, I had a thought. Maybe Billy whispered it into my ear.

"I...I just want to know what they know before I get in touch with them, that's all. Can you make that happen?" he asked.

I don't think he got the response he wanted because he threw down his phone. I made my move.

I stuck my hand into my suit pocket jutting out my finger. Maybe he'd think it was a gun. Or maybe he'd think I just had my hand in my pocket. Whatever. I needed something, and I didn't think brandishing a syringe was the way to go.

I kicked the door closed.

He stood up. "What the—"

I could only imagine what was going through his head. Nancy Reagan is a pretty foreboding figure.

"I know about Windy Willows," I said, deepening my voice just a bit. It came out even deeper, muffled by the mask.

"You—"

"I plan to tell the SEC everything if I don't get what I want."

"What, how...what do you want?"

"There's a girl in Jersey waiting for child support."

"Tess sent you?"

"She doesn't know anything about this. And I'd like to keep it that way."

Did he see me shaking? Could he hear my heart exploding in my chest?

"Who the hell are you?" he asked. The blood drained from those puffy pink lips of his.

"They call me the Badger."

I flung the door open.

Redhead screamed when she saw me. I barreled past into the hallway and headed straight for a stairwell. I went up a few flights, because if anyone decided to chase me, they'd go down. The landing smelled like cigarettes. I quickly pulled on my third outfit of the day—another one of Billy's baggy sweatshirts. At least now I wouldn't have to give away Billy's clothes.

* * *

The following Tuesday night, I was sipping weak decaf when Tess shared that she'd gotten a check out of nowhere from the deadbeat. There were nods of approval.

"It was a pretty big check. Don't know where or how he grew a conscience, but I hope they keep coming."

I did too, although I figured one of these days Randall Craig was bound to get busted for whatever scam he was running.

That night I went home. I stuck the glass that had been sitting in the sink into the dishwasher and wiped the mud off the floor by the front door. I took the baseball cap off the kitchen chair and brought it to Billy's bedroom. I made the bed and threw the dirty clothes into the hamper. I found our copy of *The Wind in the Willows* up on his bookshelf under a stack of comic books. I turned to my favorite chapter.

"What would have happened if Rat and Mole never found Portly?" Billy once asked.

"Otter would have been very sad," I answered.

"How sad, Mama?"

"I hope I never find out."

160

I could hear the hum of Bergen Boulevard in the distance. I read the book until I fell asleep.

* * *

Nina Mansfield is a Cos Cob, CT-based playwright, fiction writer and educator. Nina's short fiction has appeared in a variety of publications and anthologies including *Ellery Queen Mystery Magazine, Mysterical-E,* and *Where Crime Never Sleeps* (Level Best Books, 2017.) Her first novel, *Swimming Alone,* a YA mystery, was published by Fire & Ice YA in 2015. Nina's ten-minute and one-act plays have had over one hundred productions in the United States and around the world. Nina is a member of The Dramatists Guild, Mystery Writers of America, The Society for Children's Book Writers and Illustrators, International Thriller Writers, and she is a Co-Vice-President of the Sisters in Crime New York/Tri-State chapter.

THE WORLD ACCORDING TO LUCY

by Susie Case

The childproof cap is tricky, but it yields with a push and a twist to the left.

The retired pharmacist broke the law well. The pills are little white doppelgängers. They even have the markings of the brand-name drug, with the line pressed into the middle for easier breaking.

But no reason to worry. She will never break one in half. She takes two at a time. And this time, with luck, more.

* * *

"Mel, what's up with Shulamite?"

Mellody doesn't like it when Caitlyn, or any of her students, shortens her name, but right now, she has a more pressing problem. She needs to deal with Shulamite, face down on the floor.

The professor knows students sometimes slump forward to catch a few winks in a morning class, but sleepy students usually stay in their seats.

"Is she dead?"

"Who's calling 911?"

"Anyone know her parents?" The students cluster around the limp Shulamite for a closer look.

Most weeks, this is Mellody's favorite gig, adjunct professor at the New York Institute of Design. She grins every time she enters the classroom. What a blast to teach so soon after graduating! She'd like her job even more if she didn't have to buy her own markers or deal with a student in respiratory failure.

A strand of Shulamite's straight black hair enters one corner of her mouth, drags through to the other side, and curls around her drool. Her lips, tinted blue, complement her nail polish.

Mellody sheds her teaching voice and barks camp counselor commands. "Call campus security…don't move Shulamite…put her hoodie over her legs…someone grab her bag."

A stretcher arrives and Mellody rides along in the service elevator. She squeezes into the ambulance with the EMT and her student. The attendant's hands move in constant attentiveness. Even in trauma, it helps to be beautiful.

The ambulance pulls up to the ER door. The patient is loaded onto a stretcher and Mellody sees the tattoos. Crisp in the sunlight, they depict Lucy from the comic strip *Peanuts* cavorting, tumbling, hand standing…a dozen Lucys at play. Attendants push open the doors and take Shulamite and the Lucys away.

Mellody flops down in the waiting room until Shulamite's parents arrive from Flushing. She smooths down her pixie and pulls out her cell. The student life dean has sent a careful email to the entire campus and made a counselor available for those in distress.

Why would shy Shulamite choose tattoos of Lucy, a cartoon bully who runs roughshod over any playmate who stands in her way? Mellody read that Lucy is the most terrifying character in the history of comics. Wouldn't a sweatshirt suffice?

The parents arrive. Mr. and Mrs. Kim's eyes are red, but their faces are impassive. A nurse joins them as a translator. The pulmonologist arrives and walks over to the parents. Mellody takes half a step back, but Mrs. Kim grabs her sleeve and pulls the last person to see her daughter into the inner circle.

The doctor's tone is soft, but her message is hard. She asks, "May I have a word?" then proceeds to have many. Hypoxemic, not enough oxygen in her blood, a drug overdose, activated charcoal, an IV, a breathing tube. Not clear when Shulamite will be alert enough for questions.

The Kims collapse into the molded chairs against the wall. Mellody offers them her card to make sure the Kims understand how to reach her. She grabs her tote and heads outside.

A quick search on Yelp for the top-rated tattoo shop in Chelsea points to a place only five blocks away. She slips into a deli for a snack, then rushes back out.

Why would Shulamite ink herself with all those Lucys?

* * *

Mellody steps down and pushes the screen door. She closes her eyes while they adjust to the dimness. The man at the front desk tugs out his earbuds.

"Hi, I'm Elijah. Can I help you?"

While the artist adjusts the chopstick in his bun, Mellody gets a better look at his smokey eye makeup and black lips. They match the dark walls and the standing lamps the artists bend to light their work.

"Well, Elijah, I'm thinking about a tattoo. My birthday's coming up and I want to celebrate."

"What do you know about getting a tattoo?"

The tabby cat in the window seat jumps to the floor. "I know a tattoo stings, like a cat scratch across your cheek. But I still want one, small and private. Nothing visible on a first date."

Mellody smiles. Elijah stares back. "What comes next?" she asks.

"Look through my portfolio. We take a pic where the tattoo goes and design a mock-up."

Elijah reaches for a release form. "You sign this, pay half and wait a day. The art takes an hour or two."

"Sounds good." Mellody hangs her tote on her knees. "Would you mind if I eat my yogurt while we look at the art? Today's been a little crazy."

"Go ahead." Elijah opens his laptop to his website. Mellody grabs a folding chair from the corner and angles it to see the screen. She reaches for her Greek yogurt, peels off the top, and digs in.

Elijah clicks the spacebar. Tattoos parade by. "Butterflies are always popular. Names are out, line fragments are in." Mellody sends her plastic spoon straight to the bottom for the strawberries.

The artist clicks on. "Wings, hearts, roses, crosses, quotes." The red roses are nice. Mellody rummages around for a napkin without taking her eyes off the screen.

After two dozen images, she sees what she came for: a pride of Lucys on Shulamite's calf. They look softer without the outdoor glare. Mellody knocks over the empty yogurt, the spoon flies off.

She retrieves her spoon and chortles. "Look at these Lucy tattoos! Is *Peanuts* trending again?"

Elijah waits while the cat jumps to curl up on the desk. "One client wanted Lucy in different poses, that's all. You want something, you get it."

"But why would an adult pick a kids' cartoon character?"

Elijah's smokey eyes glare. "What's wrong with a cartoon character?"

"I'm sorry. No judgment." Mellody strokes the cat's ears. "I love Lucy's sass. A little Lucy on my shoulder could be just right."

Elijah closes the laptop. He sits with one leg tucked under and fiddles with the chopstick in his bun. "If you want a Lucy tattoo, I'll refer you to one of our other artists. I've done too many."

"No problem. I'll come back when I have it figured out." Mellody stands up and is almost through the door when she turns back. Elijah is tapping the chopstick on the desktop. "You really helped. Thanks."

Once on the sidewalk, she fishes for her phone and squints at the screen. A text tells her the next step is all set. She flags a yellow cab and hops in.

"Laight and Hudson, please."

* * *

Mellody arrives at an old warehouse chopped into studios apartments. She presses the button for "Parker." When the buzzer blasts back, she pushes through the glass door and starts up the whitewashed stairs.

On the fourth floor, Mellody catches her breath. Did turning thirty make the stairs steeper? She sees the plaque for 4B but no doorbell, so she knocks. Brianna opens the door. "Come in. Everyone you asked for is here."

Mellody sidesteps the kilim rug. "Thanks. Shoes off?"

"Fine to keep them on. Frito drags the sidewalks in. Let's get some air in here."

Brianna slips to a window too small to light the room and pushes it up. Her Chihuahua clings like a third foot. "Hey, guys, make room so Professor can sit down." Then to Mellody: "Haven't gotten around to getting chairs."

Three students–Marcus, Caitlyn, and Alex–slide from the futon to the floor. Siew Kai scoots to the end so their professor can sit in the center and Brianna can join at the other end, Frito at her feet. Mellody retrieves her water bottle before she drops her tote.

She fiddles with the metal cap. "I'm glad everyone's here since I'm sure we're all worried about Shulamite."

Before Mellody can continue, the students popcorn their questions. "Is Shu awake yet?" Caitlyn says, then attacks a cuticle. Alex, mute, works on

166

hers, too.

"What do the police think?" Siew Kai strokes his phone.

Marcus studies his slip-ons. "Is she going to get better?"

"Any ideas what drugs she took?" Brianna twirls her skull ring.

Mellody takes a steadying breath and plows ahead. "Shulamite is still in a coma. Her parents say she has never taken drugs." She pauses. "But that can't be true."

The students dive deeper into self-comfort: Caitlyn moves onto her next cuticle, Alex alternates picking at both hands, Siew Kai flips around his phone, Marcus taps his sneakers, Brianna removes her ring before slipping it back on.

Mellody pushes on. "Do any of you know where Shulamite might have gotten drugs?"

Caitlyn turns up her turtleneck. Alex's collar follows. Brianna rises to close the window.

She remains there and studies her ring before she speaks again. "Look, Shu turns in every assignment on time. She makes us look like slackers. Shu doesn't use."

Marcus shakes off his sneakers. Each toe wears a delighted shade of sorbet. "I disagree. Shu lives in the dorms. Drugs are as easy to find as phone chargers. Why would she tell us if…?"

The buzzer horns in. Brianna bolts for the intercom and listens. She holds the button down until she hears the echo of steps. Frito readies himself to protect Brianna's pack.

When Brianna hears the steps outside, she opens the door before the knock. Mellody's water bottle slides from her hand to the floor. She leaves it alone and blurts out, ahead of her students, "Emerson!"

The teacher has not seen Emerson since he graduated last year. His creamy moto jacket advertises his recent promotion. Mellody's recommendation helped Emerson land the one open job at a top branding company. His success was her coup as a first-year professor, but he has not found the time to return to school or call her since.

Emerson takes two steps into the studio and stops there. He keeps his ankle boots and his backpack on. "Good to see you, Mel. Good to see all of you."

Mellody picks up her water bottle before anyone trips, then asks Emerson, "How did you know we were here?"

He holds up his phone. "I'm Facebook friends with Bri. When I read the invite for this meeting, I wanted to be here. I think I can help."

Brianna returns to the window to crack it open. With Frito draped across her feet, she stares outside. "Em, if you knew something, why didn't you call earlier?"

"Shu made me promise to keep her secret a secret." Emerson rocks to the white noise of the street. "If it were midterm stress, why say anything? But in case it's something else…"

Alex lets out the sob she had been choking back. Caitlyn throws both arms around her friend. Marcus grabs a loose sneaker and flips it in the air. Siew Kai bites his bottom lip. Mellody's eyes lock with Emerson's.

"What do you know that could help Shulamite?"

Emerson stops his rocking and drops his gaze. "My girlfriend was working at the UN. She quit her job last month and gave bogus answers why. One night, we were doing shots and she spilled the beans about the sex trafficking run out of the embassies."

Mellody tenses. Emerson lied whenever he slid late into class. This is not his lying voice. "What do you mean?"

Emerson lifts his chin. He talks over Alex's sobs. "Shu isn't involved in the sourcing, of course. The guys in charge are a couple of higher-ups with diplomatic immunity. They pay students to escort women from JFK to massage parlors so the women can't bolt." Emerson pulls a handkerchief from his jacket pocket and blots his temples.

"We ran into Shu one night at the coffee stand next to campus. When Shu came by the UN to pick up an envelope, my girlfriend recognized her and noticed the envelope looked like the ones used for escort payments."

The students sit dumbstruck, except for Alex's low sobs. Mellody presses on. "What happened when Shulamite found out you knew?"

"She denied everything at first, but I think she needed to tell someone.

She's miserable in school, but her parents refuse to let her quit, so she's been saving up to take off. She promised to stop her job after this semester."

"How long has she been involved?"

"She didn't share any details and I didn't want to know." Emerson crumples the handkerchief back in his pocket. "She did tell me she got a tattoo after every job, because she deserved the pain."

Mellody shudders. Twelve Lucy tattoos. She grabs her tote and heads toward the door. "Emerson, if you really want to help Shulamite, come with me. When she wakes up, we need to find out more."

Emerson bites his lower lip. He stands without moving, as if posing for an influencer photo of his new jacket.

"Hey, Em, Shu needs help. Move it!" Brianna opens the door, Frito barks in anticipation. Brianna reaches down, scoops up her little one, and keeps her other hand on the knob. "Quick, move it!" The professor and her ex-student silently descend together.

* * *

Four floors later, they exit the vestibule, shaded in the early evening dusk. They head to the corner. It takes a couple of lights, but a yellow sedan pulls over and Mellody lets Emerson slide across the seat first.

"St. Mary's. Fifteenth Street entrance, please." She buckles up and pulls out her phone. While she was at Brianna's studio, a dozen new texts had popped up. "Shulamite's parents texted. She's out of the coma. Looks like we can talk."

Emerson grips the armrest and checks out the bus stop ad, the one with the latest hunk shilling Absolut. "Shu isn't going to like me being there."

"I get that. But someone may try to hurt her again. Please, Emerson, what else?"

West Fourth Street. Eleven blocks to go. The traffic is crawling. Emerson swallows hard. "Well, there is one thing…"

Two more blocks go by. Mellody grips her tote and waits Emerson out. Her students mention this stone-faced technique in their reviews, her way of Mt. Rushmoring until they answer.

Emerson shifts in his seat and studies the pedestrians. Finally, he goes on. "Shu is the student other students love to hate. She outworks everyone, she doesn't share, she makes everyone else look bad. Brianna says Shu has been disliked since freshman year."

Fourteenth Street. One block to go. Mellody looks out her window. Verizon promises 5G just got real. She turns back and raises her voice over the honking.

"Emerson, who hates Shulamite the most?

Emerson slouches in his seat. "I dunno. I'm not in her class."

The cabbie interrupts. "Okay to leave you at the corner?"

Mellody sees the gridlock of ambulances and cabs unloading the elderly and their walkers. "The corner's fine." She hands him a twenty-dollar bill for the eleven-dollar ride and waits for Emerson. They silently enter the ER.

Inside, two dozen people prevent them from finding a seat. A cursing homeless man talks over a pregnant woman's sobs. A father soothes his teenage daughter, and an older woman pretends to watch ESPN. Everyone quiets down when a young man on a gurney is hustled by as the EMTs discuss his gunshot wound.

Mellody and Emerson stand as far as they can from the misery pit while they wait for the receptionist to get off the phone.

"Ma'am, where would we find Shulamite Kim? She's a patient in the Seligman wing."

"Could I see an ID, please?"

Mellody snags her wallet from her tote and flips it open. The receptionist sets down her noodles to look at the ID, then looks back. New York saves money by not updating license photos, but Mellody is tired of double-takes because her pixie looks nothing like her high school layers.

The receptionist hands back the ID, along with a pass. "What was the name again?"

"Shulamite Kim."

She taps her keyboard. "Room 217. Visiting hours end at eight.'

"Thank you."

After Emerson gets his pass, he drags himself a half-step behind Mellody into the elevator. She reassures him. "Remember, you can stay quiet. I'll handle it."

The elevator opens. A guard sits by the nurses' station. The duo flash their passes, then head down the hall.

Mellody cracks open the door and peers into the silent room. The Kims sit upright, commandeering the room's two guest chairs. The curtain has been pulled back from the room's other bed which is empty for now.

Shulamite is staring at the ceiling. She doesn't bother to look toward the door. The Kim parents smile weakly and nod hello. When Mellody met them in the emergency room, a nurse helped translate. This time, Shulamite ignores her parents. She won't be translating.

"Hey, Shulamite. I've got Emerson with me. We've all been pulling for you. How are you doing?"

Emerson stands behind as Mellody approaches the bed. Shulamite's mother has groomed her daughter: dry shampoo in her braided hair, face cleaned of makeup, a pink sweater on top of the hospital gown. She is ready to board the junior high bus.

Mellody starts in. "I know you don't want to talk about this, but I'm really worried. I don't think you hurt yourself. Can you tell us anything?"

Shulamite's stare stays on the ceiling. Her eyes well up as she whispers. Mellody leans in closer. "I missed that. What did you say?"

"I don't want to talk about it." The patient turns toward her parents. They say something in Korean. No translation needed: Don't be rude to the professor.

Mellody pulls in inches from Shulamite's face. The antiseptic scent stings her nose. She lowers her voice. "Listen, a guard outside doesn't guarantee anything. Who wanted to hurt you?"

Shulamite raises herself on her elbows. She swivels to look at Emerson. Her rasp spits hostility. "Em, you said you wouldn't say anything. You're such an ass."

Emerson steps back. Mellody stands her ground. "Shulamite, who did this?

As Shulamite sits up, the Lucys peek out from under the bedsheets. She squeezes her eyes shut.

Mellody knows. And knows that Shulamite knows she knows.

Cornered, the patient slouches so her braids hang forward. She stares at the sheets. "I'll tell you. But you gotta promise not to tell my parents. My job had nothing to do with this."

"I swear. We just want you safe." An ice cream truck trills in the distance.

Shulamite glances at her parents, then turns back to her visitors. "My parents wanted me to be an academic star. First-generation American, only child, ticket to the future, you know the drill." She tilts her head to her parents.

"I knew in high school I liked art more than academics. But no way my parents were going to be fine with that. I was supposed to be the midtown professional, not the Brooklyn artist."

Shulamite pauses, so Mellody steps in. "So why did your parents let you go to a design school?"

"I cut myself a little, made myself throw up. Beats spending four years reading dead white guys. My parents figured I would get the art stuff out of my system, then go to grad school like a good girl."

Emerson chokes. "I'm sorry, Shu. That explains a lot."

Shulamite manages a smile. "It's okay, Em. My classes are okay, just not the constant job talk. I want to explore my art and everyone else wants a career."

Mellody's stomach knots. She has set a high bar in the classroom so her students will have a shot in the marketplace. Has the pressure been too much? "Shulamite, you've had a rough go of it. I didn't realize it and I want to hear more. But you need to tell us, how do you think you landed here?"

The patient reaches for her hospital cup and takes a sip. "The other students hate me because I don't care as much as they do, but my work is better. Caitlyn, Marcus, and Siew Kai were superstars in their high schools and thought college would be the same, but the professors praised me."

Mellody wants her water, too, but it can wait. "Okay, they were jealous, but how did that turn into this?"

"To pull all-nighters, I take Ritalin. My mom got me a prescription in high school before the SATs. Three-quarters of my classmates did the same thing. I found I could take two pills, or, in a crunch, even three."

The professor's nod helps her student continue. "I had a big project due the morning of our class. I was just so tired, I took two pills, then stupidly took two more. I swallowed them at the hallway drinking fountain, then sat down to tweak my project. You came in and asked how we were all doing, and that's the last thing I remember."

Mellody remembers her directions to the class. "Shulamite, do you have your backpack?"

"No. It didn't come with me."

Mellody reaches into her tote for her wallet. She pulls out a stack of ATM twenties and hands them to Emerson. "Please treat her parents to dinner. I've got to go check something."

She tiptoes to the door, then turns around. "And whatever you do, don't let anyone from school into the room. Okay?"

Her heels click on the linoleum. The guard never stirs. Emerson better follow her instructions.

* * *

Outside the hospital, Mellody finds an empty cab waiting. For the second time today, she asks for Laight and Hudson and hopes what she knows about students holds true.

When the cab arrives at Brianna's corner, Mellody pushes the buzzer for Parker and charges in when it blares. She takes the stairs two at a time up to the fourth floor, then bangs on Brianna's door. Frito barks three times his weight.

"Hey, Professor, glad you're back." Brianna steps aside from the door. "How is Shu doing?"

Mellody scans the room. She was right. They were all still there. Students, once at rest on a futon surrounded by classmates, will not move until pushed. "Shulamite is going to be okay. Her parents are with her and so is Emerson.

But I'm glad I caught you. Did any of you grab Shulamite's backpack? She doesn't have it and all of her midterm work is inside."

"I didn't."

"Nope."

"Haven't seen it."

"Sorry." Caitlyn, Siew Kai, Brianna, and Marcus toss off answers. Alex's "I didn't see it," slides in one beat later.

Even with only a year of teaching, Mellody's ear is already trained to detect lies.

* * *

This year, graduation lands on one of those tropical May days. The month will cool off again before the humidity rolls in to stay, but today, the students and their families are grateful for Radio City Music Hall's air conditioning.

Mellody stands clustered with the other faculty at the back of the lobby, ready to join the procession. Her academic robe hides a hydrating Gatorade inside her slim tote. She will be able to reach into it without commotion once she is on the stage.

"Okay, faculty, let's line up." The provost raises his arm and waves at all the robes to follow. Mellody is paired with an English department colleague. They stand together in their crimson-edged hoods.

Her colleague leans in to be heard over the commotion. "Whatever happened to the student who passed out in your class?"

Mellody's answer is breezy. "It was a mix-up. Two students had the same backpack, and one took the other's meds. Bad allergic reaction. Glad we got her to the hospital in time."

The situation had been handled in private. Alex confessed at Brianna's apartment to swapping out Shulamite's Ritalin for Lorazepam, so her crush Caitlyn could beat out Shu for the senior design award. The student life dean got involved and helped Alex's parents find the right residential facility.

The police weren't satisfied with Shulamite's claim that she'd mistakenly grabbed her mother's anxiety medication instead of Ritalin the last time she was home. It wasn't hard to convince her to cut a deal with the feds in exchange for her sex trafficking contacts since her options were a deal or a trial. Since she had worked with wingmen not protected by diplomatic immunity, her information delivered.

Her grateful parents funded her legal fees and promised a gap year to let Shulamite explore where her talents might take her. While waiting to hear back from the Florence art school, she anonymously donated her savings to a local anti-trafficking group. That donation made it possible for the group to hire Emerson's girlfriend as a grant writer.

Mellody beams as she reaches under her gown into the caramel tote Emerson had given her as a thank-you for his recommendation. Spending time with Frito whenever she goes over to Brianna's has tempted Mellody to get her own pup, but she will wait until her bag's new-tote smell wears off. She likes to savor her wins, one at a time.

* * *

Susie Case was born in North Dakota, grew up in Los Angeles, attended school in Boston, and has lived in NYC since. She has worked as a Wall Street research analyst, a business school professor, a writing professor for design students, and a pitch coach for start-ups, all material for her series-in-progress, *Cartoon Mysteries* from which "The World According to Lucy" *is* drawn. Susie studied mystery writing with Seth Harwood, who taught her to slow things down, and she includes an homage to Irma Bombeck in every piece she writes. Susie has been published in the New York Times and would like to be interviewed by Barbara Walters, about whom she wrote a fangirl college application essay.

INJUSTICE IN BROOKLYN

by Stephanie Wilson-Flaherty

Fall, Bay Ridge, Brooklyn, NY

Ahhh, I love my crazy neighborhood. Immigrants from everywhere. As the weather chills, I look out my window to see the Ukrainians laughing and wearing light outer coverings. And then I see the Caribbean transplants hunkering down under gigantic jackets with warm hats and double gloves.

So, maybe you can already tell that I spend quite a bit of my time at my window, looking out, and being (okay, to be honest), nosy.

Well, that's true. I am nosy. Some call me a busybody. It's okay with me. I am not easily offended. After all, somebody has to keep watch over the neighborhood.

One day, I was on my stoop and noticed a little commotion across the street and partway down the block where the newish family-sort-of-group had moved in. I say it that way because I have come to realize that not all households are married or have children. I'm totally neutral as to familial-type groups. Hey, who knows? I don't judge.

"Señora?" a kid from that familial group said a few days later, after he bicycled over to perch in front of my house as I was sitting on my stoop, watching the street scene as usual.

Well, I didn't know how to respond as my pathetic high school Spanish couldn't figure out what to say, other than:

"Qué pasa?" My uneducated reply was sort of, I think: "What's happening?"

The kid gave me a look. The kind of look that said he knew more about me than I knew about him. If so, or even not (I'm pretty neutral to most everything, as long as it's non-controversial), I decided I would play along.

But then, this kid surprised me.

"It's okay," he said. "I get that you don't really know Spanish." He pedaled back and forth. "I just wanted to speak to a person who could help us."

Well, that floored me. As a former Girl Scout, I always want to know how I can be of help. In fact, in the past when I'd helped a few neighborhood folks, it had made it into the local press.

"What's your name?" I asked.

"Diego."

"Well, hi Diego, I'm Sadie," I replied. *"Qué pasa?"*

Oh, my, I thought to myself. Why, oh why, can't I get past my stupid high school Spanish?

He laughed.

"Hola, Miss Sadie," he said and resumed his bicycle riding up and down

the street.

I could see that he was about twelve years old. Old enough in some societies to be an adult, and in some, like ours, young enough to still be a kid. And then, he stopped again in front of my stoop.

"So, Diego, what could I do to help your family, if I am able?" I still sat there. I always wait until I have a reason to move. I like my stoop. Sitting there makes me happy.

And that's when he totally stopped. Screeching his brakes and wheels, right in front of me.

"Well, Miss Sadie," he said. "My family has some difficulties in this country..."

"Whoa," I said. "Stop right there, Diego. If you are talking about immigration issues, I have no ability to navigate those policies or laws. You might need an expert instead of me."

He balanced on his two wheels and gave me the "look."

I knew that look. The one that communicated an assumption that I had some kind of superpower that could fix things in this universe.

To me, those superpowers were only available in the movies.

So, I readjusted. I can readjust to pretty much any situation. I am flexible like that.

"Diego, talk to me. Just tell me what you need."

"Gracias, Miss Sadie," he said. "I have just two problems. *Uno* is that my family would suffer even if they were born here, as I was. And, *dos*, they face deportation because they were not."

I did another "wow." How could I help this situation when it is way beyond my expertise? Luckily, over the years I have learned that research and reaching out can lead to a lot of pertinent information.

"So, Diego," I said. "Can anyone in your family, except you, speak English?"

"*Si*," he said. "A little bit. But I am best..." he puffed out his little chest as he balanced on his bicycle.

"So, is there an adult I can speak with?" I asked.

"*Si*, Miss Sadie. My *abuelo* is the head of the family. Come with me. He will be pleased to meet you." He jumped off his bicycle and waited for me by the gate to my front yard.

Well, I thought, did I really have anything to lose?

"Okay, Diego, lead me to your *abuelo*."

So, I walked across the street and partway down the block to a three-family limestone house. A typical unit in the Bay Ridge section of Brooklyn similar to my own.

There, I met Diego's *abuelo*. Even my rudimentary language skills informed me that this was Diego's grandfather. He was not tall. And really didn't seem that old. Younger even, than I was thinking. He had long, dark, thin hair and a slim build. Oh, I thought, maybe everybody is looking young to me these days…

"*Hola*, Miss Sadie," he said and gestured that I should enter the house.

"Well, hello," I said awkwardly, as my high school Spanish continued to give me trouble.

And then he said, "You are mi *amiga*, my friend."

Well, color me confused.

"I am your *amiga*?" I asked.

"*Si*," he said. "You *mi amiga*." He gestured toward his garbage cans and tapped the blue recycling bin. And then, something clicked in my brain. The recycling bin. I was forgetting the impact of my assistance when these folks first moved into the neighborhood and I noticed how they were not processing their trash correctly. The city publishes brochures that translate all the local recycling rules into dozens of languages. I merely put copies into their mailboxes. Hey, I do it automatically for any of the new people on the block; it's just the kind of thing that a Girl Scout instinctively does, especially since the fines for non-compliance are huge.

I'll admit, I had a personal motive as well. I will never forget the unbelievable racket caused by these neighbors as they unloaded a weeks' worth of bottles into the bins on Friday evenings. And then again when the sanitation workers dumped them into their trucks on Saturdays. What a headache! Interestingly, all the bottles were Guinness. Who would have suspected that immigrants from the Dominican Republic favored Irish stout?

So, I started over.

"*Hola, Mister Abuelo,* I am Sadie. I don't believe we have ever met formally. And you are…."

"Luis, *mi amiga,* Miss Sadie. I am Luis." He gave a slight bow. A very gentlemanly gesture.

So, after a bit of back and forth with Diego and Luis in Spanish, English, and a sort of Spanglish, I discerned a few critical facts. First, Luis had at least three generations of his family living in the house. Hence, all the beer bottles. Second, the older generations were responsible and law-abiding persons. And third, there was a bit of rebellion in the younger generations.

Cars would roar down the street and stop in front of the house for no apparent reason.

And then, the rumors started. Gossip about backseat sex trafficking and drug trafficking. That's when the friction became a police issue. More than once, the whole block was awakened by the late-night screech of tires, the sounds of sirens, and the flashing lights of police vehicles near that house.

So, it seems that a grandson of Luis had been accused of various crimes: drugs, gun possession, and even attempted murder.

I didn't know if the police possessed evidence of the actual cases, but I did wonder if juries could convict without it. What I now understood was that this is what prompted Luis to send Diego my way, seeking help.

Hey, I got it. I was neutral territory. Maybe that grandson was guilty as charged. But, maybe, just maybe, he was a victim of social injustice. Bay Ridge, Brooklyn, was not a hotbed of racial integration. In fact, parts of South Brooklyn were infamous for its locals harassing people of color: Brown, Black, or any other color that wasn't white.

I consulted with some friendly attorneys from the neighborhood to see what could be done. I mean, if that grandson was guilty as charged, then he deserved to feel the full brunt of the law…but, if not…

My friendly contact ascertained that the grandson in question had been guilty of some minor infractions, like smoking marijuana. As for the gun and attempted murder charges, they were serious enough to require the assistance of a local expert.

So, as a local lifer and self-proclaimed official nudge, I poked around and prodded and nudged the local police, politicians, and news people to try and get to the truth. Perhaps I should print up calling cards that read: "Sadie, Official Busybody and Nudge," I thought. It had a certain *je ne sais quoi* that I loved.

The good news was after a closer look, *Abuelo's* grandson was not actually guilty of anything more than smoking marijuana.

And, so, when fall turned into the winter cold, our immigrants from Ukraine still laughed and wore light outer coverings. And the transplants from the Caribbean hunkered down under gigantic jackets with warm hats and double gloves.

Diego, my twelve-year-old, bicycle-riding friend, just kept cycling up and down the street. Occasionally, he stopped in front of my stoop where I kept watch over my neighborhood because somebody has to do it, even when it's really cold.

And he would say, *"Hola*, Miss Sadie."

And I would say in my semi-fractured Spanish, "Hey, Diego, you are *mi amigo.*" But I couldn't figure out how to say anything else in Spanish, so I retreated to English, "Go in peace, my friend."

He would smile and keep pedaling. I like that in a kid...a hustling, immigrant kid from Brooklyn. Like so many hustling immigrant kids, or their ancestors, from so many places and countries, in so many generations...

Under my watchful eye in New York City.

* * *

Stephanie Wilson-Flaherty is a member of Sisters in Crime, MWA and RWA. She published her finalist entry in RWA's Golden Heart contest, earning a four-star review from *RT Book Review* upon its release. She has recently focused on writing short mystery stories with a humorous touch, set in her native Brooklyn, starring a busybody older woman sleuth. Three of those stories were published in the Sisters in Crime New York/Tri-State anthologies, and the second was also listed in the Other Distinguished Mystery Stories section of *2015 The Best Mystery Stories*, edited by James

Patterson.

LAUNDRY AFTER MIDNIGHT

by Nina Wachsman

N o one believes anyone in New York, especially not a twelve-year-old boy. Heck, I wouldn't have believed me either, but like many things in this city, the unbelievable turned out to be true.

"I'm going down to get the laundry," I announced to my parents, who didn't look up even though it was one in the morning. Hand on the brass doorknob,

I was about to open the front door, when I heard a noise in the hall. My view was limited through the peephole, blocked by the back of a guy in a blue sweater. When he jerked sideways, I could see the lady across the hall swinging her small purse at him by its chain handle. He raised an arm to block her attack. *Thunk!* A sickening sound, but I couldn't see where it came from because the blue sweater was blocking my view again. Bang! The slam of the stairwell door was so loud I jumped away from the peephole.

I blinked a few times with my hand still frozen on the doorknob. Then I placed my eye on the peephole again, expecting to see only an empty hall and closed doors. But there she was—the lady across the hall, facing me, her back against her door, slowly slinking down to the floor, her knees crumpling and her blond hair leaving a trail as it stuck to the doorpost. Not good.

"Mom, Dad!" I burst into the dining room banging the table so the laptops under their fingers bounced.

"Did you get the laundry, Neil?" my mother said automatically, not looking up.

"Come quickly. The neighbor's hurt. She's lying in the hall."

"What our neighbor does is none of our business," Dad muttered, his eyes on his screen.

"This is no joke," I pulled out my phone. "I'm calling 911."

They both looked up. "What's got into you?" Dad said.

I pointed a shaky finger to the hall, holding my phone, ready to dial. Chairs scraped back simultaneously, and they brushed by me as they hurried to the front door. I followed.

"Oh. My. God," my mother said, putting a hand over her mouth. Dad didn't move, just stared.

The lady from across the hall sat just as I saw her in the peephole. Up close, her eyes were open, staring at nothing, the dark pupils large and stark against the light blue of her irises. Her coat was open, and something sparkly glinted from underneath.

"I'm calling 911," Mom said, her fingers tapping her phone. "They should be here shortly."

"Neil, back to the apartment," Dad said, turning towards me. "I'll handle the police when they come."

I was not moving. A real murder, and in my apartment building! The whole thing didn't seem real. With her blond hair, blue eyes, and red lips, the lady next door looked like a broken doll. I wanted to note every detail, maybe write a story about it. Her door was open a crack, so maybe when she had been about to enter, the guy had tried to shove her inside to rob her. He had lousy aim, so she hit the doorpost. Did that mean it was murder or an accident?

Ding! The elevator doors opened, and out came two firemen. One of them carried an axe, who knows why, while the other dropped to his haunches on the floor. He reached out to take the lady's hand, feeling for a pulse.

The man with the axe turned to us. "Are you the ones who called 911?"

Dad nodded, "We live across the hall. My son was going out to get the laundry, and when he opened the door, he saw her."

Fast thinking, Dad, not quite true, but close.

"Getting the laundry at one in the morning?" repeated the other fireman, rising from the floor, facing us with his eyebrows raised. "From where?"

"From the basement. I forgot about it, and you're not supposed to leave laundry overnight," I explained.

The fireman didn't seem to be listening to me, his attention was on the microphone pinned to his chest.

"Why are the firemen here instead of the cops?" I whispered to my Dad.

The other fireman heard me and responded, "We all get the call, and whoever is closer gets here first. Here comes NYPD now."

The elevator door pinged open, letting out two uniformed policemen and a tall man in a tweed brown jacket and floppy hair.

"What happened here?" The shortest of the three addressed his comments to the firemen, not us.

"She's gone. Didn't want to move anything until you got here." The fireman pointed to the corpse.

The man in plain clothes, apparently a detective, turned to us. "Who are you people?"

"We're neighbors. We found her," Dad said, squeezing my hand in a warning to stay quiet.

"Neighbors?" the guy asked his head angled so he seemed to be peering at us through his floppy hair, "Which apartment?"

I pointed across the hall. The fireman with the axe gestured to me.

"The kid found her. Parents called 911."

All three cops turned to look at me. "You found her? Did you see what happened?"

"He heard a noise, looked through the peephole, and opened the door. When he saw her, he ran back and called us," Dad answered for me.

The detective turned his head to Dad without moving the rest of his body and said, "I was talking to your son, sir. I'd prefer he answered if you don't mind."

Dad and Mom were staring at me, but I wasn't going to lie. "I did hear something. Just before I opened the door."

"What did you do?"

"I looked through the peephole."

The detective's eyes narrowed as he looked up from his notes. His pencil poised above his notepad, he waited for me to continue. Dad started to talk, but the detective silenced him with a lift of his hand.

"What did you see?" the detective asked.

Dad's warning aside, I decided to tell the plain truth.

"I thought I saw her fighting with a man."

The detective squinted at me as if he were trying to see me better. "You *thought* she was fighting with a man? Aren't you sure?"

Sweat beginning to trickle down from my hair. I swiped my hand across my forehead, hoping the detective wouldn't notice. Then I started babbling. "She was swinging her purse at him. It happened so fast, and I was looking through the peephole, so it was hard to really see. Then I got scared and ran to my parents and by the time we opened the door, she was already on the floor. No one else was there."

"So, you didn't see where the man went? Or how she banged her head against that doorpost. It's probably that bang that killed her."

This time Mom intervened. "Look, if the lady were with someone, wouldn't the doorman have seen him? By one a.m., the door is locked, and you have to ring to get the doorman to let you in. Besides, there's video surveillance of the lobby. You can view it in the office on the ground floor, next to the mailroom."

Slamming his pad shut, the detective cocked his head on an angle, as if he were considering what Mom said, but his eyes focused on me as he answered. "My partner's interviewing the doorman now." He moved past me to our apartment door, brushing so close that I smelled cigarette smoke and sweat.

"May I?" he said as he gestured to the door. Mom nodded and he went inside, closing it behind him. I guess he wanted to look through the peephole to see what was visible from it. It didn't take long for him to reemerge.

He faced us, legs spread, and gave his assessment. "The view is distorted so I guess the boy might have *thought* he saw someone fighting with the neighbor, but for all we know he could have been helping her."

Dad was behind me and put one hand on my shoulder. I decided to stay quiet and not argue.

The detective waved to his uniformed companions and turned to the elevator, hitting the button several times. "Totally inconclusive. My gut tells me this was just an accident. Thanks for your help. We'll be in touch if we need you."

The other two policemen appeared to have finished with whatever they were doing, and the older man spoke into his radio. The elevator pinged and the detective disappeared.

"Nasty accident. Go back inside. We've got it from here," the older policeman said, clearly the one in charge. Then he turned to the firemen, "Let's get her out of here, you know the drill."

The fireman started talking into the transmitter on his chest as the elevator arrived and he and the other fireman got inside. The two policemen were blocking my view of the victim, and the older one gestured for us to leave.

Dad closed and locked the door, and Mom and I followed him to their bedroom as far from the outside hallway as you could get. I took a seat on the bed, with Mom claiming a spot right beside me.

Taking a deep breath and exhaling, I said, "Dad, I'm pretty sure the guy pushed her into the doorpost."

"Did you see him do it?" Dad asked in a lawyerly tone. "Did you actually see him push her, and see her hit the doorpost? Because if you didn't, you are just making assumptions."

"She was swatting him with her purse. So maybe he was trying to rob her, and he pushed her to get away?" I looked over at Mom, seeking validation.

She sighed. "I guess that could have happened but listen to what your father is saying. All you saw was a man with the lady across the hall, and she was swatting him with her purse. Then you saw her slink down on the floor. Correct?"

I nodded. "Strictly speaking," she continued, "that is not exactly conclusive evidence for murder." I guess now they were both lawyers.

"But he did murder her, I'm sure of it!" I burst out.

"Did you see his face? Or any clue as to who he was?" The sarcasm in Dad's voice was unmistakable.

I shook my head. "I only saw him from the back. For like a second."

"Then supposing he did give her that fatal push, where did he go? Did he just calmly waltz into the elevator and disappear?"

I tapped a finger on my cheek, trying to keep my anger in check. "I don't know. If I killed someone, I'd probably run away as fast as I could. So, I guess he escaped down the stairs. I was looking through the peephole, and then there was a loud slam. I got scared and backed away. So, who knows where he went?"

"It is also possible she fell against the doorpost. After all, she may have been drunk, and not the first time, coming home at one in the morning," Dad said as his closing argument.

"And those high heels, of course, she could fall in those," Mom added as if she were trying to convince me. "So maybe she slipped and just banged her head on the doorway."

The scene I had witnessed was beginning to blur. Only the blood on the doorpost and the neighbor's dead blue eyes remained clear in my brain. But I had to persist.

"Dad, you have to believe me when I tell you what I saw. The guy was not *helping* her. She was fighting with him, she was smacking him with her purse, and kicking him with her heels. I heard a great *thunk* which must have been the sound of her head hitting the doorpost. I saw her slide to the floor. Even if he didn't mean to hurt her, it's still murder, isn't it?"

Dad looked away, so I knew I wouldn't like what he was going to say. "You don't really know what you saw, or what really happened. Let's not open a can of worms. When we opened the door, she was slumped by her doorpost. Let's leave it at that."

Mom reached over and stroked my head. "All that blood, and a corpse. You'll probably have nightmares about it."

I flung my head back, rolling my eyes at the ceiling. They were talking to me like I was a baby. "Ma, come on. I know what I saw, even though it was through the peephole. Isn't it our duty to report a crime? You're a lawyer, Dad, so isn't that what we should do?"

Dad gave a dramatic sigh. "Forget about what you see on *Law and Order*. It doesn't work like that in real life. What you saw would not make the case for murder. The cops were here, they heard your story. They'll investigate. There's nothing more for you to do. We didn't know the victim, other than seeing her occasionally on the elevator. We don't even know her name."

Once the front door had closed, as far as my parents were concerned, it was case closed. Not for me. I went to bed with a plan to investigate.

Anything I wanted to know about the neighbor or anyone else in the building would come from the doorman, Louie. I often hung out with Louie in the lobby, and on occasion I'd see the lady next door coming home from work, tottering on her high heels, and flicking back her long blond hair. She always flashed Louie a smile, so of course, I reasoned, he must know all about her.

Louie would know if the neighbor was seeing anyone who wore a blue sweater, that's for sure. Then I remembered something. The guy I saw through the people was wearing a blue sweater, but he wasn't wearing a coat. It was like thirty degrees outside, which could only mean one thing: *he was someone from inside the building.*

* * *

The cops must have sent people to gather evidence and clean up during the night because when I opened the door in the morning, the hall looked the same as usual. It was as if nothing had happened there last night, except for the yellow tape that made a garish X over the door of her apartment. I pushed the button relentlessly to summon the elevator, determined to bring up the laundry from the basement before Mom remembered to ask me about it.

"Maybe the police have finished investigating and it may not even be considered a crime scene," Dad said when I came back upstairs and asked why the police hadn't returned. "They may have concluded it was an accident."

The detective obviously didn't believe me last night, and Dad was relieved. Unless I found something new, what happened to our neighbor was going to remain 'case closed.'

I could barely wait until 7:00 p.m. when Louie would come on. I'd learn more about the lady in 9B from him.

I was waiting for him downstairs when his shift started. He was still pulling on his uniform jacket when I greeted him, and he took his usual seat by the door.

"Whassup?" He gave me a bright smile.

"You heard what happened last night? The lady in 9B was murdered," I said, hoping he'd heard the same thing.

"You mean Laurie, the fashion designer? I didn't hear that. I heard she died in some accident." He shook his head. "Not surprising. Always stumbling on six-inch heels, and usually stewed when she came home late."

"Weren't you on last night? Didn't you see her come in?" I prompted, hoping to get a little more intel from him before I spilled what I saw.

"I was on, but I sign off at midnight. She must've come in after that since I didn't see her before I left." He pulled his phone from his pocket and started checking his texts as if I were no longer there, looking up only when one of the tenants came through the door. "I think Henry was on at that time."

I let out a moan, which made Louie stop texting. "What's wrong with that?"

"You know Henry is brain dead. I think 9B was murdered, and I was hoping you saw her come in. It's hopeless to ask Henry about it."

Louie was far from stupid and raised an eyebrow. "And you think she was murdered, why?"

"I saw someone push her."

"Seriously? Did you see who?"

"I was looking through the peephole, so couldn't see much more than his back. She was fighting with him and he pushed her against the door."

"You told this to the cops?" He pocketed the phone and gestured for me to join him outside. Lights twinkled from the wine bar across the street, and a few people were braving the crisp cold air to sit at the outdoor tables. I shivered, since I wasn't wearing a coat, but the uniform Louie wore must have been warm because he kept his jacket open. We stood just outside the building's entrance, and with his hands in his pockets, Louie leaned into me, like we were sharing a joke. "The owner's son had the hots for her."

"The owner of the building has a son living here?" That was something I didn't know. "What apartment?"

Louie bounced up and down on his toes. "On the sixth floor, on the opposite side of the building from you. A youngish guy, maybe in his late twenties. Strange dude. He works back there, in the office, and stays until real late at night."

"He had a thing for Laurie?" I prompted, now feeling entitled to use her first name.

"Yea, he did. First, he'd ask if I noticed when 9B came in and if she was with anyone. If I said no, then he'd tell me I wasn't watching the door well enough, not doing my job. What a prick." He shook his head and sighed.

"Maybe she was late on her rent, or he wanted to see if she had someone living with her," I offered.

Louie grunted. "Look, kid, it wasn't just his question. It was the way he asked it. He was in fantasyland. No lady like Laurie would ever go for a nerd in glasses and a blue sweater like him."

As soon as I heard "blue sweater" I nearly choked. I must have looked funny because Louie put a hand on my shoulder, "You okay? We should go back inside, it's probably too cold out here for you."

"The guy I saw fighting with Laurie was wearing a blue sweater."

He leaned over to my ear and kept his voice low. "If I were you, I wouldn't mention it." He aimed a look at the video camera poised above us, filming the entryway where we stood. I swallowed and kept quiet as he slapped me playfully on the back and started joking about the Knicks. I got the picture, all right, that it might be a good thing for me to take Dad's advice and cancel my investigation.

After a little more bantering, Louie pulled out his phone again, his signal that it was time for me to go. I headed towards the elevator. That's when I saw the guy in the blue sweater. From the back, just like last night in front of 9B.

He was in the little mailroom, right outside the building's office, and a few steps from the elevator. He turned toward me, but the glare from the light hitting his rimless glasses prevented me from seeing his eyes. I pushed the button again, and again, wishing the elevator would come. Until he sidled up right next to me. Leaning across me, he pushed the button and treated me to his wide creepy smile.

There was no way I was getting into the elevator alone with this guy. Without a word, I turned and ran down into the mailroom, and out the back door, my steps ringing down the metal stairway to the courtyard.

There was probably no logical reason to be as scared as I was, but my gut had told me to run, so I did. Quickly scanning the courtyard, I searched for an exit or a place to hide. The mailroom door slammed above me, and I ran towards the rear, where the garbage bags were piled up high. There must be an exit to the street, I reasoned, a way for the porters to remove the garbage. I slid my way through rows of smelly black plastic, moving faster than I thought possible in the dark passageway until I could see the street. As soon as I was clear of the building, I ran towards the welcoming lights of the wine bar across the way, hiding myself in a crowd of strangers huddled at the entrance.

I pulled out my cellphone and raised my finger to dial 911 when I saw the guy in the blue sweater emerge from the building. He turned slowly in each direction, and I was certain he was searching for me. A glint of light from the streetlight hit his glasses as he turned my way, and I hid myself behind the cluster of coated customers. He shouldn't be able to see me, I hoped, and probably wouldn't expect a kid to try and enter a wine bar. Once more he turned sideways to look up the street, before disappearing back into the building.

I let out a deep breath, just as the group I had been hiding with were ushered into the bar. I was stopped when I tried to follow them inside, but the hostess let me stay when I explained someone was following me. I called my dad.

When I saw Dad crossing the street, I ran out and jumped into his arms. There I was, like a baby, clinging to him, burying my face in his sweatshirt so no one would see the tears flowing down my cheeks. He patted my head and steered me back into our building. Louie looked up from his phone when we walked in, and his eyes widened. "I thought you went upstairs a while ago. Where'd you come from?"

"You didn't see what happened?"

"What happened?" he repeated.

I looked up at the camera recording everything, and said, "Never mind. A long story. See you tomorrow."

Louie gave me a cocky salute before turning back to his phone. I looked around the lobby, but Blue Sweater was not in sight. The elevator from the other side of the building dinged and out came a crew of leather-clad, studded punkers with spiky hair. They waved to Louie as they stomped out into the night. Despite their attempts to look scary, it was no contest between them and the guy in the blue sweater. I clung tight to Dad's hand as we went into the elevator.

I didn't let go until after we bolted the door behind us. Dad led me into the living room and sat down next to me on the couch. Thankfully, Mom wasin her room with the door shut. I had every hope Dad would understand my terror and believe my story.

"I saw the guy in the blue sweater—the guy that pushed her—in the lobby," the words rushed out before I could think about how to best say them, "He's the owner's son, and he knew I saw him, and he chased me and—"

"Whoa, whoa, hold on, you're going too fast for me," Dad said. We both looked down at my hands, which were still trembling. "What do you mean 'the owner's son'? How do you know that?"

"Louie."

Dad took both my hands in his. "Start again. Tell me what you saw last night, and what happened in the lobby just now. One step at a time. Slow and easy. You're safe now."

I cleared my throat and told him exactly what happened and what I'd learned from Louie.

"I think he was in the office by the cameras and heard me and Louie talking about the murder," I said, rubbing my chin, which usually worked to calm me.

"Don't tell me you were talking about it with Louie in the *lobby*?"

I hung my head.

My father leaned back and tilted his head towards the ceiling. Then he leveled his eyes at me. "I think you and your mother should go to the country for a few days…"

"So, do we go to the cops now?" I asked, but my hands were still shaking.

He looked at my hands and said, "Don't worry. Go to the country for a few days and I'll take care of it."

"Ohhh," was all I could say. My dad was a real estate lawyer. He knew the owner of the building. That's how we got this big rent-stabilized apartment. I wasn't going to argue because I was scared and happy to get away from there.

When we came home a week later, I heard that Louie was gone. He'd gotten a new job in one of the owner's other buildings. I kept looking over my shoulder as we entered the building, but Dad put his hand on my back and guided me calmly to the elevator.

Dad stayed with me as I unpacked and put things away. "You don't have to worry. He's gone. The guy had problems, so his family sent him away to an institution."

"It doesn't seem fair to the lady in 9B, does it?" I said.

"Life isn't always fair, Neil. Things don't always turn out the way we think they should."

When I thought of the guy in the blue sweater, I felt my stomach clench. Dad was right. What I saw would probably not convict him, or even convince anyone I saw a crime.

"He won't be coming back anytime soon, will he?"

Dad shook his head.

"Then, case closed," I said, and I meant it.

* * *

Nina Wachsman is the author of *The Gallery of Beauties*, a novel of historical suspense, to be published by Level Best Books in 2022. Inspired by family history, it is the story of a courtesan and a rabbi's daughter in seventeenth-century Venice, the city's Golden Age, and is the first of a series. Nina has been a children's book illustrator, art director and advertising executive. She raised her three children on the Upper West Side of Manhattan in a prewar apartment where she currently lives with her husband.

HARBOR LIFE AND CITY SILT

by Elle Hartford

Newspaper clipping: *The New York Harbor Times, June 10th, 2085*

Merfolk Performer Found Dead During Staten Island Ferry Show, Possible Murder!

For decades, the merfolk troupe Bridges from Land to Sea has performed daily shows along the Staten Island Ferry route as part of their efforts "to bring landfolk and merfolk closer together." Those efforts were ruined yesterday when, shortly after the 3:00 p.m. show, one of the performers was found floating in the wake of the ferry, apparently strangled by a stray fishing net. Onlookers say no fishing boats were in the area, but a small catamaran was spotted leaving a private dock at 2:30. Oliver McMean, a New York City native and frequent ferry rider, told reporters that the merfolk performer "was only one of many victims of the secret machine out to get us all." Police have yet to comment.

"Oh, dear," Pell said once he'd finished reading the article aloud to his partner. "I think I know the victim. Did you ever meet Bryne?"

"Which of the tailed and scaled was she?" Freddie crossed over to the breakfast table and sat with an affectionate grin at Pell. It had become a joke between them; many New Yorkers, who had been living with merfolk in their harbor for as long as they could remember, protested that "all merfolk look alike." Freddie, being an outsider himself—a transplant all the way from California—found this idea ridiculous, and supported merfolk celebrity Pell in his indignation over it.

"You met her in the initial dives for your project," Pell recalled. He got in a dig of his own, referring to Freddie's massive underwater sculpture, a second Statue of Liberty directly beneath the first meant to bring merfolk and "landfolk" together, as simply a "project." "Well, yesterday I do remember there being a stir in her neighborhood. Maybe the city police swam out to ask some questions."

Freddie buttered a piece of toast. "Do they really do that?"

"No." Pell sighed, flicking his long tail. "Theoretically, they work with the appointed liaison for merfolk affairs—last I checked, it's still old Tasman."

As the toast disappeared and orange juice quickly followed, Freddie turned a shrewd eye on his live-in boyfriend. "Planning a social call?"

Pell shook his dark green, scaled head.

"No sympathy visits to the relatives?"

"No, no. I know better than to pry," Pell said, folding his paper. With a smile, he added, "Besides, merfolk don't have families in the same way you landlubbers do, as you well know. No; I won't investigate this time."

"Then you should come and help me with the design. You're going to go crazy sitting here all alone and retired."

Pell looked around their beautiful waterfront apartment, one of a new blended sea-and-seafront housing development meant especially for mixed couples. It veritably sparkled, light and airy and expensive; a well-earned use of the money he'd made as a TV consultant.

"I'd be happy to," he said in answer to Freddie's request. But before he slipped from his gently curved, waterproof chair, he asked another question that weighed on his mind. "Do you think there's anything to that quote? The 'dark machine'?"

"The guy who said that's just an old madman," said Freddie dismissively. "I hear them ranting sometimes on the ferry as it passes Liberty Island. They're only there for the captive audience. Some people just can't stand the idea that things might be getting better for others."

* * *

From *The New York Harbor Times, June 12th, 2085*

Second Murder Along Staten Island Ferry Route!

This morning another merfolk performer was found dead in the water along the Staten Island Ferry route. The first one, found two days ago, was strangled by a fishing net in what was ruled to be an accident. The latest victim is suspected to have died of an unnamed industrial poison. Roberta Czech, the captain of the ferry who spied the victim, told the press that "one could be an accident, but two is a trend." The captain is a known friend of the harbor merfolk and was instrumental in setting up the Bridges from Land to Sea performances twenty-seven years ago.

Police are now looking into accusations of malignant negligence on the part of local seafront industries.

Freddie snorted as he poured espresso carefully into mismatched cups. The sun played through his red and gold hair. "Blaming industry is no better than idle speculation."

"I don't know." Pell set his paper aside to receive a steaming cup. "Merfolk have been instrumental in putting so many regulations and limits on those industries. Fishing, shipping, even industrial waste. Any one of those companies might not be so sad to see merfolk dying."

"Sure, but would they really go about it that way? Random deaths? You'd think they'd target the really outspoken merfolk." Freddie's voice faltered, but only a little. Pell qualified as one such outspoken merfolk. But Pell also had powerful friends from the TV industry and told Freddie often that he shouldn't worry about threats that hadn't occurred.

"It isn't that random if it's the performers dying," Pell pointed out.

"The performers are closest to the surface in such a busy area," Freddie countered. He set down his coffee abruptly. "It doesn't feel right."

Pell's deep eyes, eyes the color of bull kelp, softened. "What doesn't?"

"Talking about it so lightly. And how the papers talk about these deaths, too. I know things are different for merfolk and most of you don't expect to live very long, but—" Freddie broke off, staring at his brightly painted ceramic plate.

"You're right." Pell reached across the small dining table, taking Freddie's hand. "And that's why you're such a good artist, not to mention the perfect person to be working on the Seafaring Lady Liberty."

* * *

From *The New York Harbor Times, June 14th, 2085*

Third Death in Serial Merfolk Murders!

Last evening, on the 11:30 p.m. run of the Staten Island Ferry, a third merfolk victim was discovered. The victim was horribly mangled, a result of being hit by a watercraft propeller. Like the other two, the victim was a performer in the Bridges from Land to Sea Troupe. Police now believe all three murders are connected. Anyone with information is welcome to go to the special webpage set up at http://www.nypd.merfolkaffairs.report.

Freddie set down the breakfast tray. "Don't keep reading that awful excuse for reporting. They're not even naming the victims, for heaven's sake!"

Pell looked up, idly smoothing the surface of the kitchen-side pool with one long fin. "There's more of that speculation you like. This time they're thinking the 'dark machine' is someone *framing* the seafront industries, trying to make them look bad. Eh?"

"I think it's xenophobia," Freddie declared, forking some pancakes with more force than necessary. "All that talk of machines and environmental regulations is just a red herring."

"Red herring?" Pell repeated, grinning.

Freddie glanced up. "Don't you dare. I didn't mean it as a pun. You know what I—"

Pell laughed aloud, though inside he knew it wouldn't be long before they'd be pulled into the investigation. Freddie's work took place right along the ferry route. For as much as Freddie didn't want to talk about the issue—and as much as Pell would have liked to protect him—they wouldn't have much choice when the police began looking in earnest for witnesses.

* * *

When the police did come the next afternoon, they found Pell alone. Freddie had progressed to rough sculpting of his statue, a process that Pell found loud and messy and best supported from afar. He'd sent Freddie off with well wishes and a kiss and settled in to do some reading. It was, in Pell's opinion, the finest achievement of landfolk: the book.

But a heavy knock at the door interrupted his enjoyment.

Pell set aside his novel carefully and dove into the nearest saltwater channel without getting so much as a droplet on the furniture. The entire apartment had been built with channels and pools, and after six months, Pell had grown expert at navigating them. In no time at all he found himself sitting in the living room once more, this time across from an extremely uncomfortable police investigator.

Detective Francesca Miller twisted her hands in her scarf. Pell watched her, concerned but also quietly amused. It was clear to him that she'd never been to the seaside development before; or perhaps, he thought, she felt shy meeting a local celebrity.

"Thanks for seeing me." The detective's voice came out gruffly, but Pell suspected she was covering nerves. "It's about Tasman. She—well, she got the idea that maybe being Liaison's too dangerous right now."

Pell smiled. "And your department believed my celebrity status rendered me immune?"

"It's not that, exactly. I need help, Mr. Pell, sir. I can't work this case without…without—"

"Fins. It's perfectly fine to acknowledge as much, Detective," Pell said graciously. "And since we'll be working together, 'Pell' will do. Yes, yes—I'll help." Under his breath, he added, "You're lucky that Freddie isn't here."

"Thank you." Fran sighed, her hands going limp. "There's not too much you would have to do. We're fairly certain the killer is human. We just need help getting some statements from merfolk who might have been around on the days in question, including this morning. They're usually more willing to talk with a merfolk liaison present."

Pell straightened. "There's been another murder?"

"Yes. Young female merfolk, Ceta, point person in the Troupe. Found this morning trapped in fishing line. Death caused by obstruction of the gills."

"Like the first." Pell carefully looked over Detective Francesca in her tasteful if inexpensive suit, and decided he liked her. "You know, merfolk kill just as easily as humans do."

"You really think the killer's one too?" Francesca blinked.

"You think it so unlikely one might turn on his own?"

"Well—I would've thought, in that case, the murders would have more method to them. So far, the facts point to a method that's barely above random," the detective admitted.

"Method in either case would be limited by the murderer." Pell smoothed the scales of his tail with the palm of one hand.

Fran thought over the comment and then chuckled.

"Are you trying to say you think the murderer is stupid?"

"Or opportunistic. Or," Pell added more seriously, "so full of hatred that they do not care about collateral damage."

"Hmm." Fran's fingers tapped restlessly against her thigh. "I'd tried to talk to Tasman about that idea, but she has it in her head this must be some kind of predatory thing. She said its only point was to divide merfolk and humans. And in her case, it worked." The detective paused and shifted on the velour visitors' couch before meeting Pell's gaze directly. "We'll schedule a time tomorrow to take statements if that works for you. In the meantime—you live here with Freddie Herrman, the artist working on the 'Together in Liberty' project, right?"

"I do," said Pell, bemused but willing to see where the question led.

"Good. Just...make sure you stick with him." Fran rose. "Could be a high-profile thing, after all."

Pell's eyebrows rose with her. "You think *I* am in danger?"

Fran clasped her hands and looked out the window. "I'm just thinking. Maybe have him stay home with you tomorrow. There's safety in numbers."

* * *

"I knew it. I knew it. I knew it, I knew it, I knew it," Freddie muttered as he cleared up the breakfast dishes the next morning.

"Freddie," said Pell, waving an unread newspaper for emphasis, "it's not as though any direct threat has been made. The detective simply suggested we both stay home, and I happen to think it's a good idea. That way when she comes by later, you can meet her—"

"We should have seen it all along." Plates clattered, but Freddie seemed not to hear the noise. "It's because of that interview you did. Remember? You called the workings of the fishing industry a 'machine' and those poor mergirls were drowned in fishing line and—"

"And, that connection makes no sense, because I was nowhere near the murders," Pell interrupted gently.

"But they wouldn't know that. The murderer, I mean. Maybe they've just been waiting for you to come out and visit me and get caught in one of their traps! The project site is right next to the route where these murders are happening! I've been diving right next to them every day, and every time you come out too, you're in danger!"

"The murders *have* happened," Pell corrected firmly. "I have every faith that Detective Miller will put an end to this. Now, can we please enjoy our morning without thoughts of murder? When she gets here, you can speculate to your heart's content."

Freddie acquiesced, albeit grudgingly. They whiled away the hours reading and lunching and birdwatching and gaming and frankly doing anything that Pell thought might make Freddie even a little less anxious. Finally, around teatime, the knock they'd both been waiting for arrived.

"Detective!" Freddie threw open the door and greeted Fran as though she were a long-lost relative. She rocked back from the threshold; her brown eyes wide.

"Don't mind him," Pell smiled. "Come and sit."

Fran recovered herself on the way to the living room. Before they took their places on their respective waterproof or velour couches, she announced, "Actually, it's about Freddie I've come. At least in part." Turning to the shocked artist, she explained, "We've picked up our man this morning while you stayed home. You have nothing to worry about. We caught him right in the middle of a set-up. There'll be no question in court, not if I have anything to say about it."

"What?" Freddie puzzled.

Pell splashed loudly as he pulled himself up out of his waterway. "I think the good Detective is saying that *you* were the target, Freddie."

"That's right," Fran turned between her two hosts and, seeing their identically flabbergasted faces, shrugged. "I thought you realized it too," she said apologetically to Pell. "I guess I didn't make myself clear. Yesterday, while we were talking, I realized that Freddie was the target. It was something you said about collateral damage and people killing their own, and then what Tasman had told me about dividing everyone versus bringing them together. That's when I remembered there was someone who'd been preaching against Freddie and his project every day."

"*What?*" repeated Freddie.

"Not the Oliver quoted in the first article?" Pell guessed.

Freddie sputtered. "The *madman?*"

Detective Fran grinned behind her hand. "'Madman' isn't how the papers reported him, but that's about right. Yep. It was him. He'd been trying for weeks to get to you, Freddie. He was full of talk about 'desecrating the Statue of Liberty' and 'fornicating'—begging your pardon. It's awful stuff. He was even spewing some of it that first day he gave an interview, but it was lost in his rants about everything else. We should have realized it then. I'm sorry we didn't."

"It's all right, Detective," said Pell, smiling faintly at Freddie across from him. "All is well now."

"As well as it can be," Fran mused, addressing Freddie as well.

Pell cleared his throat. "My grandmother used to say that hate is like silt."

The room fell silent, until at last Fran guessed. "Because it's dirty and it gets everywhere, sir?"

"Because it's *gross,*" Freddie muttered to himself. He still had a half-wild look about him, like he couldn't believe anything that had been said.

"No," said Pell in good humor. "Because once it gets stirred up, everything becomes cloudy. Even the eyes of justice have a hard time seeing clear."

* * *

Elle Hartford has written in several genres but is currently working on a cozy mystery series with an alchemical twist. As a historian and

204

museum educator, she firmly believes in the value of stories–and fantasy in particular— as a mirror for complicated realities. Though she grew up on the beaches of the Pacific Northwest, she now lives in New Jersey with a grumpy tortoise, a three-legged cat, and a very supportive partner. Find her blog and other stories at ellehartford.com.

Acknowledgements

Many thanks to our team of judges who took time out of their busy schedules to read and select the stories included in this anthology, as well as our proofreader and photographer, who went the extra mile to help make this compilation a success.

About the Editors

Joseph R.G. De Marco: Co-Editor, is the author of the Marco Fontana Mysteries, the newest is *The Vermilion Pursuit.* He writes The Vampire Inquisitor series and the Doyle and Kord Mysteries. His short fiction is anthologized in Arsenal Pulp's Quickies series, *Men Seeking Men,Charmed Lives, Where Crime Never Sleeps,* and others. His essays appear in *Gay Life, Hey Paisan!, We are Everywhere, Black Men White Men, Men's Lives,* and *Paws and Reflect,* among others. His work appears in *Encyclopedia of Men and Masculinities,* and *Journal of Homosexuality.* He was Editor-in-Chief of *The Weekly Gayzette,* and *New Gay Life,* and contributing editor for publications including *Il Don Gennaro* (an Italian American magazine) and *Gaysweek* (NY). Currently he is Editor-in-Chief of *Mysterical-E.* (www.mystericale.com). Learn more at www.josephdemarco.com

D.M. Barr: Co-Editor—Under her real name, award-winning author Dawn M. Barclay is currently the Family Travel and Special Needs Travel Contributing Editor for *Insider Travel Report.* Past editorial positions have included Senior Editor, *Travel Agent Magazine* and Contributing Editor, *Travel Life,* as well as Meetings and Incentives Editor, *Travel Market Report.* She regularly judges contests for Romance Writers of America, including as president of her local Hudson Valley chapter. As D.M. Barr, she writes tales of suspense, satire, and sweet romance, with four currently in print and a fifth published under a different pen name. Her first short story appears in this anthology.

Lightning Source UK Ltd.
Milton Keynes UK
UKHW010640150921
390618UK00001B/23